CAST (

Ina Kell. A pretty little redh[...] hattan.

Inspector Oscar Piper. A sho[...]

Hildegarde Withers. An angular, inquisitive retired schoolteacher who's both the light of Oscar's life and the bane of his existence.

Winston H. "Junior" Gault. The playboy vice president of Gault Foods, on trial for murder.

Tony Fagan. An outspoken television personality who didn't live to regret his intemperate ribbing of his show's sponsor, Junior Gault.

Dallas Trempleau. A socialite, as blue-blooded as she is beautiful, who's engaged to Junior.

Art Wingfield. An up-and-coming young television producer.

Thallie Gordon. A bosomy singer who appears on Tony Fagan's show. She and Art Wingfield are an item.

Ruth Fagan. Tony's most recent ex-wife, who was also once married to Wingfield.

John Hardesty. An assistant district attorney and Oscar Piper's friend.

Sam Bordin, aka Sascha Bordin. A crafty lawyer and former pupil of Hildy's.

Gracie. Sam's secretary.

Vito. An enterprising street urchin who becomes Hildy's unofficial assistant.

Nikki Braggioli. A scheming young actor, half-Italian and half-English.

Ramón Julio Guzman y Villalobos. A Mexican private eye and lawyer.

Crystal Joris. A 300-pound tap dancer.

Talleyrand. An independent-minded apricot poodle, the apple of Hildy's eye.

Plus assorted cops, bureaucrats, relatives, clerks, and passersby.

Books by Stuart Palmer

Novels featuring Hildegarde Withers:
The Penguin Pool Murder (1931)
Murder on Wheels (1932)
Murder on the Blackboard (1932)
The Puzzle of the Pepper Tree (1933)
The Puzzle of the Silver Persian (1934)
The Puzzle of the Red Stallion (1936)
The Puzzle of the Blue Banderilla (1937)*
The Puzzle of the Happy Hooligan (1941)
Miss Withers Regrets (1947)
Four Lost Ladies (1949)
The Green Ace (1950)
Nipped in the Bud (1951)*
Cold Poison (1954)
Hildegarde Withers Makes the Scene (1969)
(completed by Fletcher Flora)

*Reprinted by The Rue Morgue Press

Short story collections featuring Hildegarde Withers:
The Riddles of Hildegarde Withers (1947)
The Monkey Murder (1950)
People Vs. Withers and Malone (1963)
(with Craig Rice)
Hildegarde Withers: Uncollected Riddles (2003)

Howie Rook mysteries:
Unhappy Hooligan (1956)
Rook Takes Knight (1968)

Other mystery novels:
Ace of Jades (1931)
Omit Flowers (1937)
Before It's Too Late (1950)
(as by Jay Stewart)

Sherlock Holmes pastiches:
The Adventure of the Marked Man and One Other

Nipped in the Bud

A Hildegarde Withers Mystery by

Stuart Palmer

The Rue Morgue Press
Lyons / Boulder

ISBN: 1-60187-001-9
978-1-60187-001-8

Rue Morgue Press
87 Lone Tree Lane
Lyons CO 80540

Printed by Johnson Printing
Boulder, Colorado

PRINTED IN THE UNITED STATES OF AMERICA

To NED GUYMON,
With affectionate appreciation.

About Stuart Palmer

Stuart Palmer (1905-1968) referred to Hildegarde Withers as that "meddlesome old battleaxe" but he was as fond of her as were the readers and moviegoers of the 1930s. She debuted in 1931 in *The Penguin Pool Murder* where she met Inspector Oscar Piper of the New York Homicide Squad. Set in 1929 shortly after the collapse of the stock market, *The Penguin Pool Murder* was filmed a year later with Edna May Oliver as Miss Withers and James Gleason as Oscar Piper. The lighthearted movie became one RKO's biggest hits of the year. Oliver was perfect in the role, perhaps because Palmer was inspired to create Miss Withers after seeing Oliver on stage during the first run of Jerome Kern's *Showboat*, although he also used other people from his past to round off her character, including a librarian from his home town of Baraboo, Wisconsin, who disapproved of his literary tastes, and a "horse-faced English teacher" from his high school days. He credited his father as the inspiration for Miss Withers' Yankee sense of humor.

Miss Withers appeared in eight novels between 1931 and 1941 and then went on sabbatical for six years while her creator labored in Hollywood where he eventually wrote 37 scripts, including several in the Falcon and Bulldog Drummond series. In 1944 at nearly the age of 40 he enlisted in the army and was sent to Oklahoma where he produced training films on field artillery. In 1947, Palmer revisited Miss Withers in *Miss Withers Regrets* and went on to produce four more books in this series during the early 1950s. The last Withers novel, *Hildegarde Withers Makes the Scene*, was completed by Fletcher Flora after Palmer's death in 1968. Jennifer Venola, Palmer's fifth wife, whom he married when he was 60 and she just 21, called his death a "rational suicide" following a diagnosis of terminal laryngeal cancer. At his wish, his body was donated to the Loma Linda Medical School for study.

For more information on Stuart Palmer see Tom and Enid Schantz' introduction to The Rue Morgue Press edition of *The Puzzle of the Blue Banderilla*.

Nipped in the Bud

"From ghoulies and ghosties
And long-leggitted beasties
And things that go Boomp in the night
Oh Lord deliver us!"
            —*Old Scottish Book of Common Prayer*

1

The noises were ugly and a little unreal, like sound effects left over from a nightmare. Only Ina knew she hadn't been sleeping. She had been too highly charged with the wonder of it all to close an eye, because tomorrow—if it ever dawned—would be her first day in the city, the beginning of a new life all in glorious Technicolor.

She had been lying awake hour after hour, listening to the night symphony of Manhattan and from each chord weaving dreams in which a certain little girl with fire-blonde hair played the starring role. Every foghorn on the Hudson or the East River was from a luxury liner taking her to Capri or the Bahamas; every siren was clearing the way for a squad car full of personable young policemen coming to rescue her from some vague but deliciously shuddery doom; the planes that roared overhead to and from La Guardia were bearing her to Casablanca or Carcassonne. Even the rattle of the milkman's cart and the tinkle of his bottles lent themselves to the game, for Ina saw herself and a Gregory Peckish young man in white tie and tails sitting on the rear step of that homely vehicle, singing "Shall I Wasting?" and "Mavourneen" and the rest, and splitting a quart of homogenized Grade A as an antidote against hangovers. So had passed the night, the happiest of her life.

Left behind forever was Bourdon, Pennsylvania (1950 pop. 3,495) where nothing ever happened except the biweekly change of program at the Bijou. Ina had come to the greatest, noisiest, cruelest, dirtiest, most generous city on earth to seek her fortune, equipped with a reasonably nice face and figure and quite exceptional hair and skin, some sixty dollars in cash, and no training or experience of any sort; but still filled with the firm conviction that she was a very unusual girl destined for a wonderful and exciting future, starting now.

The hand of her watch had crawled past six, though there was still no sign of dawn at the east windows. She had been lying there in the strange bed in the borrowed one-room apartment, loving the night and loving the city as she never could again. At the moment all Manhattan, down to the last sooty snowflake, belonged to her by a sort of divine right. Above her the heavy future hung like a rain cloud over the desert, like ripe purple fruit ready to be plucked.

"Just let things happen to me!" Ina prayed to her own special deity. "Anything at all as long as it's different and exciting and soon!"

At the same time something warned her that if she intended making the proper impression on the men who interviewed models and showgirls and mannequins and perhaps (heaven forbid) even secretaries and receptionists, she really ought to be getting some sleep. Only maybe dark shadows around her eyes would be intriguing. Girls weren't supposed to look too innocent these days, even if they were. Oh, she thought, to be like the wise, dreamy minxes in the Marie Laurencin paintings she had seen reproduced in the art magazines back in the Bourdon Carnegie Free Library; those girls so faintly but definitely dissolute!

They looked as if they wouldn't be surprised at anything. They wouldn't have popped up in bed like a jack-in-the-box at hearing strange muffled noises in the night. The sounds must be coming, Ina decided suddenly, from the next apartment, where a late party had been going on until a couple of hours ago. She had eavesdropped shamelessly, straining her ears in an attempt to catch the words of the tantalizing songs they were singing, the point of the long involved jokes they told. All she had been sure of was that they sang, and laughed. Finally they had broken it up and gone home, with much slamming of doors and many loud farewells. But that party *couldn't* be reviving itself, not now.

Then she realized what she was hearing. It was almost too simple. Men were fighting there, on the other side of the wall—at a quarter past six of a winter morning!

Perhaps Ina was the only one in the entire apartment house to hear the battle, though it is fairly certain that any seasoned New Yorker, wakened in the night by noises up to and perhaps including the Last Trump, would only have turned over and gone back to sleep. Not Ina. Wild horses could not have kept her a moment longer in bed.

She smiled in the darkness, wondering just how wild horses could possibly keep anybody anywhere. Slipping out of the warm covers, a slim white naked virginal ghost, she found her old wool bathrobe. Then she pattered barefoot across the room, holding out her arms so she wouldn't stub a toe on the television set or on Crystal's little spinet piano, and finally made the hall door without mishap. With an ear pressed to the panel she could hear that the fight was still going on.

Dry smack of hard fists on soft flesh. ... Feet stamping like the hoofs of rutting stags. ... Wordless exclamations, smothered gaspings for breath.

Once a male voice blurted out a name coupled to a black obscenity. Whoever they were, they weren't fooling.

Ina was trembling now, and not with cold. But she softly turned the knob. Just as the latch clicked there was a muffled crash, louder than anything before, and then silence as thick as cold molasses.

With one eye against the tiny crack in the door she waited, filled with an unreasoning impatience. She shivered there for what seemed an hour, and was never able later to swear whether it was really only a few minutes, or ten, or thirty. But she never took her eyes from the door at the end of the hallway, and at long, long last it opened and a man came out.

He was a stocky, youngish man in rumpled dinner clothes—what Ina called a *tuck*—hatless, and carrying a dark overcoat. His face was paper-white, his dark hair plastered across his damp forehead, and his bow tie was loose. He looked utterly spent, breathing heavily through swollen lips, his eyes blank and unseeing. Indeed, he almost threw his exit into low comedy by stumbling over the milk bottles outside the door.

As he came forward Ina saw that his right fist was jammed into his coat pocket; his left held a gold lighter, its flame inches from the cigarette dangling from his mouth. He went past and on down the hall, walking like a zombie, limping a little. Like Lord Byron, Ina thought. His face was something like the engravings of Byron, too—handsome, arrogant, demon-haunted. It was only as he reached the elevator at the other end of the hall that he succeeded in setting fire to his cigarette, and then he absently tossed the lighter into an urn filled with sand, as if the golden toy had been only a burnt match. Then the door of the automatic elevator slammed shut behind him. Curtain.

Excited and disappointed at the same time, Ina closed the door. But this couldn't be all. Maybe he would come back. Maybe ...

Pausing before the bathroom mirror, she decided that the tiny red spot on her nose wasn't going to be a pimple after all. And a good thing the fascinating young man hadn't turned and seen her peeking around the door, with her hair this way. She came back into the room again, surprised to find that she was listening so hard that her ears ached, listening for something she'd heard ... or almost heard. Were there sounds outside, sounds anywhere? Even the city seemed suddenly muted.

And especially was everything quiet in the next apartment. The other man in the fight should have been up and around, ministering to his cuts and bruises, pouring a comforting drink or straightening up the wreckage.

Then she suddenly remembered. The man she had seen leaving *hadn't* shut the door behind him, or she would have heard the click. It must be—it was!—ajar. Ina started impulsively out into the hall just as she was, and then almost too late remembered to stop and release the lock so that she wouldn't be trapped out in the open with no retreat. A few steps and she was just outside that other door. No light showed inside. "Hello?" Ina said softly.

There was the ghost of a sound somewhere inside. It could have been a groan or a snore, the rustle of a Venetian blind in the morning breeze or an inner door softly closing. She touched the panel, which swung easily inward, and a fan of yellow light from behind her began to widen across a formal foyer, across a scuffed and rumpled rug. She saw the slipper first, and then a man's leg.

"Excuse me, but is anything wrong?" Ina waited a moment and then pushed the door hard, and then the hall light blazed in on the body of a man wearing cerise pajama pants. The upturned face was not recognizable, even though she had seen it a hundred times in her own stepfather's living room back home. Blood and bruises had altered it, smeared it inhumanly.

Ina didn't move. She knew she had to do something, but what? She was missing her cue. Here she was forced into the role of heroine, standing before the footlights in front of a waiting, if yet invisible audience, not knowing what the tragedy was about or what lines she ought to be improvising. She was caught like a fly in amber, stiff with stage fright, unable to take her eyes from the thing smashed against the wall. It was a bloody atrocity, crying mutely to have its limbs decently composed, to be covered up. ...

Any minute now there would be policemen swarming all over; the cold white light of publicity would expose her. In this bathrobe, and her hair ...

Ina sighed. As she slowly went forward to bend over the crumpled man in the corner she had a clear preview of herself on the witness stand, wearing a demure black suit and her sheerest nylons. The prosecutor was roaring, "Miss Kell, you have testified that you knew the man was dead! How did you *know* that?"

"Because I forced myself to touch him—this artery right here on the throat—and there was no sign of a pulse!"

There was a little ripple of applause from the spectators in the courtroom, among whom were talent scouts from MGM, Fox, and NBC-TV.

"Why should I strive to set the crooked straight?"
—WILLIAM MORRIS

2

It had been a deceptively quiet afternoon, as afternoons at Centre Street go. Only ten minutes more and Inspector Oscar Piper would have closed up his office and taken off for greener pastures. Then to his unbelieving ears there came the sound of scrabbling paws in the outer room, and through his doorway there descended an avalanche of dog.

"Judas priest almighty! Get down, you damn silly beast!" But the inspector, even as he fended off the big poodle's attempts to lick his face, was flattered at being remembered after all these months. As might have been expected, the dog's mistress was not far behind—a weather-beaten spinster armed with a black umbrella, who had the general appearance of having dressed hastily in an upper berth.

"Oscar!" she cried. "As I live and breathe!"

Speaking of breathing, he thought, the poor old girl still wheezed a bit. And for all its sun tan, her face seemed thin and tired. "Well, Hildegarde," he said heartily. "So California's finally lost its charms, eh? About time."

"Not at all," Miss Withers told him, as she settled into a chair like a nesting Buff-Orpington. "California is a good place to vegetate. The climate is mild, and my asthma is much improved. Probably it was only caused in the first place by an allergy to those awful stogies you chain-smoke from dawn until midnight."

"This happens to be a clear-Havana *puro-puro* out of the box you sent me for Christmas," the inspector protested mildly. But he put it out. "Anyway, it's good to have you back. I'll confess that in a way I've sort of missed—"

"Why, Oscar!" she bridled.

"—missed that hat," he concluded wickedly.

"But I'll have you know it's a brand-new one, from Bullock's-Westwood!"

"No! I'd have sworn you borrowed it from the Smithsonian. It looks like all the others you used to wear, only more so." He grinned. "Okay, okay. Why didn't you let me know you were coming? I'd have met you."

"More probably you'd have mislaid my wire and left me stood up in Grand Central. But thanks anyway for the gallant thought." She surveyed him critically. "You need a haircut, Oscar. And you look a bit peaked. Overworking?"

"Nothing special. The homicide index is up a few points, as it usually is when temperature and humidity get in the eighties. But most of the stuff is routine, and can be taken care of at precinct level. Today's been dull—I was just about to shut up shop." The inspector stole a quick glance at his watch.

"But I am keeping you from an appointment or something?" Then Miss Withers snapped her fingers. "Of course, I'd forgotten. This is Thursday, and you're planning an evening of bowling and a few hands of stuss with your raffish cronies; now, don't try to deny it."

"The Third Avenue Schooner and Pastrami Club," he told her, "has a rather distinguished membership—aldermen, attorneys, doctors and civic leaders."

"I can imagine. But you just run along and be distinguished, then. Don't mind me. I'll be here a week or more, and there'll be other times for us to meet."

"Yes, but I can just as well—" Suddenly Piper's jaw dropped, and he did a broad doubletake. "A *week* or more? You're not actually going back out West?"

She nodded. "I just returned to close up my apartment and sell my furniture, all but the walnut table and some books and things I'm having shipped."

"But—" he said incredulously. "But—but—"

"Stop making noises like an outboard motor, Oscar, and listen. As Emerson once said, 'It is time to be old, to take in sail.' "

"Why can't you furl your sails right here in civilization?"

Miss Withers sniffed eloquently. "Like most New Yorkers, Oscar, you make the mistake of thinking that everything west of the Hudson is a howling wilderness."

"That description," he told her firmly, "fits Los Angeles like a glove! And you could never be happy away from the bright lights of the big town."

"No, Oscar, New York is for the young. It's for people who are still fighting. It's a beehive, with no place for a retired old drone like me."

With admirable restraint the inspector refrained from telling her some of the facts of life about drones and beehives. For many years his secret fondness for this courageous, preposterous old biddy had grown and deepened, and it cut him to the quick to hear this new note of defeat in her voice. Of course, retirement often did that to people. He fiddled absently with some reports on his desk and then said very casually, "By the way, there's a couple of interesting new cases in the open file."

" 'Two blockheads to kill and be killed,' " quoted Miss Withers. "Murders aren't what they used to be, and neither is anything else. Come, Talley." She caught the end of the leash and dragged the big apricot-colored poodle away from the office wastebasket, where he had been foraging for scraps of the inspectorial lunch. Then, almost in the doorway, she paused. "By the way, Oscar, do you know what tomorrow is?"

"Friday," he said blankly. "All day."

"Friday, *and* the sixteenth of August." She waited expectantly.

"Let me see. Can't be your birthday, because you stopped having those years ago. Say, is it the anniversary of the day we *didn't* get married?"

"It is not. I jilted you in the autumn, as you well remember. Tomorrow happens to be the day set for the opening of a certain murder trial, I believe in the Court of General Sessions. Can you fix me up with a ticket of admission?"

"Trial? What trial?"

"A young man named Winston H. Gault, for the murder of Tony Fagan, so-called radio and television comic. Your memory, Oscar ..."

"Sure, sure! Junior Gault, the radio sponsor who got tired of being ribbed on his own program and did something about it with a blunt instrument." Piper sat up straight. "How come you're so interested?"

"It's a very *mild* interest, Oscar. You wrote me about the case at the time, and even sent me some laudatory press clippings. I gathered you handled the investigation personally, and that it was one of your major triumphs?"

The inspector nodded, almost complacently. "I knew from the first moment that Gault was guilty. His alibi didn't stand up for ten minutes, and almost as soon as we arrested him he made a confession. No rubber-hose stuff either, so don't go getting any ideas."

"Relax, Oscar. I have no intention of trying to upset any applecarts; my days of sleuthing are over. And if it's too much trouble getting me admitted to the courtroom, no matter. I can while away my lonely hours here in town by going up to the American Museum of Natural History and studying their sea shells. Since I've been out in California I've become something of an amateur conchologist, you know." She reached into her handbag and produced visual evidence. "Here is a Hairy Triton I found at Malibu, unusually well-marked. This is a Ravenal's Scallop, and the spotted one is a Junonia."

"Snail shells, yet!" muttered Oscar Piper, with ill-concealed distaste. Something had to be done for poor old Hildegarde, and soon. If he could only keep aflame this one feeble flicker of interest in her old-time pursuits. … He reached for the telephone and dialed a number. "John Hardesty, please. Piper, Headquarters. Hello, who's this? … What? You people keep banker's hours, don't you? Where's John, out getting warmed up for the big court job tomorrow? … What?" He listened for a moment, said "Judas!" and hung up. "No dice, Hildegarde."

"Oh, dear. No seats left?"

"No trial. That was one of the other assistant D.A.'s. He says that Hardesty is going to get up in court tomorrow and ask for a postponement."

"But why?"

"The fellow either didn't know or couldn't tell me over the phone."

"Oscar, is it true that Sam Bordin is the defense attorney?"

Piper nodded. "With all the Gault dough, Junior would only hire the best. Further proof that he's guilty, as if we needed any. Innocent men don't retain Bordin, a legal magician who's a combination of Darrow and Steuer …"

"With a dash of John J. Malone, who never lost a client either?"

"You've heard of him, then. Yeah." Piper sighed. "The trial can be set back on the docket for thirty or maybe sixty days, but Bordin will be hoping to get a nol-pros. Somebody's slipped up somewhere." He shook his head, scowling.

"Well, Oscar," said Miss Withers, shrugging, "let me know sometime how it all comes out." She edged toward the door again. "And do give me a ring when you're not so tied up. I'll be at the Barbizon."

"Sure, sure," said Oscar Piper. "Just for my own satisfaction I'd like to get the lowdown on this new development. Hardesty will probably be dropping in at the club tonight as usual, and I'll twist his arm."

But Miss Withers and the poodle were gone. The inspector gnawed on his cold cigar for a moment, then cleared his desk by shoving all the official papers helter-skelter into a top drawer. In three minutes he was on an uptown subway.

"Botheration!" remarked Miss Hildegarde Withers somewhat later that evening. She had just lowered her angular frame into a steaming tub, and of course there was no surer way on earth to make a telephone ring. Swathed in an insufficient towel, she made her moist and dripping way out into the little hotel bedroom, stepped over Talleyrand, picked up the offending instrument and said wearily, "Yes, Oscar?"

"How'd you know it was me?" was the blank response.

"*I*," she corrected absently. "Perhaps it was ESP and perhaps it was just that you're the only person in town who knows where I'm staying."

"Okay, okay." His voice was jumping. "Had dinner yet?"

"Why, I was just going to order up a tray ..."

"Don't. Hell's a-popping. How about meeting me and John Hardesty somewhere for a bowl of soup?"

"But, Oscar, I'm tired from the trip, and ..."

"This is right up your alley, and we really need your help. That poor girl ... But I can't tell you any more over the phone."

Curiosity had always been her besetting sin, and Miss Withers hesitated only a maidenly moment before she said, "Very well. But after months of Los Angeles cooking you're very much mistaken if you think I'll settle for anything less than duckling *bigarade* at La Parisienne or perhaps sauerbraten at the Blue Ribbon."

"Anything!" conceded the inspector. "A car will pick you up in ten minutes."

So it was that theater-bound Manhattanites that evening were amused by the spectacle of a large and whimsically-plucked French poodle, with a bit of green hair ribbon in his topknot, sitting regally enthroned beside the uniformed driver of a police limousine illegally parked half a block off Times Square. Talleyrand was not in the least bored with the long wait. He listened with interest to the radio as it droned forth interminable lists of the license numbers of stolen cars; he shared with polite enthusiasm the lunch of the embarrassed policeman beside him; hamburgers, onion, pickle and all. Talley was a dog who took things as they came, especially food.

Inside the pleasant old *Bierstube* the dog's mistress had been slowly paying less and less attention to her excellent sweet-and-sour pot roast while she listened to the official tale of woe. "You see, Hildegarde," the inspector was saying earnestly, "it's a matter of my personal pride. They're always saying around town that a rich man can get away with anything, even murder. If Gault goes free the wise-guys will nod and wink and whisper that the fix was on. He's simply got to be tried and found guilty and take his punishment, or the law and the department and my whole career are just so much dust and ashes. Isn't that so, John?" His voice trembling faintly, Oscar Piper busied himself with his bratwurst.

"That's—that's right," John Hardesty agreed, swallowing. He had turned out to be a tall, snub-nosed man in his thirties with unruly hair and large hands, who looked somewhat like a prosperous farmer. "Now, none of what I'm going to tell you must go any farther," was his cautious beginning.

Miss Withers tossed her head indignantly. "The inspector here will bear witness that when necessary I can be twice as silent as the grave."

Oscar Piper choked suddenly on a bit of sausage, but Hardesty was already outlining the highlights in the Fagan murder, on the surface at least a black-and-white, open-and-shut case if there ever was one. It seemed that at eight-thirty on the evening of December 17 last, Tony Fagan had started his eleventh weekly video program for Gault Foods. While on the air he had said certain unkind things about his sponsors under the thin guise of humor, the barbs particularly aimed at Winston H. Gault, Jr.

The same evening a little after midnight, Fagan had run into Gault sitting alone at a table in a well-known night club, and had gone over to apologize. Gault had refused to accept the apology and had said something indicating an intention to assault Fagan, but as the younger man was rising from his chair and off-balance, the comedian had swung first and lucky-punched him colder than Kelsey.

Fagan had then left for his apartment at the Graymar, on East Fifty-fifth, where he was later joined by some friends and business associates, including his divorced wife Ruth, the party breaking up around four. A little after six in the morning Gault had shown up and, when Fagan made the mistake of answering his door, had given him a severe beating and then smashed his skull with something heavy—possibly a blackjack. Or it might have been a vase or a piece of bric-a-brac from the apartment, which was as crowded as a museum. With Fagan dead, there was no way to check whether or not anything was missing.

"No fingerprints," put in Piper. "But everybody knows about them nowadays. And Gault had plenty of time to clean up his traces afterwards."

Hardesty nodded, and went on to say that Junior had then walked home to his bachelor apartment on Park and had given the night elevator man fifty dollars to say—if anyone asked—that he'd come home about two. When arrested next morning just before noon he had said, "Then I really did go kill the bastard—I thought it was only a bad dream. Well, he had it coming…" or words to that effect.

"If you can prove all that—" Miss Withers nodded thoughtfully—"I don't see what the prosecution has to worry about. Why postpone the trial?"

"When you go up against a smooth defense lawyer like Sam Bordin," the assistant D.A. explained patiently, "you've got to have something more than just motive and circumstantial evidence. You need witnesses." He rubbed his high forehead, imparting still more disorder to his hair. "There were three important witnesses against Gault, like the three legs of a milking stool. Our case rested on them. First was Ernest Pugh, the waiter at the Stork Club who saw the one-punch battle—"

"But Pugh happens to be a lieutenant commander in the Naval Reserve, and got called back to active duty six weeks ago," the inspector put in. "Now he's on the U.S. *Boxer*, somewhere in the Pacific."

"Second leg," Hardesty went on, "was the taxi driver, Maxfield Berg, who picked Gault up outside an after-hours bottle club on Second Avenue around six that morning and drove him to Fagan's apartment house. Berg swore that his passenger was crazy drunk; that the young man told him to wait, he'd just got to run upstairs a minute and beat somebody's brains out. Hearsay evidence, but valuable since it shows intent, and thus is properly part of the *res gestae* ..."

"Only it was discovered that Berg had spent time in a mental hospital a few years back," Piper said. "You can't put a former schizophrenic on the witness stand; Sam Bordin would tear his testimony to shreds."

The schoolteacher looked puzzled. "But if you have their sworn statements ...?"

The two men exchanged a knowing fraternal smile. "Of course," Hardesty went on wearily, "depositions, and also any testimony given at the hearing or before the grand jury, are admissible. But they don't carry much weight even when they are read into the record. Juries always have a feeling that if the prosecution has witnesses they should be right there in court, so that the defense can cross-examine."

"I see." The schoolteacher nodded, frowning. "But what about the third witness? Perhaps a milking stool should have three legs, but from my girlhood days out in the Middle West I seem to remember some stools with only one."

"Sure," said Hardesty bitterly. "The third and most important witness of all was one Ina Kell, a little country cousin camping out in the next apartment who heard the fight, peeked out into the hall and saw Gault sneaking away after the murder, and then who went on in and discovered the body. Only ..."

"Only what?" demanded Miss Withers. "You don't mean that something's happened to her? She's not—?"

"Disappeared," Hardesty said flatly. "Like a soap bubble. Now you see it shining and floating, and then—pouf!"

"Well!" said the schoolteacher, in a tone that Oscar Piper had not heard her use in a long time. "A fine kettle of fish! So a brutal, ruthless killer is going to get away with it because you men hadn't sense enough to keep an eye on an important witness. Why, she may even be dead!"

"I thought of that," nodded the inspector solemnly, avoiding Hardesty's eye.

"More details," demanded Miss Withers after a moment's deep thought. "And more coffee."

"... There ariseth a little cloud out of the sea, like a man's hand ..."
—I Kings

3

"I knew you'd be interested," the inspector was saying. He took the perfecto out of his mouth and smiled wryly. "I was telling John here earlier about the Bascom case and how you set out to solve the disappearance of three thousand women all at once."

"And ended up by disappearing myself?" Miss Withers sniffed modestly. "But never mind the good old days just at the moment. Do go on. If you want me to try to help find Miss Ina Kell, I'll have to know more about her than just the fact she reported finding Fagan's dead body."

"That's just the point," Hardesty put in. "She *didn't*."

"But you said—"

"Inspector, you take it from here, will you?" The lawyer gestured. "After all, you were on the scene and everything."

"Okay," said Oscar Piper. "It was the boy on that paper route on Fifty-fifth who phoned in and reported that he had just discovered a dead body while in the act of leaving the usual copy of the *Herald Tribune* outside the door of Fagan's apartment. The door had been left open, so naturally he peeked in. Our radio car got there in a few minutes, the precinct men soon after, but I was called over on account of the victim being a sort of public character. The body was a mess of blood and brains, but I learned that it had been found partly covered by a Persian rug. Right away I concluded that somebody else must have found it *before* the paper boy—presumably a woman."

"Mercy," said Miss Withers. "I've seen several corpses in my time, but I never had the slightest impulse to throw rugs over them."

"A certain type of woman," the inspector explained, "always wants to cover up horrible things, to get them out of sight. Of course, when the rest of Fagan's apartment was searched and Ruth Fagan, the ex-wife, was found asleep in a back bedroom, we figured it was her. Only she claimed that she had just had too much to drink at the party, had wandered off alone and fallen into a deep sleep."

"A likely story!" Miss Withers decided.

"But it stood up. We found that Ruth Fagan had never wanted to go to Reno in the first place. She still loved her husband and hoped to get him back someday; carried his picture around in her handbag and saw all his video programs. Besides, she got nice fat alimony that of course would cease at his death. She must have been under considerable strain that night, to be suddenly called up and asked to come over and then find that all he wanted was for her to help celebrate a sort of wake over the corpse of his television career. Because after that broadcast, and then popping the sponsor on the jaw, it was a cinch that Tony Fagan would be blacklisted on the air waves. He knew by then that he was through, and of course he wanted to cry on her shoulder. And she came running. "

"The more fool she. She should have spat in his eye!"

Piper shrugged. "Anyway, it seems that Ruth wasn't used to drinking—she's the pleasant, housewifely type—and she had little or nothing in common with the entertainers and radio and television people who were there. She'd never fitted in with that crowd, which was one reason for the divorce. So in self-defense she drank more than she could handle, and instead of getting gay she got sleepy. It actually took the boys ten minutes to wake her after they discovered her in bed, and they're pretty good at spotting fakes. Besides, there was enough concentration of alcohol in her blood when we tested it that morning to indicate that she was absolutely blotto."

"But, Oscar, mightn't she have knocked herself out with liquor *after* she found and covered the body, or for that matter even after she did away with ..."

"Stop leaping at conclusions, Hildegarde! She had no motive. Anyway, by that time we'd found small, presumably feminine fingerprints on the outside of the door of Fagan's apartment, which the murderer had evidently left ajar. The prints weren't Ruth Fagan's, they didn't belong to any of the people who had been guests at the party earlier. It was apparent that somebody else in the building, somebody who wasn't dead to the world like poor Ruth, must have heard the fight and come over to see what was wrong. But who?" Piper sighed. "Because the apartment underneath was vacant, being redecorated. The people upstairs were in Florida for the winter. The only adjoining apartment belonged to a tap dancer named Crystal Joris, and the manager of the building told us that the girl had closed it up a week before and gone out to Hollywood to test for a role in a musical picture."

"Aha!" cried the schoolteacher. "I'm away ahead of you!"

"Wrong again," Piper told her. "We checked immediately with the Los Angeles police, and Crystal was out there all right, registered at the Beverly Wilshire."

"Then who—"

"I decided," said the inspector, "that the woman we were looking for must be very young and unsophisticated, probably fresh from the sticks, or else she wouldn't have gone barging out into the hall to see what was wrong. Anybody who'd lived in New York for any length of time would have minded their own business, or at most would have called SPring 7-3100 and reported a disturbance. So, anyway, on a hunch I phoned Miss Joris long distance, finally locating her on a test stage at Mr. Zanuck's studio. Sure enough, she admitted that she had lent the key of her New York apartment to her cousin when she stopped off for a day's visit at her home town out in Pennsylvania on her way west. So now we find out about Ina Kell, a kid who wanted to try her luck in the big city."

"And you mean to say that all during the hullabaloo the Kell girl had been playing possum in the next apartment, unbeknownst to your detectives?"

"She had not. Ina was playing a different game. It turned out that she'd arrived in town on a bus the previous evening, and come to the apartment after the manager had left the lobby. Little Ina went in and upstairs, using her borrowed key, unseen by anyone. But sometime next morning she made up the bed, removed all traces of her ever being there, took her bag and sneaked out. It must have been while the boys were busy inside the Fagan apartment and before anybody had time to post an extra man on the front door of the building."

"But why would the child decamp like that? It seems out of character—"

"Wait. We had the girl's description from Miss Joris, and a cute little redhead wandering around the city that early in the morning is as easy to trace as a circus parade. We found the coffee shop where she had breakfast, and the counterman remembered she'd been carrying a suitcase and studying the want ads while she ate. So we checked the *Rooms for Rent* columns and that same day we picked her up, a wispy, eager, scared little girl from Bourdon, Pennsylvania, with hayseed in her hair. ..."

"And with stars in her eyes," said John Hardesty dreamily, and blushed at the look the schoolteacher gave him.

"Anyway," continued Oscar Piper, "little Ina turned out to be deeper than she looked. At first she got into a panic and denied everything, even her own name. You can't be rough with a girl like that; it took the whole bag of tricks before I could get her to let down her hair and admit that she'd spent the night in the Joris apartment. I had to threaten to turn her over my knee and spank her before she confessed that she'd been awake and heard the fight, and had got up and gone out into the hall to see what was going on. The murderer had left the door ajar, and she peeked in and found the body. Then, according to her, she covered it up with a rug because 'it looked so lonely and terrible and messy!' "

"Poor child! And then she tried to run away because she was afraid of being accused of the murder?"

"Wait a minute," cut in Hardesty. "You must understand that Ina was as green as—as chlorophyll. All she knew of life was what she'd got from romantic movies and soap operas and sensational fiction. She wanted to play it heroic. Nobody could get her to admit that she'd seen Junior Gault actually leave the scene of the murder until she knew he'd already been arrested and had confessed—even though we found his gold cigarette lighter in her handbag, that he'd dropped on the scene and she'd picked up as a sort of souvenir, I guess."

"She should have been spanked," Miss Withers observed firmly.

"Ina claimed," continued the assistant D.A., "and I for one believe her, that after covering the body she went rushing back into the Joris apartment to phone the authorities. But Crystal had had the phone disconnected before she left, and Ina either didn't know it or had forgotten it. She kept trying to get the operator and of course she couldn't. Probably the only phone she had ever seen was one on the kitchen wall, with a crank. Meanwhile outside in the hall the paper boy had looked in the half-open door and rediscovered the body, or at least the feet that were sticking out from under the rug. He sounded the alarm, and then suddenly the place was swarming with cops. She realized she had missed the boat, and ..."

"Ah!" objected the schoolteacher. "But even if the paper boy arrived just as Ina popped back into her own apartment, it still must have taken him some time to sound the alarm, and five or ten minutes more before the police could get there. A rather long time to sit and jiggle the phone, don't you think?"

"Not for her," Hardesty said. "Don't forget she'd probably never seen a dial phone; probably she was expecting the operator to say, 'Number, please.' Anyway, when she heard the police arrive she realized that matters were out of her hands. She thought she might get into trouble for not being the one to report the body, so her only thought was to run and hide."

"A funny kid," Piper agreed. "After we picked her up she claimed that twice that morning after she had thought it over she started to call Headquarters and confess, and each time she hung up because she got cold feet. There's evidence that she did try to make a couple of phone calls in the restaurant. But down at my office she finally identified Junior Gault's photograph out of a dozen others as the man she'd seen leaving Fagan's apartment after the fracas."

"So, you see, Ina Kell is really the key witness for the prosecution," John Hardesty pointed out. "She's the one person who can actually put Gault at the scene of the murder at the right time. We didn't dare take chances with her, for fear of showing our hand. We got a signed statement, but she wasn't allowed to testify at the preliminary hearing or before the grand jury; we kept her under wraps and strictly away from the press and everybody. I got her a place to live at a nice respectable rooming house out in Brooklyn Heights; I even got her a job as a file clerk down at the Hall of Records."

"And," suggested Miss Withers hopefully, "you took her out now and then?"

Hardesty stiffened. "Oh, no. I knew then that I would probably handle the prosecution when the Gault case came to trial. It would be unethical for me to have any personal contact with a witness. Until after the trial, of course." He sighed. "Maybe I should have held her in custody as a material witness, or required her to put up a bond. But if you'd seen Ina Kell you'd realize why nothing of the kind was ever thought of. She was—different."

"I am," observed the schoolteacher, "growing more intrigued with little Ina every moment. For a simple, unsophisticated little girl from the country she seems to have done a pretty good job of winding you men around her pinky. And to top it all, she had suddenly disappeared? How and when and why?"

"She was fine and dandy," said Hardesty, "when I last phoned her a couple of weeks ago. Just to check up, you understand, nothing personal."

"Of course not!" Miss Withers beamed.

"Our operatives were keeping an eye on her, too, though we didn't have men enough to spare so we could have her shadowed twenty-four hours a day. It wasn't as if her story had got into the papers—nobody knew about her at all. And then last Monday when we tried to serve a subpoena on her, we found her gone."

"Gone? Gone where?"

"Just gone. Quit her job and moved out of her room, the preceding Saturday. Told her landlady she'd write and give her the forwarding address, but she hasn't. So if you can help us on this thing in any way…" Hardesty smiled brightly. "Of course, there mustn't be any fanfare. I don't mind so much having it known that I let an important witness slip through my fingers, but we're still hoping to bring her back and spring her as a surprise on the defense when the case comes up again."

"I see," said Miss Withers slowly. "I suppose you yourself talked to her landlady and the other roomers? Was her room searched?"

Piper nodded. "Nothing."

"Her friends?"

"She seems to have been a shy little thing; kept pretty much to herself. No dates. When she wasn't at the office she was either at a movie or window-shopping along Fifth and Madison or with her nose buried in a library book."

"Probably scared stiff, and after what happened on her first day in the city I hardly blame her. I see I shall have to start from scratch. But three heads are better than one, and you gentlemen had the advantage of meeting the young lady. Mr. Hardesty, yours is the first guess. Where would you say little Ina has gone?"

The assistant D.A. paused to light a cigarette, his big hands surprisingly dexterous. "I think she's in hiding," he said. "Probably not far away. Ina has a powerful imagination, and I think she brooded over the impending trial until she just couldn't stand it. She may have had a sort of long-distance crush on Junior Gault—many nice girls are fascinated by scoundrels—and she couldn't face swearing his life away on the witness stand. Since she wouldn't lie, and anyway could hardly retract her own sworn statement, I think she just decided to drop out of sight until after the trial."

"The girl would have to have a heart soft as butter, to say nothing of her head. But, very well. Oscar, what is your hypothesis?"

"I hate to say it," pronounced the inspector, "but it's possible she was bought off. The girl was dying to get into the big time, and maybe being a file clerk in New York wasn't much improvement over the home town. Somebody got to her—there could have been a leak somewhere in the D.A.'s office or mine. Junior Gault, or his family, or his attorney, could have learned how important Ina's testimony would be to the prosecution. A few thousand bucks and a plane ticket dangled in front of Miss Ina Kell..." Piper grinned. "Maybe those stars our young friend here saw in her eyes were only star sapphires!"

"You'll eat those words," Hardesty said quickly, "when we find her."

"If we find her," put in Miss Withers. "Of course, we are all aware that there are still other possibilities. Ina might have been frightened away, or kidnaped, or even worse."

"Relax, Hildegarde," advised Piper. "She hasn't been murdered. The only person with the faintest motive is still safe behind bars."

"Relax, yourself," she countered snappishly. "And, speaking of motives, I am still far from convinced that Junior Gault really had sufficient reason to kill Fagan. Just because of a poke in the jaw, and some snide remarks on the air. ..."

"Well, now!" The inspector nodded genially at Hardesty. "Listen at her! And only a couple of hours ago in my office she was swearing that this time she had no intention of upsetting any applecarts. John, don't you agree with me that this is the time for us to fix it up so Miss Withers here has a look at exhibit A?"

The assistant D.A. shrugged, but Miss Withers sat up straight. "If you're thinking of showing me a lot of gruesome photographs of a dead body ..."

"Not at all, Hildegarde. You're going to have a look at the motive, and then you can decide for yourself if it's sufficient or not. Know anything about television?"

She looked blank. "From what I've seen it's mostly wrestlers and puppet shows and old Hopalong Autry movies seen through a blinding snowstorm."

"Forget the good old days of the family stereoscope, will you? Time marches on." The inspector winked at Hardesty and rose from the table. "Come, Hildegarde. ... Just a minute while I make a phone call, and we'll be on our way."

"Hmm," Miss Withers said. "Oscar, I think you're up to something. But I'm just curious enough to trail along."

"You'll get curiouser and curiouser," he promised, with a too-innocent smile.

"What will you do to yourself, who have added insult to injury?"
—P<small>HAEDRUS</small>

4

The police limousine was turning east toward Madison, though, as Miss Withers pointed out, the Barbizon was straight uptown. "Who said I was taking you home?" the inspector countered. "This is New York, and the night is young."

"But I'm not. And it's getting on toward my bedtime."

"Nonsense. Tomorrow may be too late. You want to help us find the Kell girl, don't you? Hardesty wants her found pretty bad, and not only because she's an important witness. I think he's a little sweet on her, don't you? Not that I blame him. She had a pixie face and hair the color of a Wyoming sunset, and there were times—"

"Times when you found yourself wishing you were thirty years younger and had all your own teeth and hair? Well, Oscar, you aren't and you haven't. Face facts."

"Okay, *you* face some! I found out over the phone that young Wingfield is still over at WKC-TV. He's one of the bright young men of television, and if he isn't too tied up I'll get him to show you a film which is now something of a collector's item. When you see it you'll realize why."

They pulled up outside that vast cathedral on lower Madison Avenue which is consecrated to the dream-makers, to a nation's collective, commercialized escape from reality. Piper, Miss Withers and Talley the poodle were all whisked up to the twelfth floor, and as they approached the information desk the brittle blonde on duty took one look at the schoolteacher and said, "Sorry, no casting tonight." Miss Withers started an indignant sniff and then warmed at the implied compliment, having always felt that she had latent Thespian talents.

"Dogs," the receptionist continued, "are auditioned only at ten Monday mornings. He talks, of course?"

The schoolteacher recovered quickly. "Yes—and sings baritone." Then she flounced off after the inspector, who across the room had just caught sight of a thinnish young man in well-cut but rumpled flannels, coming through a doorway. Piper slipped quietly up behind him and put a heavy hand on his shoulder. "This is it, Wingfield. Will you come quietly or do I use the handcuffs?"

The young man jumped as if somebody had given him a hotfoot. "Yipe!" he cried, and then managed a feeble sort of grin. "Please, Inspector. My *nerves!*"

Oscar was getting corny, Miss Withers felt. The feeble joke had made poor Mr. Wingfield turn quite green for a moment. He was obviously relieved when they were introduced and he learned the reason for the visit. "Why, certainly," he said in a rather threadbare Harvard accent, "I'll dig up a print of that thing somewhere and get you set in a projection room right away; no trouble at all."

Piper said they could count him out, as he'd seen the film several times, and besides he had to get back down to the office and start some wheels turning at Missing Persons. "See you later, Hildegarde. And thanks, Wingfield—I'll fix your next two parking tickets." He waved cheerily and was gone.

Miss Withers found herself being ushered down a wide corridor filled with scurrying people, vaguely suggestive of a disturbed anthill. She was a little worried as to Talley's welcome, but, as Art Wingfield pointed out, in a television studio she could have been walking a saber-toothed tiger on a leash and nobody would have given a second look. She and the poodle were soon deposited in a small, slanting room where a dozen or so big leather chairs faced a screen, and left briefly alone. Then their guide and mentor was back, with a flat, round tin can about the size of a pie plate. "You want to see the whole thing, ma'am, or just the last reel with all the fireworks?"

"All or nothing. But first could you tell me just what it's all about?"

"The background? Yes, yes, of course." Wingfield must have trained for his job, she thought, on Benzedrine and jumping beans. "You're about to see a kinescope, which is a TV program recorded on film. This particular broadcast, the last one Tony Fagan ever made, was a live show—but there was a studio audience and also a recording on film, to be used later on the West Coast." He mopped his forehead. "Sit tight, Miss Withers. There never was a program like this before, and God grant there never will be another." Wingfield shuddered, and then signaled the projectionist.

The room darkened, the screen lightened, and then after a few identifying credits and numbers had flashed past they were suddenly looking at a big, balding man who sat sprawled elaborately at ease with his feet on a desk littered with papers, props, and even a bottle of milk. If this was Tony Fagan, Miss Withers decided, he had a most unusual face, vaguely suggesting a personable gargoyle, with the peaked eyebrows and the wide slit of a mouth. "He's smiling, but he's nervous as a cat on hot bricks," the schoolteacher murmured.

"*Was,*" corrected Wingfield. "Tony Fagan's been in a box for eight months, remember. I went to his funeral, and he drew twice the house he ever had at any other personal appearance."

"The Gault Foods Show!" came the offensively booming voice of an invisible announcer, and then a fanfare of distant trumpets. Fagan looked up, nodded, and slid his feet off the desk. Then he picked up a small package with the firm's name prominently displayed. He ostentatiously dropped the box and blew on his fingers with elaborate pantomime. "*Cold!*" he confided, shivering.

Over applause from the studio audience, Fagan said easily, "All right, as if you good people out there didn't know, this is old Mother Fagan's little boy Tony back again, brought to you tonight through the courtesy of Gault Zero Foods, which are the very best frozen foods, it says here in the script. ..."

"He'd learned about an hour before this broadcast that the Gault people had decided not to renew his contract," Wingfield explained.

The man on the screen was smiling his wide thin-lipped smile, chatting about one thing and another, smoking a dollar cigar and tossing off quips about current events—current last December. Now and then, as casually as if they had just dropped in for an impromptu audition, he introduced his guest talent—an Italian boy who worked himself into a lather squeezing opera from a mammoth piano accordion, and a little later three lush, dead-panned girls who wore sunbonnets and Gay Nineties bathing suits and harmonized "Silver Dollar." While they were giving their all, Fagan leaned back in his chair and nodded approvingly, now and then taking a swig from the bottle on his desk. "A milk addict, wasn't he?" observed Miss Withers.

Art Wingfield snorted. "Panther milk," he told her. "Nobody suspected it then, but Fagan had spiked the bottle with a pint of bourbon. Cute kid, Fagan."

The program rambled along in a breezy, informal sort of way, and it was hard for the schoolteacher to realize that for all its cheery glibness, its carefully calculated lightness, the Dark Angel was already beating his wings overhead. Now an earnest, ferret-faced little man who whistled duets with a bedraggled canary had his crowded moment and withdrew in confusion, with Fagan holding his nose and crying for "the hook."

"That was poor Joe Fernando," Wingfield explained. "Always trying the amateur shows, and always getting laughed off. Takes himself seriously, too." He lighted a cigarette from the end of the one half-burned in his mouth. "Anything went on Fagan's show—his stuff was out of Henry Morgan by Arthur Godfrey with a dash of the old Major Bowes routine, but it went over."

Next the three lovelies returned, dressed in wispy French bathing suits, to render a slightly purified version of that Dixie college classic, "Cold as a Fish in a Frozen Pool," after which the studio orchestra continued the theme with variations while the cameras swung to a brisk young woman miraculously preparing dinner for four out of different Gault Food packages, the only part of the program so far which Miss Withers enjoyed. Even Talley, who had been snoozing comfortably in his chair, perked up his ears and then subsided as his nose told him that the steak and pheasant and lobster and so on were only phantoms after all.

The first commercial over, they were back with Tony Fagan again as he told a couple of long and fairly funny stories about what happened to him on the way to the studio tonight. "Those papers on the desk in front of him were supposed to be a script," Wingfield explained. "But Fagan was his own producer and director, and he always ad-libbed most of his stuff anyway, switching it all around. Nobody ever knew what was coming next."

A big flashing-eyed brunette appeared, in a dress whose plunging neckline had turned into a high dive. While she rendered a comedy number, "I Come Here to Be Kissed With," in what she fondly imagined was a Pennsylvania Dutch accent, Fagan nodded encouragement and then toasted her in panther milk.

"Thallie Gordon," Wingfield said. "A regular on the show." Miss Withers thought the girl had a voice like a rusty hinge, and said as much. "Voice?" the young man came back. "Who cares about her voice?"

Miss Gordon obliged with "Careless Hands" as an encore, and the schoolteacher sighed. "By any chance does she do imitations, too?"

"You guessed it. In just a minute she does impressions of Dinah Shore and Merman and, of course, one of Hildegarde—"

Miss Withers sat up straight, and then realized that of course he meant the other one, the girl with the gloves and the handkerchief and the Milwaukee French accent. With the impressions finally over, the camera returned to Tony Fagan, who took a last hearty pull at the emptying milk bottle and said, "It is time for a brief word about our sponsors, bless their black, money-mad little hearts."

"He always panned his sponsors," Wingfield explained. "It was supposed to be all in fun, but he'd lost several good contracts that way before. This time he'd been out of work a good while, M.C.ing around the hinterland in supper clubs, and he'd sworn to be good. But just listen."

"... because Gault Zero Foods are really deep-freeze frozen, folks, cold as a well-digger's armpit, locking in all the nice fresh vitamins and calories. Why, I don't suppose there's anything in the world colder than Gault Foods unless it's the heart of their first vice-president in charge of paper clips and advertising, who happens to be Junior Gault himself. You must have heard of Junior, folks; you've probably all seen his picture in the funny papers—oops, I mean on the society page, standing next to his polo pony." From his desk Fagan produced and held up before the camera an enlarged photo of a smiling, almost too handsome young man dressed for the ancient sport of the maharajahs, white breeches, helmet and all, evidently in the act of changing mounts between chukkers.

"That's Junior there. No, *no*, not that one. That's the south end of a northbound horse. But there is a sort of family resemblance, isn't there?" There was a lot more of the same, with the comedian building Gault up as a sort of half-witted Lord Fauntleroy grown to man's estate and playing pint-sized dictator with the family business and bankroll to back his play. Fagan spoke of the nose bob Junior had had performed by a celebrated beauty surgeon, of his special shoes with built-up heels, of his wartime 4-F status, and of a showgirl named Bubbles something, to whom had been given a diamond bracelet and who had settled a breach of promise suit out of court. It was all sophomoric, but fast and barbed and really rather funny.

"Funny," Wingfield conceded, "if you didn't happen to be Junior Gault, who was paying for all this. An estimated six million sets that night were tuned in to this channel—it would have been ten million if the coaxial cable had been extended all the way to the Coast."

Fagan was still talking very fast, with a wild light in his eye. He had the bit in his teeth and evidently couldn't or wouldn't stop. He lowered his voice and confidentially let the audience in on the secret that Junior Gault was engaged to Miss Dallas Trempleau of the Social Register and Dun and Bradstreet Trempleaus, a very lovely girl who fancied herself as a singer, and as a singer she was certainly a very classy girl to *look* at. He delicately held his nose.

"She wasn't *that* bad," Wingfield put in. "Even appeared on this program once, for some Junior League charity or other. That was when Gault met her."

Behind her Miss Withers fancied she heard the door open and close again, and took her eyes from the screen long enough to notice that a young woman had come into the room and was blindly feeling her way along in the darkness toward the nearest chair. "Art?" came a throaty contralto. "You in here? They said—"

"Yes, darling, I'm busy—"

Which evidently gave the newcomer time to recognize what was on the screen. "Art, what are you running that old thing for, tonight of all nights? Do you know who was snooping around the studio just a few minutes ago?"

"Excuse me," murmured Wingfield, and bounced quickly out of his chair to seize the tall girl by the arm and lead her out into the hall again. But not before Miss Withers, whose eyes had become adjusted to the dimness, had seen who it was.

On the screen Tony Fagan, the smile frozen on his face, was asking the TV audience to send in twelve Gault Food box tops as a wedding present to Junior and Dallas, obviously improvising desperately. But even the sheeplike studio audience had stopped laughing now, and suddenly in the middle of a sentence the screen went blank. The room lights picked up and Art Wingfield came back in alone, looking more harried than ever. "Women," he said, thus disposing of the interruption. "Well, Miss Withers, you've seen the picture, what—"

"That particular young woman who just came in was Thallie Gordon, wasn't she?"

"That's right. She just wanted to tell me that there was somebody from a rival agency hovering around, probably trying to steal one of my clients…"

"Young man," said Miss Withers with a look, "I have been lied to by experts. We both know to whom she referred."

"Okay," Wingfield said easily. "So Thallie doesn't like our good friend, the inspector. I guess her mother was scared by a badge before Thallie was born." He grinned. "Well, so you see what I meant about Fagan's last program?"

"Yes, but I don't see why he wasn't cut off the air much sooner."

"You have a point. But all of us there in the control room—"

She perked up her ears. "*You* were there?"

"Ma'am, you didn't know?" Wingfield shuddered. "I was monitoring the program. I sat in the control room, and I was the one who should have done something about shutting Fagan up, even if I had to go down on the sound stage and hit him over the head with his own milk bottle. Only I got buck fever. It was just too awful to believe. And of course for a while we all kept thinking that he would work himself out of it somehow as he had always done in the past, and wind up by saying a lot of nice things about Junior, taking out the sting."

"You were an eyewitness, and you just sat there?"

"Believe me, cutting a show off TV isn't like it is on radio. You don't have a standby studio orchestra to carry on with. We couldn't believe what we were seeing and hearing. The stunt was likely to finish off Fagan's career, but I guess he just didn't give a damn."

"A sort of compulsion, an irresistible impulse?"

"Right. All radio and TV people hate sponsors, the necessary evil of this crazy business." Wingfield looked at his watch.

"I'll not keep you, young man," said Miss Withers. "I suppose that Miss Gordon is waiting? Romance is a wonderful thing, or so I've heard. Do you have an understanding with her?"

"Yes," he said glumly. "But we understand it two different ways." He went up the steps to the door of the projectionist's booth and took back the can of film.

"By the way," asked the schoolteacher, "I suppose that the district attorney has a print of this picture, and plans to show it to the jury at the trial?"

"If he does," Wingfield told her, "he's apt to get a verdict of justifiable homicide, don't you think?" They came out into the corridor, Talley in the lead.

"In your opinion, what we have seen would constitute motive for murder?"

"But definitely. I could have strangled Fagan myself. Only don't get any ideas; I didn't. It wasn't until the next day that I found I'd lost my job over this wing-ding, and even then I didn't think it would take four months to get back on salary."

"But the things that Fagan said about Junior were true, weren't they?"

"Basically," Wingfield admitted slowly. "Or else they wouldn't have hurt so much. Only Fagan put them in the worst light. And, you see, Junior was sitting there in his big duplex over on Park, with the Virginia-born blue-blood, Miss Dallas Trempleau, and some other café-society pals, and of course they'd tuned in the program. Junior saw what was happening and came busting over here with blood in his eye, but by the time he arrived the show was over and Fagan had taken a powder. Young Gault was really frothing at the mouth—he even took a poke at me and then rushed out looking all over town for Tony."

"And found him, or so I gather?"

"Other way around. Some of us got hold of Fagan first and fed him some black coffee and straightened him up. We made it clear to him that the only hope for his career was to square himself quick, even if he had to eat dirt. A few strategic phone calls to headwaiters around town produced the information that Junior had wound up at the Stork, one of his old hangouts, so we rushed Fagan over there and sent him in to apologize. Only you know what happened, don't you?"

Miss Withers nodded. "Mr. Fagan added insult to injury by landing a sucker blow to Mr. Gault's chin. Then he went home and threw a party. I'm interested in that party, by the way."

"So were the police at the time. But it was perfectly natural that Fagan wouldn't want to be alone at a time like that. I can't tell you much about it, though I dropped in for a while, along with Thallie and the three Boyle sisters and a couple of writers and some other riffraff. But it wasn't very gay. Most of the people there made their living one way or another out of Tony Fagan. It was like dancing on deck after the ship has hit an iceberg, and it didn't help any to have Tony's ex-wife there, mooning over him and patting his shoulder. Ruth is one of the 'this is *our* song' girls, solid schmaltz and sentiment. Pretty soon I got tight and went home, or vice versa."

"Taking Miss Gordon with you, of course?"

"N-no, Thallie wouldn't leave. I guess she thought she had to stick around and play loyal, just in case Fagan got another sponsor sometime. She was a regular on the show, remember—and she didn't realize yet just how badly Tony had loused up his prospects."

"So she stayed to the bitter end?"

"How should I know?" said Wingfield cautiously. "Thallie said later that they all left around four. Except Ruth, of course, but she'd disappeared earlier and everybody took it for granted that she'd gone home. Actually, according to the newspapers she was only asleep in the spare bedroom, where the police found her next morning and gave her a rather bad time of it, I expect." He fidgeted a little, looking at his watch again.

"Just one thing more, young man. What is Mrs. Fagan's present address?"

"Her address? How should I know? I suppose she's in the book. And now, if you'll excuse me, I'm overdue at a rehearsal."

This vein of high-grade ore had petered out. She thanked him for his trouble, and departed. But young Wingfield couldn't have been in too much of a hurry to get to his rehearsal, for when she stole a quick look back from the other end of the long hallway he was still standing there by the projection-room door, scratching his head. Miss Withers went out into the reception room, thought a moment, and then went back to the doorway and peeked again. Art Wingfield was just disappearing into a phone booth at the other end of the hall, a rather queer place to hold a rehearsal.

"All of which has been fairly informative," the schoolteacher observed to Talleyrand the poodle as they came out of WKC-TV again onto the avenue, after pausing by the phone booths in the lobby long enough to make sure that no Mrs. Ruth Fagan was listed in any of the Greater New York directories. "But we are still no forrader in finding out what happened to little Ina Kell, are we?"

Talley answered only with a wide yawn, being a dog of regular habits—at least as far as eating and sleeping were concerned. He would, however, have enjoyed the long walk uptown, and was somewhat less pleased than his mistress to find that the inspector had gallantly left the official limousine waiting. Miss Withers sank gratefully into the cushions and murmured, "Home, James."

"The name is Patrolman Gerald Van Dusen, ma'am."

"Very well. The Barbizon Hotel for women, Gerald—I mean Officer." But being Miss Withers, she changed her mind again. After all, it was only a little after ten o'clock. She rapped on the glass and asked to be taken to the Graymar Apartments, on East Fifty-fifth.

By the time they arrived, Talley was curled up in a fuzzy brown ball and fast asleep. His mistress left him so, not knowing just what might be in store for her inside. There was a canopy outside the entrance of the somewhat forbiddingly plain building, but no doorman in sight. Inside was a marble lobby, but nobody at the desk. Miss Withers found the mailboxes, and on one of them a card reading "Joris, Miss Crystal—803," and was about to resort to the old dodge of pressing a number of other bells in order to get in when suddenly an effervescent party of four came out, dressed to the teeth and swaying slightly. The schoolteacher had no difficulty whatever in getting the toe of her number-ten Walkover in the door before it quite closed.

Junior Gault could have gained admittance this same way on that fatal morning, she realized. Taking the little automatic elevator to the eighth floor she went down the hall to the Joris apartment—and then ran bump up against a stone wall, for nobody answered the bell. "Tarnation," murmured Miss Withers. She was about to turn away, somewhat more than baffled, when she remembered that she must be standing at this particular moment only a few feet from the actual scene of the murder. From this doorway Ina Kell must have peeked out and seen—it could only have been the door of the farther apartment, the door on which the corridor ended. And the door held on its upper panel a small brass frame and a card. ...

Surprisingly enough, the card was lettered "Fagan." Miss Hildegarde Withers nodded sagely. She had had a hunch that something would come of this, and her hunches were of iron. " 'There is a destiny ...' " she quoted to herself happily. It was time she had a break. Somehow the murder apartment had been kept vacant all this time. It couldn't have been at the behest of the inspector or of any authorities; not this long. Possibly the place had been tied up in litigation, or else it might have been proved unrentable because of the tragedy.

The schoolteacher could not have explained, if pressed, just what she hoped to find out on a trail so cold. But all the same she listened outside the door of the Fagan apartment for a moment, just in case. Everything was as still as death inside.

Miss Withers gave a furtive look behind her, making sure that for the moment the long corridor was deserted, and when she found that she was really alone the impulse to have a quiet peek at the murder scene was too great to be resisted. She felt in the recesses of her capacious handbag and came up with a bit of metal, her mouth set in a grim line of satisfaction. Oscar Piper was always ribbing her about trying to open locks with a hairpin, but this flattened, slightly straightened-out button-hookish device had once been the property of a professional thief. The inspector had made the mistake of showing it to her and explaining its purpose, then leaving it unguarded on top of his desk.

Miss Withers had practiced with the gadget and read up on the subject. There was really nothing to picking the average lock. All one had to do was to line up the tumbrels, or whatever they were. The maiden schoolteacher worked busily, making soft, clicking noises like the romping of a dozen or so metal mice, yet in spite of her best efforts the lock refused to cooperate. "Drat it all," vented Miss Withers in an angry whisper. "One might as well try saying 'Open sesame'!"

And the door opened.

"The third day comes a frost, a killing frost ..."

—Henry VIII

5

The door opened, as Miss Withers immediately realized, not from her success with the picklock nor as a result of any supernormal forces invoked by Ali Baba's ancient gibberish, but simply because the knob had been turned from the inside. It was a comely young woman of about thirty wearing pajamas obviously designed to be slept in rather than admired. Her hair had been arranged for the night in two flaxen braids the color of oleomargarine, she wore no makeup whatever, but still there was something about her.

Frankness, perhaps. "You didn't need to go to all that bother," she was saying. "You could have just knocked."

The best defense is a good offense, or so the schoolteacher had always heard. She pointed an accusing finger and said, "Then *you* must be Ruth Fagan!"

"Of course." The voice was a little nervous, but not very. Miss Withers elbowed her way forward into the foyer, a small bare room whose floor was covered with a fine Kermanshah rug. A moment later she was seated on a large and almost too comfortable divan in a heavily overfurnished room; a man's room filled with knickknacks, oddments, strange weapons, curios, pictures, objets d'art—a jumble of types and periods and schools. Tony Fagan, the schoolteacher thought, must have been the sort of man who could never bear to throw anything away.

"My name is Withers," she said. "I didn't expect to find *you* living here!"

"It isn't so strange, really," Ruth Fagan was saying. "A gal has to live somewhere. This was my late husband's apartment and after his death it came to me so I stayed on, the housing shortage being what it is."

There was really no arguing that. "But you were divorced, were you not?"

"Not really. Only the interlocutory." Ruth's gesture indicated that interlocutories were accidents that could happen in the best-regulated marriages.

"An interlocutory—in Reno? Come, come."

"Oh, I didn't go through with the Nevada thing. I changed my mind. I'd been to Reno once before and it's grim. But later I got my decree back East, because Tony insisted. He even got some girl to be photographed with him in her nightgown in a hotel room—I don't mean that, I mean *she* was in her nightgown. I never wanted the divorce, but Tony was very difficult sometimes. These artists—"

"Difficult how, Mrs. Fagan?"

"Well," said Ruth bluntly, "there were other women. That wasn't so bad, but finally it settled down to just one other woman."

"Who?"

"I never knew, and never wanted to."

"Was it the girl who played corespondent in the nightgown?"

Ruth shrugged. "I really have no idea. She gave her name as Jane Doe, they say."

"I see. Naturally you felt very bitter about this?"

Ruth looked at her cuticle. "I was hurt. But I knew he'd come back to me when things went wrong. Just as he eventually did. But then I failed him when he needed me most. If only I'd been more tolerant and understanding that night! But I had expected to be here alone with him, and I couldn't stand watching those girls putting their arms around him and calling him *Darling*. And dancing with him when I was playing *our song* on the combination! So I took a drop too much, and topped it off with the allonal tablets, so I was dead to the world when he needed me most."

"I heard about that," admitted Miss Withers. "I understand that you heard nothing of the fight that preceded the actual murder?"

The woman hesitated. "Not exactly. But I seem to remember bad dreams, very frightening dreams. I didn't quite wake up—of course there were two closed doors and the entire length of the apartment between. But I'll never forgive myself for not waking. If I'd got up and come in ..."

"You might easily have been murdered, too," the schoolteacher comforted her. "But I still fail to understand one thing. Even though you were divorced, was Mr. Fagan's will in your favor?"

"There was no will. Tony was too much in love with life to ever believe he would die. But, you see, we had what they call a decree *nisi*—a decree *unless*. Unless there was a reconciliation during the twelve months before the decree became final. Our spending the night in the same apartment constituted just that little thing. You see, his bed hadn't been slept in!" There was a definite note of triumph in Ruth Fagan's tone, even as she reached for a lacy handkerchief and dabbed at her prominent, pale-blue eyes. It had all, she seemed to feel, worked out for the best.

"Mrs. Fagan," said the schoolteacher soberly, "are you satisfied—do you agree with the police that Gault is guilty?"

"*What?*" Ruth's voice was flat and gritty. "But of course. Who else? I was watching television that night, and I saw Tony's show. He got carried away—he always hated sponsors anyway. He did needle Mr. Gault, but I only hope that the jury doesn't take that as sufficient provocation and let that awful man get away with life imprisonment. He deserves to die."

"It would certainly seem so," admitted Miss Withers. "I'm sorry to have to bring up painful memories, but in my work—" She sighed. "I have no official standing, of course, but I understand that there seems to be some difficulty in bringing Junior Gault to trial."

"He's trying to wriggle out of it, with the help of his money," said Ruth slowly. "But he must pay the penalty! I have some money, too—most of my husband's programs were transcribed, and the kinescopes are still being played around the country on a royalty basis. And if it takes my last red cent. ..."

"Naturally," agreed the schoolteacher.

Ruth was looking at her strangely. "You're not working on this case for the Gault family, are you?"

"Good heavens, no!"

"Because it would be worth a good deal to me to see Junior Gault found guilty. Say, five thousand dollars, and expenses ...?"

"My amateur standing!" murmured the schoolteacher. "But I'll keep it in mind." She moved toward the door, walking carefully so as not to sweep her skirt against any of the bric-a-brac. "By the way," she said, "I understand that the police never have found the weapon. Did you notice anything missing?"

"No," said Ruth. "But I wouldn't have known. Fans were sending him stuff all the time, all sorts of stuff. I have no way of knowing what loot came in after our separation."

"Of course not." Miss Withers hefted a weighty alabaster vase, and set it down again. "Of course, the weapon may still be here—the room is full of blunt instruments, and Junior Gault had time to wipe off any blood or fingerprints. ..."

"He was seen leaving here that morning," the woman told her. "You know that?"

"Oh?" The schoolteacher tried to look surprised. So much for the district attorney's office and their carefully guarded secrets. "By the way, Mrs. Fagan, you said a moment ago that you didn't ever know the name of the woman with whom your husband was having an affair; I mean the important one. He must have broken up with Thallie Gordon sometime before, then?"

"*Thallie?*" Ruth laughed, not pleasantly. "Whatever gave you that crazy idea? Tony never messed around with the girls on the show; a bird doesn't foul its own nest. It was somebody else, one of his worshiping little fans, I suppose. He used to get thousands of mash notes at the studio, mostly from small towns."

"I see," murmured the schoolteacher, somewhat elated. She paused in the doorway. "By the way, the next apartment belongs to a dancer, doesn't it? Odd that being neighbors and all, your husband never put her on one of his programs."

"Crystal Joris? Oh, but he did. A year and a half ago. The Joris girl was good as a novelty act, but, of course, tap dancers are tap dancers."

"Which nobody can deny," agreed Miss Withers, suddenly anxious to leave. Ruth Fagan said if there was anything she could do to help, money or anything ... "There is," said the schoolteacher crisply.

"What?"

"You can call Mr. Wingfield back and thank him for preparing you for my surprise visit. Don't bother to deny it, Mrs. Fagan—you knew too much about me, and didn't even think to ask for my *bona fides*. But it has all been, in a strange sort of way, most illuminating." She went out, smiling a smile of modest triumph.

There was more to this case, she decided, than met the eye. And it was nearly midnight when she sat facing her old friend and antagonist, the inspector, across a booth in a little delicatessen just off Fifty-seventh and the Avenue of the Americas, over doughnuts and coffee.

Oscar Piper was bright and chipper, and seemed very pleased with himself. "You know, Hildegarde, you're looking better already. A new light in your eyes. But why the Mona Lisa smile?" He cocked his head. "Found Ina Kell already?"

"No, Oscar. That will have to be up to you. I imagine that the usual hue and cry, with her picture on thousands of placards, should produce results."

"You out of your mind?" he cried. "Ina is a surprise witness ..."

"The surprise is on the other foot. I haven't had time to fill in all the blanks, naturally. But I want to give you a new slant on this crime."

"New slant, my eye!" he yelped indignantly. "Didn't you see the film of that broadcast? Aren't you satisfied that that's motive enough?"

"Enough and to spare. The trouble is, Oscar, that too many people knew, hours before the murder, that there was a perfect case against just one person. If Fagan died by violence, Junior Gault alone would be suspected. It was therefore a perfect setup for any other enemy Fagan may have had."

"Oh, *no!*" winced Piper. "Why must you do everything the hard way?"

"The rocky road to truth? Oscar, it never seemed to me quite sensible for a man to go to all the trouble of beating up an enemy before killing him. That would be piling Ossa on Pelion. And there is no proof that Junior Gault ..."

"No proof? But I tell you the Kell girl saw Junior leaving!"

Miss Withers nibbled daintily at a doughnut. "Listen. Tony Fagan was a wolf; he could hardly have avoided it in his profession. His wife leaned to the opinion that he never fooled around with members of his cast; I believe she said something about a bird never fouling its own nest. Which proves that she hadn't ever taken a good look at a bird's nest close up. Anyway, I am reasonably sure that Fagan trespassed at least once—I refer to the bosomy Miss Thallie Gordon, who otherwise could hardly have obtained or kept her job on the show."

The inspector shrugged. "So maybe Thallie did have an audition by courtesy of Beautyrest. She had no motive to bump off her—her meal ticket."

"Perhaps not. Then there's the girl who played corespondent in the Fagan divorce, being caught with him in a hotel room with nothing on. Suppose she really wasn't forewarned about the deal, and felt strongly about being compromised?"

"Fiddle. Two out of three girls who hang around the TV studio would be tickled pink to be photographed anywhere with Fagan, in a nightgown or out of one."

"I'd still like to know who was with him that night, if you can find out. And I also suggest to you, Oscar, that Fagan had a fling with Crystal Joris, the tap-dancing neighbor who appeared on his program a year or more ago."

"We know all that. She did a one-shot on his show. But as for the rest ..."

"Please listen. Isn't it possible that through Crystal he somehow met her little cousin, either on a visit here or perhaps when he accompanied the Joris girl back to the old home town? A man like Fagan, wearied by the stereotyped glamor girls of show business, might be extremely attracted to a naive little thing like Ina—who must have had unusual charms, or you and Mr. Hardesty wouldn't speak of her as you do. But of course he was the type to grow tired quickly, a man used to orchids would soon be bored with a simple violet."

"Go on," ordered the inspector with grim patience. "Say your say."

"I suggest to you that the reason Ina wanted to come to New York was to see Tony Fagan again, to be at least in the next apartment to the man she worshiped. Or perhaps she had revenge on her mind when she came. 'Hell hath no fury …' "

"Your blushing little violet is poison ivy now?"

Miss Withers sniffed again, prodigiously. "Perhaps after the party was over Ina came tapping at his door, begging just for a kind word, and got laughed at—Fagan not even pretending that he wasn't tired of her, through with her. …"

"You ought to write soap operas."

"So Ina went back to her borrowed apartment, furious. Then she heard the fight, came out into the hall in time to catch a glimpse of Junior Gault hurrying away after having given his tormentor the beating he so richly deserved, and was curious enough to investigate the open door and find Fagan lying there unconscious. He was in her power …"

"Better and better," conceded the inspector. "Dream on."

"So, having seen the television program earlier that evening and realizing that this was the perfect opportunity to revenge herself on the man who had wronged her, Ina picked up a nearby vase and finished the job. Then she washed off the weapon, covered the body, sneaked back into the other apartment and made her getaway." Miss Withers paused, leaning back in triumph. "That would explain why she didn't call the police. She didn't want to appear at all, even as a witness. She was afraid that on the witness stand, with Sam Bordin cross-examining her, she might trap herself. Well, Oscar?"

He nodded admiringly. "Nice try, old girl."

"What do you mean, *try?* It's the only hypothesis that fits the facts."

The Inspector's smile was pitying. "Now *you* listen!" he said.

Some years before, during the period when Miss Withers had been devoted to the raising of tropical fish, a friend returning from Army Air Force duty at Karachi had presented her with a tiny replica of the Taj Mahal made of intricate bits of white marble; a delicate, lovely, incredible thing not five inches high. It had occurred to her how striking the little temple would be if placed at the bottom of her largest aquarium, framed by the green of the water plants and reflected in a little mirror set in sand for the foreground.

So she had arranged it, had carefully siphoned back the warmed, cured water and replaced the hundred tiny, jeweled fish, turned on the concealed overhead fluorescent lamp and then had sat herself down in rapt admiration to gaze upon her handiwork. The *betta splendens*, the neon *tetras*, the mollies and guppies and hatchet fish and *scalares* had all swum inquisitively around the new addition to their green wonderland, and a snaky *dojo* had even writhed its way, like a minuscule boa constrictor, into a doorway …

And then, in front of her eyes, the Taj had begun to shimmer and change, like faery gold. Nightmarishly, the thousand intricately assembled bits of marble drew in upon themselves, assumed strange, ungeometric attitudes contrary to all the rules of architecture, and then slowly, inevitably, collapsed into a pile of rubble.

Now, as Oscar Piper talked, Miss Withers began to feel the same shock of incredulous disappointment. The case she had built up in the last few hours, like the miniature of the Taj Mahal, had lacked waterproof glue.

The inspector, in short, was telling her not to try to teach her grandmother to suck eggs, nor the police to follow obvious lines of investigation. First of all, Tony Fagan's love life, involved as it might have been and probably was, could not possibly have included an affair with Crystal Joris. Miss Joris was billed in nightclubs as "300 Pounds of Rhythm," and her weakness was calories, not cuddling. Nor had she ever had a chance to introduce her little country cousin to Tony Fagan. Ina Kell had never been more than fifty miles from Bourdon, Pennsylvania—except perhaps in dreams—nor had any of her infrequent trips away from the drab home she shared with an invalid mother, a stepfather, and three half-brothers ever taken her near a city where Tony Fagan might have been making a personal appearance at some theater or night spot. Her life was an open book, and Tony Fagan—because of the business he was in—came under the same category. It was absolutely impossible that the two had ever met until that moment—*la hora de verdad*, as the Spanish put it—when her curiosity had led her to push open his door and look upon his bloody ruin.

There were many times when Miss Withers had doubted her old friend the inspector, and with reason. But not about things like this. She subsided slowly, letting her coffee cool.

Moreover, every point in Ina's story that could be checked had been—and rang true as a bell. There had even been enough prints of her little bare feet recovered from the floor of the hallway to show that she had tiptoed cautiously from her door to Fagan's and then had gone back considerably faster, almost running. Her fingerprints were on the Joris phone, backing her story about trying to call the police.

"Oh," said Miss Withers, in a very small voice indeed.

"And just to top it all," Piper added gently, "Junior Gault, after repudiating his confession, agreed to a lie-detector test. Like so many other smart boys who read recent articles in *Esquire* and *True* and other men's magazines explaining how it's so easy to beat the machine, he did his best and it wasn't good enough." The inspector drew one finger across his Adam's apple. "Guilty. Of course we can't bring that evidence into court—a man can't be forced to testify against himself—but we're satisfied. Gault killed

Tony Fagan. But unless we can find that Kell girl and bring her back to testify, he's going to get off scot-free."

The schoolteacher nodded, a very chastened nod.

"And Gault *has* to be convicted. There can't be one law for the rich and another for the poor. The Department has had enough criticism, what with the bookie scandals and all. So far homicide hasn't been smeared with the tarbrush, and I mean to see that it doesn't get smeared. Now, will you go out and find Ina Kell for us?"

"I'll do my best; angels can do no more," said Miss Hildegarde Withers. "Obviously, with so much money and influence involved, and so much depending on her testimony, the girl is in danger. She may be out of my reach, as well as beyond subpoenas or extradition papers. It occurs to me that you and Mr. Hardesty are more interested in Ina's testimony than in her safety."

Piper was reaching for his hat. "She's safe enough, as long as Junior Gault is on ice. Now it's late, and tomorrow is another day. How about my walking you home?"

"You took the words right out of my mouth," snapped Miss Withers. "But then, as you were probably about to say, I have plenty left!"

The inspector merely looked sheepish.

"Oh, thou child of many prayers!"
"Life hath quicksands; life hath snares!"

—LONGFELLOW

6

"I am not seeing any clients this morning," said Sam Bordin in as firm a tone as one dares use to an attractive employee with whom he has been rumbaing until two A.M. "Gracie, you know I'm up to my hips in the Gault thing and I've no time to tackle anything new—not even if it's a beautiful widow with a smoking pistol in one hand and a fat checkbook in the other."

The tall rangy girl looked down at him fondly, in spite of the fact that the tubby little lawyer had not shaved that morning and obviously had a hangover. "If she was beautiful I wouldn't *let* her in," she told him. "This one is the intellectual type, and I don't think she's a client. She just wants ten minutes of your time."

"For some worthy cause," Sam Bordin said, wincing. *"No,* Gracie!"

The tall girl sighed, and then went out of the room with a practiced waggle of her lips. A moment later she bounced back, bearing an envelope. "The lady said perhaps you'd like to have this anyway, to look at when you're not so busy."

Bordin glanced at the two sheets of yellowing paper inside, started to drop them into the basket, and then his eye was caught by something in the handwriting. He read on a bit and then cried, "What did you say her name was? Never mind—run after her! No, give me five minutes and *then* send her in!" Starting out, Gracie noticed that her employer was reaching hurriedly into the top right-hand drawer of his desk, where she knew he kept a loaded .38.

The drawer also held an electric shaver, with which Sam Bordin had just finished touching up his blue jowls when the visitor entered. He stared at her for a moment, rather as if she were a ghost. "Miss *Withers!*" he said wonderingly. "I didn't connect the name at first—but you haven't changed a bit. Even the hat, and the umbrella!"

She smiled, and nodded toward the yellowed sheets in his hand. "I thought perhaps a glimpse of your own handiwork might remind you. '*What Being an American Means*, by Sascha Bordin, aged nine.' Prize third-grade essay of the year. I thought you might like to have it back, perhaps to show your own children?"

"Well—" He laughed nervously. "I'm married to my law books, I'm afraid."

"Really? Then I'd watch out for that girl in the outer office; she has a certain glint in her eye." They talked for a few moments about the old days at P.S. 38. "Not," Miss Withers admitted, "that I'm surprised at the way you've risen in the world. The child is father to the man, and as I look back on it I can see very clearly how you were meant for the law. You used to argue interminably, whether you were in the right or the wrong, and perhaps best when you were in the wrong. I've watched your career from a distance, and when I heard the other day that you are to appear in another big murder trial, I suddenly thought it might be possible for me to see you in action."

"Oh, the Gault case. But it's been set back on the calendar, or I'd be happy to fix it so you could have a front seat. When the time comes—"

The schoolteacher thanked him. "But I'm afraid I won't be in town. I've retired, you know, and am living out in southern California."

"Too bad. There'll be some legal fireworks, if the case ever comes before a jury. I'd like you to see the fun."

"*If?*" said Miss Withers sharply, cocking her head.

He looked at her with an added respect. "You don't miss much, do you?"

"Sascha, you haven't answered the question!"

"Yes, ma'am. Well, personally I don't think that the D.A. will press. They haven't a very strong case against my client, you know." He waved his hand. "Except for the circumstantial evidence."

"And except for—" began the schoolteacher, and bit her tongue.

"Except for a so-called surprise witness for the prosecution who has suddenly turned up missing?" At the look on her face Sam Bordin broke into a wide grin. "Wait a minute, don't get me wrong, I haven't been tapping wires or listening at keyholes, but those things get around."

Across the desk the maiden schoolteacher looked hard at the little boy whom she had once assisted over the bumps and potholes of the third-grade curriculum. There were not many among her thousand and more pupils for whom she had once held higher hopes. "You never used to cheat, Sascha," she finally said softly. "Not in my classroom. You might argue that black was white, but you never cheated."

He bowed. "Thanks. But why bring that up now, ma'am?"

"Because somebody in this Fagan-Gault affair has cheated and still is. Where is the Kell girl, Sascha?"

It was a clean miss. "You tell me," he came back swiftly. "Because I have a subpoena here ready to serve on Ina Kell if she ever shows up. Even if the prosecution doesn't want her on the stand, I do."

Miss Withers' sniff was eloquent of doubt, but she said, "You are, I suppose, quite satisfied in your own mind that your client is innocent?"

Bordin hesitated only a moment. "I could hardly express an opinion—"

"Then you think he's guilty?"

"Not until proven," said the little man stubbornly. "Listen a minute. It's an attorney's job to make the best defense possible for his client. *I'm* not the judge or the jury. I use every means at my command to get the facts, particularly everything on *his* side of the story, and to present it all in the best light. I don't know how you happen to know so much about the Fagan murder—"

"Justice is the problem of every good citizen," she informed him. "And sometimes my friend Oscar Piper, down at Centre Street, talks to me about his cases."

The famous Bordin smile congealed a little. "So? I'll bet you the inspector didn't tell you that the autopsy showed that Tony Fagan had an abnormally thin cranium, a skull so frail that it might have been smashed during a man-to-man fight by slamming against a wall or other hard object?"

Miss Withers said nothing.

"At the moment," the lawyer went on, "I have almost decided to base the defense on the fact that while Gault may have been responsible for Fagan's death, he never premeditated murder but meant simply to beat him up. Manslaughter while in a state of temporary emotional insanity caused by malicious persecution ...."

"Been reading up on the Harry Thaw case, Sascha?"

It was Bordin's turn to say nothing.

"You know perfectly well the man is guilty. There's the confession, and the lie-detector tests."

He brightened, like a chess player confronted with a difficult gambit. "But neither is admissible as evidence. The confession, if you can call it that, was verbal and never formally signed or sworn to. As for the polygraph, even Professor Leonarde Keeler, who invented it, always said it must be used by trained technicians, of which there are perhaps a dozen in the nation. But the police, as you probably know, use it as freely as if it were a pencil sharpener, just as they are always using sodium pentothal and the other truth drugs. I don't mind telling you that I have every hope of being able to satisfy a jury, in spite of everything, that Gault is no murderer at all, and that there is at least a reasonable doubt that he caused the death of Tony Fagan. Gault *may* have only left his enemy unconscious from a deserved beating, and then some other person or persons happened along and finished the job knowing it would be blamed on Gault anyway."

"Ingenious," Miss Withers admitted with a wry smile. "Sascha, you haven't changed a bit since you were nine. You argued hardest when you were trying to convince me that two and two weren't necessarily four." She sighed. "Would you like to do me a favor for old time's sake? I want an interview with Gault."

"What?" Bordin was incredulous. "You want me to fix it up for you to talk to Gault in jail—and you lined up with the opposition?"

"I am only with the opposition if he's guilty, remember."

The lawyer thought it over a moment. "Hmm. Junior is not what one could call an especially cooperative character. He seems to have certain antisocial tendencies."

"So many murderers do, don't they? But I still have, I hope, an open mind. I don't like to see killers get away, but I also have a deep disinclination to see an innocent man rot in prison—or for that matter an innocent young girl tangled up and perhaps destroyed in what is no real concern of hers at all. Don't you think this whole affair would be the better for stirring up a bit?"

"You mean you want to play Hawkshaw?"

"The inspector says I'm no detective, simply a catalytic agent. What real harm would it do for me to have a few well-chosen words with Junior Gault?"

Bordin picked up the desk pen. "I'll see what I can do." He carefully wrote down the name of her hotel.

"And if it isn't possible for me to see the accused, could I talk to his family and his fiancée?"

"Whatever for?"

"Why not? There might be facts that haven't come out."

"Forget it, Miss Withers," the lawyer advised earnestly. "Just forget the whole thing. The old couple have taken their son's arrest very hard, and they've crawled back into their shells. Junior's previous mix-up with a showgirl was bad enough, even if the court did throw her breach-of-promise case out of court, but this was the last straw. You couldn't get the time of day from them." Bordin shook his head, lower lip thrust out. "And as for Miss Dallas Trempleau—those socialite dolls have their fine blue blood cut with vinegar. The engagement was quietly broken before Junior got settled in his cell. I even went out and crashed the gates of the big Trempleau house on the North Shore, trying to suggest to Miss Dallas that it would help the defense considerably if she would be there beside Junior in court, and what do you think she said? She said she wished her friend Mr. Gault the very best of luck, but that unfortunately she was about to start out for a trip abroad and so she wouldn't be able to make it!"

"That does sound rather heartless, doesn't it? But—"

"They're all alike," said Sam Bordin with deep bitterness. "They have no flesh and blood in them—only straw. Just lens lice for the society photographers."

"Obviously she thought him guilty," the schoolteacher observed. "Then nobody really believes in Gault's innocence!"

"Nobody but me," Sam Bordin countered, almost too quickly.

"*I*," Miss Withers corrected. They parted with expressions of mutual esteem, and promises on the lawyer's part to get in touch with her.

Perhaps he would, but the schoolteacher was glad she didn't have to hang by her thumbs until Mr. Bordin kept that promise. It had not been a wholly happy interview for her, what with one thing and another. She had preferred Sascha as a nine-year-old. When she came out into the other office, Gracie was smiling up at her from the desk. "I promised you he'd see you, didn't I?" she said brightly, one woman to another. "His bark is worse than his bite."

Miss Withers sniffed indignantly. "Sascha Bordin knows better than to bite or bark at me, or I'd take a ruler to him as I have had to do once or twice in the past. He used to be one of my prize pupils, you know. And now he's a famous criminal lawyer. ..."

"*Trial* lawyer, we say," Gracie corrected. "The best."

"He's never lost a client, I understand?"

"Never a death penalty yet."

"It must be nice," observed the schoolteacher, "to have so many innocent clients." She peered down at the old-fashioned gold watch pinned to her old-fashioned bosom. "My, it's after twelve! Is there a good place to have lunch around here?"

Gracie said there was a nice cozy little tearoom in the next block. Somehow she wound up showing Miss Withers to the place, and facing her across a little booth in the rear of the restaurant. "The pot pie special," said Gracie. And, "So you were Mr. Bordin's teacher once! Imagine that!"

"Yes. But now I think he could teach me things. About getting people out of trouble with the law, for instance. Tell me, my dear, would it be much of a blow to his prestige if he really did have a client go to the chair?"

"Jeepers, yes!" Gracie had had a double dry Manhattan, for medicinal purposes, before lunch. "We really need a break right now. Twice in the past year Mr. Bordin had bad luck with his cases. One client got ninety-nine years, and one twenty to life. We just *got* to get this Junior Gault off, believe me!"

Miss Withers expressed a mild interest in the case, implying that Sam Bordin had discussed it with her casually in passing. "Too bad that Miss

Trempleau proved such a broken reed."

"Oh, he *told* you?" Gracie sighed. "But you can take that with a grain of salt. I saw Dallas and heard her sing at a charity thing once—very natural and pretty and ladylike; everybody liked her."

"But Mr. Bordin intimated ..."

"Oh, *him!* If she didn't want to appear in court on Junior's side she had some good reason. My boss is sour on that one subject—he has a grouch against everybody on the society page. He's an idealist, see? And a couple years ago, after he was so brilliant in the Whitfield case, he got taken up by some of the Barberry-Morocco-Stork crowd. Invitations to dinner every night, white tie and tails, Newport and Aiken and so on. Only he had to go and get serious about one of those gilt-edged gals who turned out to have been playing winter rules. Sam Bordin didn't enjoy the idea that he'd been kept around for laughs."

"He wouldn't," nodded the schoolteacher.

"So he threw away the fancy clothes and settled down to work again. My boss is really an awfully good lawyer when he sticks to it."

"I believe you," said Miss Withers dreamily. "And never lost a client! It's rather a shame, then, that poor little Ina Kell wasn't one of his clients. ..."

"Is *she* lost?" cried the tall girl sharply. "I mean ..."

"About as lost as one can get, I fear. I see you recognize the name."

Gracie nodded. "Why, yes, I wouldn't say this if you weren't practically a member of the family, and don't breathe it to a soul, but there was a Miss Kell who called up in a dither one day when the boss happened to be out of the office. She had to see him right away, and I gathered it was about something that might help free Junior Gault, though she wouldn't say what. She didn't even want to give me her name, but I wormed it out of her and promised that if she'd leave her number I'd have him call her back. I put a note on the boss's desk when I went home, but he didn't get around to calling her next morning and then it turned out to be only a pay phone somewhere. Isn't that a shame?"

"I rather think so," agreed Miss Withers gravely. "And when did all this occur?"

"A couple or three weeks ago. But—"

"Shortly before Ina Kell became officially lost," the schoolteacher mused. It was odd that Sascha Bordin hadn't mentioned anything about this to her—or on second thought, perhaps it wasn't. "Did you try to locate her?"

Gracie nodded. "Everywhere, but she'd just dropped out of sight. The boss thinks that the D.A.'s office found out their prize witness was going to give them the wrong sort of surprise, and got rid of her—"

"Well!" said Miss Withers, somewhat more than baffled, and transferred her attention to her lunch. She seemed to be going around in circles, like a traveler lost in the North Woods.

What was indicated, she decided, was an hour or two of deep cogitation.

But when she got back to her little hotel room she was met head-on by Talley the poodle.

Talley had had a dull morning, little brightened by a turn around the block with a bored bellboy as anchor. Long used to the limitless beaches of Southern California, Talley desired lots of exercise.

"Later. Can't you see that I'm thinking?"

The big apricot-colored poodle had thoughts of his own. With a sort of frenzied resignation he set out to curry favor in every way he knew. He brought his mistress's slippers, which she did not want. He tossed his beloved rubber rat in the air and caught it; he knocked the telephone off the hook, and barked cheerfully when the operator answered. Then in desperation he went through his entire repertoire of tricks; walked on his hind legs, played dead dog on the carpet and circus dog sitting on a table, chased his pom-pom of a tail and knelt to pray. Finally, clearly implying that he had been silly enough to please any human however unreasonable, he brought his leather lead and laid it firmly at Miss Withers' feet.

"Oh, very well, you dratted nuisance," conceded the weary schoolteacher. They fared forth into Central Park, and had already done a fast mile or so when the belated inspiration struck her. "Talleyrand!" she said sharply.

The poodle stopped short, searching his conscience. Then he sat up and pawed apologetically with both furry forefeet.

"Relax. It just occurred to me that French poodles, like gold-headed canes and electric broughams, carry a certain cachet of respectability in some circles. Talley, for once in your life would you care to do something to earn your salt?"

Talley lolled a long, very pink tongue, his eyes hopefully searching her face for some trace of meaning in all those words. He was, he made clear, ready for anything that wouldn't immediately take him back to the hotel.

"First we must find a phone," Miss Withers observed thoughtfully. Talley barked, plunging eagerly ahead of her as she altered their course, obviously entering into the spirit of the chase. Only, the schoolteacher told herself, he probably thought her last word had been "bone."

" *'The living should live, though the dead be dead,'*
Said the jolly old pedagogue, long ago."
—GEORGE ARNOLD

7

Miss Withers tracked down a telephone, and the coffin-like booth and chain-bound directory that went with it. Somewhat to the puzzlement of the poodle she made no phone call, but headed north again, up Fifth Avenue, to turn east near the Metropolitan Museum and finally wind up in front of an old-fashioned four-story house crowded between looming apartments. But the place still stubbornly clung to a tiny yard on one side, with patches of yellowish-green grass and brown rosebushes that had long since given up the struggle against Manhattan's fumes. The garden was heaven-sent, and swiftly the schoolteacher rearranged her plans to include this useful stage property.

Shutters were drawn on all the windows of the Gault house, but Miss Withers somehow had a feeling that it was still inhabited. The knobs were polished, and the steps swept clean. She loosed Talley's leash, then pointed at the iron fence surrounding the deserted little garden. "Do you suppose, Talley, that you could possibly scramble over that thing and get yourself trapped inside?"

The poodle cocked his furry head, politely interested in her conversation but still waiting. Then she remembered that dogs, even poodles, best understand sentences of no more than two or three words. "Go!" she commanded. "Over!"

Talley launched himself, sailed up a good part of the way and then scrabbled a bit, coming down on the other side of the barrier.

"Dig!" said his mistress.

Talley looked around until he found a reasonably soft spot and then began excavating in an uninspired sort of way, casting out earth and stones between his hind legs. His heart obviously wasn't in this game. No bone had ever been buried here, and the last mole had given up decades ago. But his not to reason why.

"Stay!" ordered Miss Withers, and then climbed the steps and firmly rang the bell. When a nervous little woman in cap and apron answered the door the schoolteacher spoke her own brand of double-talk in a cultured Bostonian accent, and ten minutes later she was sitting on the edge of a needlepoint chair in the stiffly formal living room full of heavy mahogany and obscure oil paintings, facing a little old gentleman and a little old lady.

The bewildered hostess wore black satin and pearls, the host a velvet smoking jacket; both had an odd resemblance to one another and to certain illustrations in old popular magazines. Junior Gault must have been a late child; no great wonder that he had more or less broken with his family and gone in for a Park Avenue duplex and all that went with it.

"Forgive me," said Winston H. Gault, Sr. "I do not hear very well, and what the maid said makes no sense to me whatever. You say that your name is Weevil, and there is some problem or other about damages to your lap dog?"

The schoolteacher carefully avoided meeting the sharp little black eyes, which belied the fumbling voice. She corrected him about her name. "Somehow," she sailed on brazenly, "my dog has got into your garden, where I am unable to follow him because of the fence. He is, I believe, at the moment digging among your rosebushes."

"Oh, is *that* all!" It was obvious that the rosebushes were of no moment.

"Not quite, Mr. Gault. I must admit that when it happened I was lurking in front of your house, trying to get up enough courage to ask you to see me. I am looking for a missing relative—"

"In our garden?" gasped the little old lady, who wasn't, Miss Withers decided, quite so old as at first she had seemed.

"No, not in your garden. But Ina Kell has disappeared."

"I am very sorry. But I still don't see—"

"Ina Kell is supposed to be the principal witness against your son at his forthcoming trial," Miss Withers said gently. "She admitted to the police that she had seen him leaving the apartment in which the murder of Tony Fagan took place—"

Mrs. Gault clutched at her pearls, but the old man drew himself up sharply. "You are quite mistaken, madam," he said clearly. "We *have no son.*" Then he stood up, as a sign that the distasteful interview was over. Miss Withers was shown into the hall and her poodle was returned to her by the strait-lipped maid through the side door, whereupon both departed in some confusion.

And that was that. It was not one of Miss Withers' more successful forays, though it proved that, apart from his lawyer, nobody in the world seemed to have a good word for Junior Gault. The schoolteacher said as much to Oscar Piper when she dropped in at his Centre Street office next day, which was Saturday. "Nothing, Oscar, is ever that open-and-shut. Do you suppose that something could be just a *little* rotten in Denmark?"

He heard her out. "Okay, Hildegarde," he said finally. "You have the type mind which always leaps to the conclusion that when we have arrested somebody and the grand jury has found a true bill, it must necessarily be a mistake. You forget that while you've successfully kibitzed on a dozen or so of our more fantastic cases in the last decade or more, the department has wrapped up thousands without your help."

"Perfectly true, of course," admitted Miss Withers with unaccustomed meekness.

"You were asked to lend your talents, such as they are, to hunting Ina Kell, not reopening the investigation."

"Yes, Oscar. But Ina's disappearance is all part of the same thing. And I still would like a talk with the prisoner."

"I don't think—"

"Perhaps you don't. But listen a moment. Junior Gault has been in prison for months. During that time he has been questioned and interviewed and heaven knows what. Do you suppose there is any possible harm I could do with my innocent queries?"

"But why?"

"Ina Kell," she pointed out, "is still missing."

The inspector frowned. "She'll turn up. It's only a question of time."

"Time, Oscar, is of the essence. I have a hunch—"

There were moments, and this was one, when Oscar Piper could be surprising. "Okay," he reversed himself reasonably. "Go ahead. Some of your hunches have worked out in the past. We have Gault over in Detention. He has as yet been convicted of no crime; he is technically innocent until proven guilty. He can write checks, he can vote, he is still a citizen. We certainly can't prevent him from having an interview with a representative of the press, for instance."

"Why, Oscar!"

"I can fix it up for you to be taken to his cell, introduced to him as Miss Whoozis of the Daily Whatzis, and from then you are strictly on your own. What more can you ask? After all, you're on the other side."

The maiden schoolteacher had given him many an askance look in her day, but this was one of the askancest of all. "*Et tu, Brute?* Everybody takes it for granted that I'm necessarily on the other side, even when I'm only trying to get at the truth!"

The interview with Junior Gault took place that same afternoon in a grim and ill-smelling building overlooking the scummy waters of the East River. The warder escorted Miss Withers through two gates, down a long hall, motioned to a particular cell, and then withdrew almost but not quite out of earshot. And then at long last the schoolteacher was face to face with Junior, or at least with such portions of him as could be seen through heavy steel grillwork.

It was not quite as she had expected. In the back of her mind she had been romantically anticipating something like Bert Lytell in the famous old one-act play, the one where he denied his identity to his long-lost sister and then walked off bravely to the electric chair, saying, "Cowards die many times before their deaths; the valiant never taste of death but once." Here before her was a pasty-faced, sullenly handsome young man smoking a cigar bigger and blacker than any the inspector had ever sported. There was nothing heroic about him, no trace of graciousness in his manner. He did not even bother to stand up.

"So you're a reporter," Junior greeted her. "What paper do you write for, the *Hobo News?*"

"Frankly, I am not a reporter at all," Miss Withers broke the news to him. "I only said that so I could get in. I'm here to help you."

"Okay," he told her. "Leave the Bible tracts with the warder and run along."

She sniffed. "I don't happen to be passing out tracts, though it would appear that you are in need of some. You seen very bitter, young man, which is quite understandable. I'll come to the point. You have already caused one death—with some provocation, I'll admit. But isn't that enough to have on your conscience?"

"Maybe you know what you're raving about," Gault said. "I don't."

"Just who would kidnap or perhaps even murder a key witness in a misguided attempt to save your skin, young man?"

"What?" Now he stood up.

"Just what has happened to the young lady who was unfortunate enough to happen to see you leaving the scene of the crime?"

"There wasn't anybody—" he began quickly, and stopped. "Nobody has yet proved that I was even there!"

"Whatever happened to your gold cigarette lighter, by the way?"

"Whatever happens to all cigarette lighters? They get lost. You couldn't get lost too, could you?"

"But if you will only listen—"

Junior Gault was calling to the waiting man in uniform. "Look, isn't it bad enough to be locked up in this crummy cell without having you turn loose one of the Whoops sisters on me?"

The warder approached, jerking a grimy thumb. "All right, ma'am."

"I was just leaving," vented Miss Withers indignantly. "And I'll remember to send you the tracts, young man. I also hope to have a front seat at your trial for murder!"

"Don't count on it." Junior Gault was smiling, not pleasantly. "And if there is a trial I'll bet a thousand bucks against your bustle that I get an acquittal." He said a good deal more too; as she took her hasty departure the schoolteacher kept both hands pressed over her maidenly ears.

"What did you expect, chimes?" demanded the inspector reasonably when he heard about it. The two ancient friends and sparring partners were holed up in a little spaghetti joint a few blocks from Headquarters, over plates of scallopini of veal and tossed green salad redolent of olive oil and garlic and grated Parmesan cheese. "Of course Junior Gault is a louse. Murderers aren't nice people—and murder isn't a chess problem; it's a cruel, ugly mess. You should have stuck to your conchology or whatever it was."

"Yes, Oscar. I wanted to, but you seemed anxious to have me return to the fray. Anyway, I feel sorry for that young man."

"Sorry? But I thought you wanted to wash his mouth out with soap?"

"That, too. But he is a soul in torment, or he wouldn't talk and act as he does. Even in my classrooms, Oscar, I never made the mistake some teachers do of saving all my attention and affection for the teacher's pets. The problem children need help much more. And so what if Junior Gault did commit a murder? It was in hot blood, and he had unusual provocation."

"Sure, the television ribbing he got. But ..."

"It went deeper than that. Rich men's sons can have inferiority complexes too. Junior was born to a stern, rock-ribbed father who must have been more than fifty when his one child was born, with an almost insurmountable gap between. Junior was only trying to express his individuality in all his early life—in his college athletics, his polo, his fling with the chorus girls. He finally found himself in business and even then they called him the Wonder Boy, the boss's fair-haired son. But he was going great guns, he had made a success of the moribund family business and was even engaged to a glamorous postdeb. And then he was cut down by ridicule, the oldest and cruelest weapon known to man."

"I thought Cain used a stone," murmured Oscar Piper.

"The stone was no sharper than Tony Fagan's gibes. Remember, Junior was sitting with his new fiancée and some of their—meaning *her*—friends when he had his mildly vulnerable past dragged out and held up for half the world to laugh at. Everything that Fagan said about him was cleverly calculated to hurt, to strike below the waist ..."

"Belt," corrected the inspector.

Miss Withers' sniff was almost a snort. "Don't quibble. I happened to notice during the interview in the prison that Mr. Gault actually does wear built-up shoes, but one of them is built up an inch or so more than the other. I checked with the newspaper files—and he had a triple fracture of one leg in a spill from a wild horse some years ago. That would account for his wartime 4-F status. And the crack about the beauty doctor—according to an old picture of him taken during his junior year at New Haven, when he played the last five minutes of a Yale-Army game, he had a very Byronish profile, quite like his father's, even then. The nose must have been rebuilt after some other smashup, or one might even say restored. Don't you see? Fagan's ribbing, which even had to include cracks about Dallas Trempleau's nice but presumably untrained voice, was all what my children at P.S. 38 used to call 'dirty pool.' "

"So maybe the charge should be reduced to second-degree murder," Oscar Piper said with a medium-sized shrug. "That's out of my hands. You should talk to Jack Hardesty about that—we just catch 'em and assemble the evidence."

"I might just do that," Miss Withers told him. "Except that I'm not sure about Mr. Hardesty. For a vigilant assistant district attorney, who also makes it clear that he has a slight crush on an important, but missing witness, he isn't half enough worried about Ina Kell. Mr. Bordin's secretary, whom I shamelessly pumped at lunch yesterday, is of the opinion that it is the prosecution which has spirited Miss Kell away, under the impression that she has come around to the idea that perhaps Junior Gault isn't guilty after all!"

"Forget it," said the inspector seriously. "Hildegarde, I mean it. You know I cut corners sometimes, and so does the D.A.'s office, but nothing like that. We don't hide witnesses. And Junior Gault, as you well know, is guilty as sin."

"I know," said Miss Withers. "Only I'm still sorry for him."

"You women are all alike. Always full of mawkish sympathy for some no-good killer—"

The schoolteacher frowned. "Oscar, during that few minutes when Junior Gault sat in front of the television screen, watching his own program that he was paying for, he lost just about everything he had to lose. Including his girl. Miss Trempleau, I understand, couldn't take it and bowed out."

"Sure. Out of town."

"Hmm. Then it wasn't just a polite excuse? Dallas is really traveling abroad?"

"Sort of. She's traveling in Mexico. Europe probably looked a little hot to her, with the political situation what it is."

Miss Withers peered into her coffee cup, as if looking for tea leaves with which to read a fortune. "I can understand that. The whole world is hot, and I wouldn't exactly blame her if she had taken off for the moon. But, Oscar, how do you *know* she's in Mexico?"

"Relax, we're sure. If you must know, one of the D.A.'s men went out to check on Miss Trempleau; he's a smart, curly-haired laddie who makes friends easily. The place on Long Island is closed down, except for a caretaker and his wife who've been with the family for years. But their little boy was found playing with a horse and rider made of plaited straw that still bore a tag, 'Souvenir of Tijuana.' The young mistress had remembered to send it along for his sixth birthday a few days before."

"Oh," said the schoolteacher flatly. "Then what about the Gault Foods offices? What did his business associates think of Junior?"

"About what you'd expect them to think of the boss's 4-F son who'd shot up to being practically head of the firm in a few years, and tripled the business. Grudging admiration, respect, some jealously and resentment. He had no close friends. ..."

And at that moment Emilio, who usually stayed put behind the cash register, came waddling toward their table. It was the custom of the genial host to pour out for favored visitors a few drops of *strega*, a particularly vile cordial which the inspector thought must have been aged in an old kerosene can. He was about to explain that the lady didn't drink and that he himself was still on duty, when Emilio said, "Signore Inspector, it is your office on the phone—a Sergeant Smeety. You are here, *sí?*"

"I am here, *non!*" snapped Piper. "Can't a man finish his *zabaglione* in peace?"

"But he said to tell you, if you happened in, that it is a *twenty-three.*"

The inspector suddenly stood up, almost knocking over his chair. "Sorry, Hildegarde," he mumbled, and was gone. Leaving Miss Withers with his dessert, his almost-unsmoked perfecto, and the check. *Twenty-three* obviously meant "skidoo" in his private office code.

Oscar Piper was a fast walker, but in spite of his lead she drew up alongside before he was halfway down the block, and came across the finish line at the entrance to his office a length and a half in the lead, just galloping. John Hardesty, his hair rather more windswept than usual, was pacing up and down the room, giving a better-than-average imitation of a cat on hot bricks.

"Well?" demanded the inspector.

"It's Ina Kell!" blurted out the assistant D.A.

"Oh, my prophetic soul!" cried Miss Withers. "They've found her body?"

"No!" the young man barked. "She's *gone!*"

Piper sat down wearily at his desk, looking dazed. The schoolteacher said brightly, "I think this is where I came in? Hasn't she been missing for a week or so?"

Nobody answered her. The inspector was staring at Hardesty. "You mean your man who went out to Ebensburg to get her let her get away?"

"It *wasn't* her," confessed the younger man. "Just a nightclub floozie who'd been stranded in Pittsburgh and who was working her way back here. Had the right colored hair, except at the roots, and fitted the general description. A smart cookie, too. Somehow she found out what it was all about, and accepted service of the subpoena and the free trip back to New York, laughing up her sleeve. She was *really* named Mary Smith—she proved that, and also the fact that she'd never heard of Ina Kell, in my office just now. Nothing we could hold her on."

"Judas priest on a merry-go-round," gurgled Oscar Piper. "So all this time you've been so sure you could lay hands on Ina whenever you wanted her—" He stopped short. "Hildegarde, I'm feeling woozy. Would you mind running down to the drugstore and getting me a bromo?"

"I would be happy," the schoolteacher snapped, "to run and get you a dose of Rough-on-Rats. But you're not getting rid of me until I have a full explanation. What's all this, Mr. Hardesty, about little Ina?"

"Don't blame John, blame me," put in the inspector, squaring his shoulders. "I meant it for the best. It was for your own good. You were so determined to die a slow death out there in California among your silly snail shells or sea shells or whatever they are—"

"Never mind the conches. Just exactly *what* was for my own good?"

"The little act we put on. Getting you all worked up over the Gault case and the missing witness." Piper studied the cigar butts in his ash tray, and selected the most promising. "I figured it was a natural for you to amuse yourself with—and you were interested in it anyway on account of the defense attorney being a former pupil of yours. You couldn't do any harm or get into any trouble, because we already had the murderer locked up. Even if you succeeded in tracing Ina Kell back to Pennsylvania, where we had her—we *thought* we had her located and under surveillance, it wouldn't have mattered. We could have had a good laugh over it."

"Ha ha," said Miss Withers coldly.

"The inspector's intentions were good, anyway," offered Hardesty hopefully.

She told him what was paved with good intentions, and they all sat in a stiff, uncomfortable silence.

Oscar Piper smiled sheepishly. "But nothing's changed, really. What we told you as a gag turned out to be true, that's all. Ina Kell really has disappeared. All we know is that on the day she moved out of her room *somebody* bought a bus ticket to Bourdon, Pennsylvania. She never arrived there, anyway, so we started quietly alerting the police at all points between. Ebensburg thought they had her, but—" He shrugged.

"You'd better alert Missing Persons, and have some Wanted flyers printed," the assistant D.A. offered. "The time for secrecy is past—"

"The time for almost everything is past," Miss Withers snapped. "You two sit here like bumps on a log and talk about posters and Missing Persons. Why aren't you out interviewing Ina's landlady, the other roomers, the people she worked with? Where did she have her hair done and what rinse did she use and has any girl with pretty red curls had it bleached or dyed recently? What cigarettes did she smoke and what type of movie did she like, and what sort of books did she take out of the library?"

"Yes, but …"

"Is Ina dead at the morgue, or unconscious in some accident ward, or locked up in some private mental institution?"

"But, Hildegarde …"

"Don't but Hildegarde me, you son of Ananias!" Miss Withers flounced out of the room, closing the door behind her with unnecessary firmness. But as she went down the hall toward the stairs she suddenly smiled, shook her head, and said softly, "Bless his black Irish heart!" It was almost flattering on the whole.

She would have been more flattered still if she had waited around to see how meticulously the two men followed her suggestions re: Ina Kell. Only one of them, however, paid off to any noticeable degree—the public library branch.

It had been a busy Saturday evening—the clock in the inspector's office was showing ten to midnight when the returns on Ina Kell's literary tastes were all in. He and John Hardesty bent over the list of titles, in a blue haze of tobacco smoke, with paper cups of coffee cooling forgotten on the battered, old oak desk.

"To sum it up," Hardesty said, "Ina started out on novels, long sentimental novels of the Faith Baldwin type."

"Cinderella stuff," Piper agreed.

"Then about six weeks ago she switched to travel books. Books about Scotland and Norway and France and the Orient and South America, first. Then she began to narrow it down to the West Indies. In the two weeks before she disappeared she took out every book in the branch library that had to do with the Virgin Islands—which, if you don't know, have become a very fashionable resort for important society lights who want a quiet divorce or just a nice, quiet tropical rest. It happens that the Islands are under the American flag, so there wouldn't be any difficulty about passports." He nodded grimly.

"Nor about extradition, once she's been served." The inspector grinned.

"That's where she's gone, obviously," Hardesty said. "We could check airlines and steamship companies and so forth, but she probably used a phony name, and I think it would be quicker and simpler if I flew down there at once. I'm sure she'll come back willingly, once I explain the situation and promise her complete protection from whatever scared her off."

"You better take the subpoena along, just in case," Piper told him dryly.

"I'll grab the first plane in the morning," continued the younger man eagerly. "Just as soon as I throw some lightweight suits into a bag. It'll be warm down there, and I may have to be in the Islands some time—tracing her down, and getting her to agree to come back voluntarily."

"A few nights with a beautiful, starry-eyed, red-haired lovely under a great big tropical moon?" The inspector snorted. "I'd take a week or more, if it was me."

John Hardesty said good night and streaked out of the office, but the back of his neck, Piper noticed delightedly, was flaming red. He must remember to tell that to Hildegarde when he called the old girl up tomorrow.

But when he rang the Barbizon just before noon he learned that Miss Withers had checked out and gone, dog and all, early the previous evening. No forwarding address, but if this was Mr. Piper there *was* a message. The girl obligingly read it over the phone.

> Dear Oscar,
>   Don't think it hasn't been fun because it hasn't. You are still in my bad graces, but you'll hear from me. In the meantime, I suggest that you curl up with a good book—an atlas.
>
>   Hildegarde

An atlas! That would be one of those big, unwieldy books full of maps. And there'd be a map of the Virgin Islands in it somewhere. The inspector scratched his head, having a vague feeling that his best friend and severest critic had somehow got ahead of him again.

"Every sweet has its sour; every evil its good."

—EMERSON

8

On Monday mornings the inspector's temper was always likely to be a little uneven. The weekend's crop of major crimes was usually heavy, and whenever Manhattan's citizens had at one another with gun or axe or blunt instrument the reports piled up on his desk, making paperwork and still more paperwork.

This particular Monday morning he found himself more often than not looking idly out of his window—which faced a plain brick wall. John Hardesty, that lucky young cub, must be in St. Thomas by now, combining business with pleasure and no doubt chasing a pretty redhead along the tropical beaches beneath lacy, fluttering palm trees.

And there still had been no phone call from Miss Withers. There was no doubt of it, the old girl was showing her years at last. The time had come when she couldn't take a joke. And, besides, the harmless little hoax which had turned out not to be a hoax at all had been only for her own good.

His morning cigar was burning unevenly, and Oscar Piper paid only cursory attention to bright, up-and-coming Sergeant Smith, who was explaining that he had finally solved the mystery of the identity of the anonymous lady who had acted as technical corespondent in Tony Fagan's divorce case. The photograph which had been exhibit A had shown only a curvaceous lady in a nightgown, with her arm across her face. Smitty had got a print, had it blown up to show a ring she was wearing, and had matched it with a similar ring that Thallie Gordon had worn in a studio publicity photo.

"So she did her boss a favor," the inspector said, "to help him get divorced. Okay, file it and forget it. That's all."

Sergeant Smith said that wasn't quite all. There was a telegram that had just come in, probably from some screwball. ...

The wire had been filed at Tijuana, Baja California. Piper read it, reached into his desk drawer for his glasses, and read it again. Then he bit through the cigar.

HAVING WONDERFUL TIME. WISH YOU WERE HERE. HAPPY HUNTING GROUND FOR AMATEUR CONCHOLOGIST. HAVE FOUND A MEASLED COWRY, A LEFT-HANDED WHELK, TWO HAIRY TRITONS, A SPIKED TREMPLETTE AND A RED HAIRY KELL. WOULD PROFESSOR HARDESTY LIKE THE LATTER FOR HIS COLLECTION?

HILDEGARDE

"Yipe!" cried the inspector. "When did this come in?"

"Maybe half an hour ago, sir." Smitty gulped. "I didn't think it was important. It's signed 'Hildegarde' but your friend Miss Withers couldn't be there already."

"Damn and blast," said Oscar Piper. "She could be. She must have caught a plane shortly after she walked out of here Saturday evening. That woman has a double-barreled intuition sometimes. She must have seen something that we missed, that's all."

The sergeant had been to some extent involved in the search of the libraries to trace Ina Kell's reading habits. "But there wasn't a single book about Mexico in the stuff she took out of the library!"

"That's the point. It was a plant, a false trail carefully laid to lead us in the wrong direction. Now Hardesty is to hell and gone in the Virgin Islands, and the witness we want is in Tijuana. Out of the country, out of our reach."

Sergeant Smith said, "No chance of extradition, sir?"

"There's no treaty with Mexico. Anyway, there's no question of extradition for a witness. She isn't even a fugitive from justice. If she stays there below the border—" Piper stopped suddenly. "Wait a minute. That wire's from Tijuana, isn't it? Hasn't that name crept into this case once before?"

"Yes, sir. It was in the report. There was a straw toy marked 'Souvenir of Tijuana' that Miss Dallas Trempleau sent to her caretaker's little boy."

The inspector snapped his fingers. "That's it! The Trempleau dame didn't really break her engagement after all; she just said she did! Suppose she has a yen for Junior Gault, and having learned somehow—we must check that leak, by the way—that the case against him rests on the testimony of one witness, she decided to make sure of saving his precious neck by taking the girl out of the country until after the trial!"

"Could be, Inspector. The Kell girl was bought off. And she seemed like the kind you'd take home and introduce to your mother."

"There's somebody smarter than little Ina behind all this. Smarter than the Trempleau girl. A certain high-class shyster named Sam Bordin, maybe." Piper picked up the telephone and after some slight delay spoke briefly with John Hardesty's superior. "That's that," he said, hanging up. "Bordin is being summoned to the D.A.'s office first thing tomorrow morning."

"He'll wriggle out of it," Smitty said.

"Maybe not. Anyway, the thing to do is to somehow get the Kell girl back on U.S. territory, and then slap her with a subpoena."

"It would take a magician," said the sergeant.

"Well, I've seen Hildegarde Withers pull rabbits out of her funny hat several times in the past," the inspector said softly. "She's right there on the scene, and for once she's on our side." He nodded. "Say, what's Tijuana near?"

"Somewhere along the border, sir. Near Arizona, I think. Or New Mexico." Eventually they did have to look it up in an atlas, to find it a tiny speck in the very northwest corner of the Republica. The map was detailed enough so that both policemen saw at once why Hildegarde had smelled a rat. Tijuana was across the border, but still only a suburb of San Diego. No real railroads, no through highways, led out of it into Mexico proper. And nobody touring through the beautiful and exotic land of the Aztecs would ever be likely to go within hundreds of miles of the place. Yet Dallas Trempleau had purchased a toy horse there.

"Book me on the first plane to San Diego," ordered the inspector.

"But, sir—"

"Don't but me! I haven't had a vacation in three years, and if the Commish won't okay it I'll pay my own way! Now get going!"

Smitty got, but his superior officer had barely swept off the top of his desk and put on his hat when the younger man poked his head in the door. "Ten-forty out of La Guardia for Chicago, Denver, L.A. and San Diego," he said. "Flight Six."

"Okay."

"And the *Daily Mirror* is on the phone."

"I don't care if it's the *Times*; somebody else will have to handle it."

"Okay by me," said the sergeant. "Only I thought you'd want to know that it's Walter Winchell's Girl Friday at the *Mirror*. She wants you to confirm or deny a report that you know the whereabouts of Miss Ina Kell, the supposedly undercover witness in the Gault case. They've just had a hot tip that she's you guess where." Smitty nodded wisely. "There's been a leak somewhere."

"A leak? The goddamn dam has burst! How'd they find out what only you and I know?"

"The tip came from Sam Bordin, sir. He'd like to have it known that he wants to call Ina Kell as a witness for the defense."

"Get Bordin's office on the phone."

A few minutes later inspector Oscar Piper was listening to the dulcet if slightly Brooklynesque tones of Gracie, Sam Bordin's secretary, who was very sorry to say that Mr. Bordin was out of town and not expected back for some time. Was there any message?

Was there! Apt and well-chosen words rose in the Inspector's throat, but luckily he bit them off just in time.

"Everybody wants ta get inta da act!"

—Jimmy Durante

9

Miss Withers knew all about Tijuana and anticipated no difficulties whatever in proving or disproving her wild hunch about Dallas Trempleau in the first half-hour. She remembered her other visit here—it had been on her first tourist trip west shortly after her gory misadventures on Catalina Island. The little border village had been a sleepy ruin, wrecked by the repeal of prohibition in the States. She had walked the drowsy Main Street, where a few bars and restaurants and tourist traps were still trying to keep open for the *yanqui* dollar, had seen the Foreign Club with its roulette wheels shrouded in cobwebs, dead grass rippling on the course where the great Australian Phar Lap had triumphed and been murdered in his stall, the once-famous gardens of Agua Caliente's dead hotel bleak and sterile in the white sunlight.

That was then; it must be a veritable ghost town by now. American tourists would be as conspicuous as a caravan on the desert.

Confidently the maiden schoolteacher, with Talley beside her on the front seat of a little drive-it-yourself coupé, had headed south on U.S. 101 early that Sunday evening less than an hour after she had landed at Lindbergh Field, pausing only to leave her un-unpacked suitcases in a room at the U.S. Grant. Out of San Diego the highway cut past gasworks, tuna canneries, acres of junked and rusting Navy landing craft; it wound through unlovely industrial towns, dead lemon groves, and finally into barren, open country with here and there a crowded trailer court or motel.

Soon she found herself caught in a solid column of cars all moving in the same direction, mostly filled with uniformed sailors. Passing between ever bigger and better billboards, the parade moved steadily onward until suddenly they were all piled up at the gigantic fence of the international port of entry. At long last her turn came, and Miss Withers drove up beside a sleepy dark man in a half-unbuttoned uniform. She reached into her handbag for her passport (*circa* 1936), her proof of vaccination and other papers.

"*Con su permiso, señor, Yo quiero—*" she began, in her high-school Spanish.

Horns were blaring behind her. "You're blocking trafeek!" the border guard cried, waving her on. "Get the lead out, lady!" And then, with a fanfare of crashing gears, she was suddenly in the romantic land of roses and guitars.

Crossing the long bridge over the muddy trickle of the Tijuana River, Miss Withers sniffed sharply, remembering Coleridge's poem about the city of Cologne and its two-and-seventy stenches. The way led up a steep, narrow street and suddenly burst into the town itself, no town at all now, but a booming city that had somehow exploded all over the surrounding hills. The glare in the hazy sky of early evening seemed brighter than that over Broadway during the theater hour; the sidewalks were spilling with humanity of all ages, conditions and colors.

A thousand blinding, flickering neon lights offered information on mail-order marriage and divorce, girl shows, curios, *licores*, food and amusement—almost every conceivable kind of amusement. The spinster schoolteacher bewilderedly clung to the wheel and let herself be carried along by the tide of other cars down what she remembered as the sleepy Main Street of the town—now it had become the *Avenida de la Revolución*.

This wasn't Tijuana at all; it was Reno and Skid Row and Coney Island gone mad. Signs implored her to attend the *jai-alai* games at the Fronton Palace or the greyhound races or the Foreign Book (track odds anywhere) or to see the death-defying girl *matadorables* at the Torero; to purchase tax-free gasoline or duty-free perfumes; to drink half a hundred brands of beer or tequila or whiskey.

Miss Withers was borne along for three or four blocks past blaring, blazing dance halls, honky-tonks, saloons, all interspersed with curio stores, divorce mills, arcades, more curio stores, more honky-tonks. Even on a Sunday everything was wide-open. People, mostly young males between eighteen and thirty, swarmed the sidewalks and poured recklessly back and forth across the Avenida, jaywalking with a magnificent disregard for life

and limb and fender. Whenever traffic slowed or snarled dozens of hawk-
ers rushed out from the sidewalk to offer trays loaded with junk jewelry,
plaster animals, belts and billfolds and poisonously hued blankets and can-
dies.

As soon as possible the schoolteacher edged her rented car up a darkish
side street, and pulled into the curb with a sigh of relief. Even here the
blare of cantina orchestras, the mingled roar of voices and laughter and
barkers' cries and auto horns was almost deafening. It occurred to Miss
Withers that finding anybody in this hurdy-gurdy atmosphere was going to
take a bit of doing. "Talk about your needle in a haystack!" she murmured,
and prepared to disembark.

A smallish brown ghost materialized suddenly out of the shadows, a
ghost wearing a ragged T-shirt, blue jeans, and an electric-orange jockey
cap. Thrusting his face into the car window he cried, "For one quarter I
watch your car, lady?" He might have been eleven or twelve, but the dark
mestizo eyes were older.

"No thank you, little boy. My dog will watch the car very nicely."

"I watch the dog, no? Fine dog like that, somebody could steal it for the
big reward."

"No." She started the motor, and the car lurched backward. But the boy
clung to the door. "I am Vito," he said cheerfully. "I show you much better
parking place. I show you anything you like in town, anything at all. I
speak good English, because one year when my father is alive he pay to
have me go across the line to American school." He had somehow con-
trived to open the door, and was within. "You want nice curios, fine leather
huaraches twenty percent off?"

It was the time for Talley to play the protecting role, but he had obligingly leaped over into the back seat and was licking the intruder's neck in
welcome. "Now, young man—" began Miss Withers severely. Then she
thought of something. "Do you happen to know what store here in Tijuana
sells little toy horses and riders made of plaited straw?"

"You make fun, lady." Vito looked searchingly up into her face. "Two,
three hundred curio stores here—every one sells the *caballito de paja*." He
lowered his voice. "Maybe you want sleepy pills, no prescription? You
want Paris postcards, absinthe, maybe Mary Warners? You want dorty
books? I take you to one very fine dorty bookstore, you can buy *Fanny
Heel* and *Life an' Loves of Frank 'Arris?*"

"No! Get out, you nasty child. Must I call a policeman?"

"But, lady, no policeman even can show you anything in thees town I
can't!" Vito insisted proudly. "Tell me, what you really come for, eh?"

Miss Withers hesitated, looking down on her self-appointed guide with
sudden compassion. He did look rather hungry. "Vito," she said, "is there a
place nearby where we can get a nice chocolate ice-cream soda?"

It was her theory that a boy is a boy anywhere. The dazed youth gave her
directions, and a few minutes later—leaving Talley locked and unhappy in

the car—they were inside a little *botica* which looked exactly like a corner drugstore anywhere. Craftily the schoolteacher waited until Vito's straw made sucking sounds in the glass, and then over her own coffee she remarked casually, "Young man, you have guessed that I did not come down here for ice cream. I am—I'm looking for someone, and I don't know just where to begin."

Dark eyes comprehended. "Your man, he run off with some pretty *ramera?*"

"Er—no, Vito. I am looking for a girl, or more probably two girls. Americans, but they do not go back across the border, even to sleep."

"I catch. You are the mama, or the relative. You do not like that the gorls work in one of the hook shops over on Negrete or maybe do the strip tease in some *cantina.* You wish to find them and take them home."

She explained somewhat. Vito frowned. "They are hiding here, yes?"

"Yes. At least if they are here at all they won't exactly be advertising their presence. Perhaps a bright boy like you could help me to locate them, without their knowing." She added, whispering, "I am something of a detective."

Brown eyes bugged. "A detective like Deek Tracy?"

"More, I hope, like Sherlock Holmes." Miss Withers went on to outline the functions of the original Baker Street Irregulars, and never did seed fall on more fertile ground. "Five bucks," said Vito firmly. Then, as she nodded, "And five more when I find out what you want, okay?" Nor were pesos acceptable; only American dollars were legal tender here. But the boy scorned her card with the hotel address scribbled thereon. "You come with me, we find 'em now if they're here."

"But how? This must be a city of at least fifty thousand—it's spread out all over the hills and both banks of the river. There must be hundreds of apartments and auto courts and rooming houses."

He grinned wisely. "Maybe so. But you say they are rich gorls. They know how to cook? They make all their own meals?" Miss Withers had her doubts about that. "Then you listen, lady. Such high-class *turistas* would only go to extra-special place to eat, which here in Tijuana we got very few of. Let's go!"

Doubtful but willing, Miss Withers found herself out on the Avenida again, playing chauffeur to a big, sleepy poodle and a small, alert Mexican boy. She stopped the car outside half a dozen restaurants—Caesar's, Chez Goldman, Nacho's, The Original Nacho's.

Each time Vito would pop hopefully inside, and then come out smiling and shaking his head. "If only you had a peecture of the gorls!" he said finally.

"No picture," Miss Withers admitted. "But they are very pretty girls—and one of them has bright-red hair, or at least she did have. And even if it's dyed the roots should be showing by now."

He nodded, and tried again at a place called Los Coyotitos, drawing another blank. "They all say maybe so, maybe no," he confessed. "Now we try the last shot in our locket. Is the Primero Hotel restaurant, where my cousin Carlos is busboy." They went back down the Avenida for over a mile and turned into an almost-filled parking lot in the shadow of a block-long cathedral whose pink towers and buttresses were illuminated by mammoth floodlights. It looked, she decided, as if the architect's mother had been frightened by a Moorish pastry cook. "Don't tell me that is the hotel!" Miss Withers gasped.

"No, lady. That is the Fronton, where they play handball with baskets. Very fast game, much big betting. Another cousin of mine, he is locker boy in the dressing rooms, he get many hot tips …"

"Some other time," said Miss Withers firmly. Vito pointed out to her a small hotel across the street, a teetering, five-story building bristling with sagging ornamental balconies, whose gap-toothed electric sign spelled out "—OT— — —RIM—RO," and beneath that the words, "*Cuisine Célèbre.*" "I think," said the schoolteacher, "that this time I shall join you. I could do with a bit of that *cuisine célèbre* myself."

The boy was already leading her across the street. Doors swung shut behind them, cutting off the noises of the town. She found herself being guided across a wide and almost deserted lobby, past flaking marble pillars and dusty potted palms. A desk clerk looked up from his newspaper, photographed her with one blink of his bulging, ophidian eyes, and turned away forever disinterested.

They passed the wide arched entrance to a bar—obviously a respectable bar, for there were more women than men in the place, young women in sedate black gowns whose eyes were intent on the small glasses of vermouth before them. Then on into the dining room, a vaulted space somewhat smaller than Grand Central Station, filled with white empty tables and lined with booths, some filled with family parties. A few waiters hovered about, like seagulls looking for a place to light. There was a patina about the place, an ancient, mellowed odor of oil and garlic and spices like that of a fine old salad bowl.

Vito led her to a booth at the rear of the room. "Better I talk to Carlos alone," he said softly. "My cousin has not much of the English. Order the family dinner. And lay off the Peruvian wines, they're sour."

He left her, and Miss Withers tapped her toe impatiently for some time. The family dinner, when it arrived, turned out to be a superb venison steak with an odd orange sauce, browned potatoes, new asparagus, and a mammoth romaine salad. The schoolteacher, who had resigned herself to the usual steaming platter of traditional Mexican dishes consisting mostly of chili peppers, set to with a will. The cooking, she decided, would compare with the best Manhattan could offer. So, unfortunately for her peace of mind, did the check when it came.

Yet even that shock was forgotten when she saw Vito slipping back across the long room, arriving at the booth at the same instant as a smallish, worried man with buck teeth, who immediately set about cleaning up the table with considerable clattering of china and glasses. "My cousin Carlos," said the boy proudly.

Miss Withers nodded, and Carlos burst into a flood of *sotto-voce* Spanish, of which the schoolteacher caught not one word in ten. "He says yes," Vito translated.

"Yes *what?*"

"Yes, he knows the young ladies. You want to give him something?"

The schoolteacher produced another five-dollar bill. "He says," continued Vito, "that they are a Miss Jones and her companion. They eat here almost every night. One very sweet and *simpática*, one very proud and haughty and difficult to please. He noticed them particularly because of what he calls the peenk hair—*color de rosa*."

"Eureka!" gasped Miss Withers. Never until this moment had she actually believed that her hunch would come true. "And does your cousin know where they live?"

Vito shrugged. "No. But he will try to find out for us later, perhaps. Anyway, there is nothing more to be done now. Nobody would be at home on Sunday night. They would be at the *jai-alai*, or the greyhound races, or ..."

"We'll look for them!" decided the schoolteacher, picking up her pocketbook. Vito looked pleased at the evidence that this oil well was not going to run dry on him, but Carlos' worried face brightened even more. He spouted Spanish again.

"He says," translated the boy, "that when the young ladies were having dinner here earlier this evening, he happened to notice that they were studying the list of entries for the *corrida de lebrel*, the greyhounds. It is only two small miles, lady—"

"Off to the races!" decided Miss Hildegarde Withers. It would, she felt, be most valuable to have a quiet look at her quarry while they were still unaware of her interest. She followed Vito out of the place, at the doorway giving a quick backward look toward the busboy. Carlos still stood by the booth with his tray of dishes, smiling an odd smile. Probably, she thought, the poor little man was dazed with his sudden wealth.

Coming back to the car, the schoolteacher found Talley the poodle howling softly, in a way he had of indicating that he was at the end of his patience. She placated him with a paper napkin filled with the remains of her dinner, and ten minutes later was pulling up toward the Agua Caliente race track, which at night rather resembled one of the country clubs in the Los Angeles area.

"The fifth race just comes up," Vito advised her. "We hurry."

As they stopped at one end of the parking lot, Talley made it very clear indeed that he was having no more of playing prisoner. It might have been different if he had had his beloved rubber rat along for company, but he was all for getting out of the car and staying out.

"No, Talley," said Miss Withers. "Be good for just a bit longer, and I'll bring you a hamburger or something." Hardening her heart, she pushed the eager apricot-colored face back inside and slammed the door, leaving the windows down on each side enough to give the dog plenty of air. He whined softly, then subsided and fell to worrying the paper napkin.

As they approached the turnstiles, Vito gallantly produced a pair of passes to the track, explaining that they were given away in Tijuana with any purchase of five cents or more. Late as it was, people were still hurrying in. Miss Withers and her young escort moved along with the current, winding up on a lower level of the sparsely filled grandstand. The wide slope between stand and rail was filled with a few thousand spectators milling thither and yon, people of all conceivable colors and conditions. There were whole Mexican families, from the proud *papacito* to the smallest *niña* sucking a *dulce*; there were impassive Chinese with fistfuls of pari-mutuel tickets; there were groups of well-dressed Negroes obviously enjoying themselves, and a great many white norteamericanos—most of them in uniform—who were feeling no pain.

It was not the easiest place in the world to locate two girls, as Miss Withers observed to her companion. Vito grudgingly tore his attention away from the track—a smaller oval which had somehow been mysteriously superimposed upon the larger *hipódromo* in the hour or two after the horse races wound up this afternoon. Out there the greyhounds were being paraded around the track at a pace slow enough to permit every last *yanqui* dollar to pass into the mutuels before they were locked into the starting gate. Each starved, humped-looking beast was led by a handler. Ahead of them waltzed a dapper zoot-suited clown in straw hat and spats, swinging a cane. From the public address system a record blasted "Good Night, Irene."

"I like Number Three," said Vito. "His tail has just the right curl."

Miss Withers sniffed. "I don't believe either of the young ladies we are seeking is running in this race. Get busy, young man."

He sobered at once. "We never find them just wandering like this. In the stands there is a man; he rents binoculars. If we had them, and stood down there by the rail—"

"An excellent suggestion." Miss Withers nodded. "With all the lights blazing, it would be an easy thing to sweep the entire grandstand and the betting area." It was no sooner said then done, or very little sooner. While every other person in the throng watched the parade of dogs, the posturing master of ceremonies, or the odds board, a maiden schoolteacher and a Mexican school boy stood against the rail near the judges' stand and watched them, face by face, row by row.

They were so engrossed that they did not see their doom until it was upon them.

Outside, in the parking lot beyond the turnstiles, Talleyrand had long since finished with the paper napkins in which his meager lunch had been wrapped. He had searched both front and back seat of the little rented coupé without finding anything of interest, not even any comforting belonging of his mistress. The small prison was narrow and chilly and lonely—and the sound of the crowd so near and yet so far set the big poodle's heart to beating strangely.

Talley was an unusual poodle, who had led an unusual life. It would not be fair to say that he was a spoiled poodle, since he was usually more than willing to meet humans halfway. But he was a gregarious dog; moreover, a dog who had inherited certain mental traits and physical abilities from a long line of theatrical ancestors. A few minutes of careful research told him that the door latches were beyond his best efforts, but something might just possibly be done about the narrow space at the top of the window. ...

He went up, got head and paws out, and wriggled through, landing handily on his forefeet like a tumbler. Then without hesitation, without any stupid bloodhound's sniffing for tracks, he was off. His hot brown eyes had seen his mistress pass through a certain gate. Like an apricot-colored streak of lightning he was after her. The gateman glimpsed only a moving shadow, the merest ghost of a dog, swore softly and then crossed himself. No more *pulque* tonight.

Inside the enclosure of Agua Caliente's racetrack the stentorian voice of the announcer had just called the attention of the crowd to the fact that the greyhounds were nearing the starting gate. There was a rush of last-minute betters toward the pari-mutuel windows, and an equal rush outside to see the final odds. Of course there were guards and other track employees about who should have seen and headed off the determined poodle, but their attention too was in the other direction, toward the odds board or the starting gate.

Through the ramp, through the clubhouse building, out into the crowd Talley trotted, sniffing now for all he was worth. He worked his way up into the grandstand, along past the mezzanine boxes, and down the other side. Once on the stairs a man in uniform did cry after him, but Talley neatly reversed his field and darted back down the slope toward the fence, under and sometimes between the legs of the crowd, causing mild hysteria here and there in his abrupt passing.

And then the judge on the platform waved his program and crossed over the track to the other side. The grandstand lights went dark, and far across the oval a white bouncing object—a mechanical robot which could have suggested rabbit only to an animal like the dog whose eyesight is his poorest faculty—started its bouncing trip around the track.

It circled and came closer, past the racing greyhounds trapped in their wire cages, on and on in its first trip past the finish line. "They're off!" cried the announcer's voice, magnified a thousand times, and the crowd tensed as gates snapped open and eleven greyhounds poured forth.

Talley, having viewed the entire procedure from between the legs of an excited man at the front of the crowd, poured too. It was not that he mistook the robot mechanism for a real rabbit—indeed, he had seen rabbits only in dreams. But with a poodle's quickness he caught the general idea and decided to enter into the spirit of the game. Over the fence he went, in the effortless leap of his loose-limbed breed. He was out on the track a stone's throw ahead of the field, even ahead of the rabbit. But he angled cleverly toward the other side, to head off the quarry.

The excited screams of the crowd died suddenly into a mass gurgle, above which the announcer's mechanically charged voice boomed, "At the start it's Five, Two, and—urp!" There was nothing for anybody to say. Out on the track a comic, fantastic interloper was sprinting, timing himself so cleverly that he met the rabbit almost head on. Talley even managed to get a mouthful of cloth before the momentum of the thing flung him tail over applecart. Nothing daunted, he collected himself and set out bravely after it at a full gallop. Behind him, unnoticed in his joyful excitement, came the eleven frenzied hounds. ...

"Oh, *no!*" screamed Miss Hildegarde Withers, dropping the binoculars and pressing both hands over her face. She was speechless for perhaps the first time in her life, having momentarily forgotten how to pray and never having learned how to swear.

"*Jesús, María y José!*" cried Vito helpfully. "Lookit the sonofabeech go!"

Peering through her fingers, Miss Withers saw that Talley was still in there trying, but falling off the pace. Head down, brown legs flying so fast that they blurred in the white floodlights, the poodle stuck to the inside rail, waiting for that rabbit or whatever it was to run itself out.

He was still driving when suddenly he was rammed from behind by eleven greyhounds, was overcome and trampled and submerged in a mad flurry of entangled dog. The rabbit forgotten, a number of the leaders set upon Talley as the next best thing, and suddenly the night was rent by horrid sounds. It was a free-for-all, with the poodle underneath.

"I can't bear to look!" moaned Miss Withers. "Vito, tell me—"

"Is okay," the boy told her. "Four of 'em still running. I think number Three is in the lead—yes!"

"But—" The schoolteacher opened her eyes. There was still pandemonium out on the track, with the handlers rushing back to try and separate the dogs. No sign of Talley anywhere, not even when the fracas had been resolved. She sagged back against the fence. "They can't have eaten him whole!" she protested. "There should at least be some brown fur—"

"*Three* wins!" observed Vito happily. The four dogs who had managed to avoid the melee had circled the track and crossed the finish line, "And I put the five bucks you paid me right on the nose!" he added.

"Not even his collar left!" Miss Withers was saying. She remained disconsolate, even when Vito pointed out to her that racing greyhounds run in leather muzzles, and that with his teeth and fuzzy protective coat Talleyrand had had rather the best of it.

She shrugged. " 'Life must go on ...' " said Miss Withers dully. She had suddenly lost all interest in the proceedings, though she waited while Vito returned the rented binoculars and cashed his win ticket. They passed out through the turnstile.

"Perhaps if we wait here, and watch while people come out?" the boy suggested.

"Very well, but I feel in my bones that it won't do any good," the schoolteacher told him. They waited, and it didn't. After the last race was over, and the last of the crowd had trickled forth into the parking lot and the waiting taxicabs, Vito had to agree with her. No pair of pretty young Americanas fitting the description of Dallas Trempleau and Ina Kell had been at the greyhound races this night.

Slowly the schoolteacher and the Mexican boy went back across the almost-empty parking lot to the little coupé parked at the far end. "He was only a dog, after all," Miss Withers was saying, mostly to herself. "Companionable enough, in his way. But often a nuisance, and a considerable expense with meat prices as they are. I should have a cat anyway, or perhaps go back to tropical fish. ..."

They came up to the car, and she unlocked the door. "Hop in," she told the boy, and he hopped. From beneath the car came a sheepish, bedraggled brown shadow, who hopped too. Talleyrand sat on the front seat, wagging his stump of a tail furiously, aware that he had transgressed the mysterious laws of humankind but confident of being scolded and forgiven.

"*You!*" she cried. "What have you to say for yourself?"

Talley wagged wider, unable to explain that when the press of greyhounds had become too great he had wisely withdrawn from the fray, vaulted the infield fence, and then circled around until he found a way out through the enclosure.

They drove back into Tijuana, and as they came past the Hotel Primero Vito put a hand on her arm. "We stop here, no? Maybe my cousin Carlos has found out where the gorls live?"

It was Miss Withers' considered opinion that his cousin Carlos couldn't find his own pants pocket, but she prided herself on keeping an open mind. "Very well," she said, and drew over to the curb. "You may go and see."

In a moment the boy was back, grinning. "You come with me, lady. My cousin Carlos has found where the gorls live." He gestured. "Right there!"

"Right where?"

"In the hotel!"

"I see," said Miss Withers grimly. "*Now* he tells us." She paid Vito his remaining five dollars, patted him gently but firmly on the head, and sent him on his way.

"But, lady—"

"Enough is enough," said the schoolteacher, who had had a difficult day and a still more difficult night. She watched the boy out of sight and then crossed the Avenida and again entered the hotel. Nothing, it seemed, had changed except that some of the lights in the lobby were dimmed and the palm trees in their pots were even dustier.

This time she went directly to the desk. The same young man was there, reading the same newspaper. "I am sorry, but we have no vacancies," he said firmly.

"Oh?" Miss Withers hastily replanned her strategy. "I had so hoped that you would have something for me. You were so well recommended."

"By who?"

Resisting the impulse to correct his English, she said, "Why, by the two American girls—"

"*Norteamericanas?*" It was a mild reproof, but definite.

"Of course. Miss Jones and her companion—they do live here?"

The ophidian eyes were ever so faintly amused. "They did, señora. But they checked out a little while ago."

"Oh?" Miss Withers blinked. "But that was very sudden, wasn't it?"

The padded shoulders shrugged delicately. "Perhaps. But death is always sudden, is it not?"

"*Death?*" Suddenly there was a new scent in the schoolteacher's flaring nostrils, drowning out the dusty odor of the potted palms, the musky reek of the man's pomade. It was an acrid, bitter scent—the smell of defeat.

"Be bold, Be bold, and every where, Be bold ..."
—EDMUND SPENSER

10

The oily young man at the desk waited patiently, obviously enjoying the impression he had made. But then Miss Withers remembered the affinity that all Spanish peoples have for *la muerte*, even to the extent of giving their children grinning skulls of candy and gingerbread to play with. "Let's back up and start over," she said crisply. "Whose death was it? Not one of the young ladies?"

"Oh, no, señora." There was almost a trace of regret in the soft, chocolaty voice. "But Miss Jones said they had to leave suddenly because of a death in the family."

The schoolteacher relaxed. Whose death it had been and how long ago it had happened were not hard to guess at. The ripples made by Tony Fagan's splash into eternity were still moving outward, as they would move forever.

Dallas and Ina—it could be nobody else—had obviously fled in a panic because somehow they had learned that questions were being asked about them. Vito, of course! The little scamp had taken her money and then, while she was eating dinner, had dashed off to turn another fast dollar by warning the quarry. But at least she was on the right trail. "Can you tell me where they've gone?" Miss Withers pressed hopefully. "I'm most anxious to reach them, because they are relatives—nieces of mine. Did they make reservations anywhere?"

The clerk shrugged. "They only throw everything into a so-beautiful big blue Cadillac and go. I suppose maybe they go home."

Miss Withers had reasons for supposing maybe not, but she did not voice them. "But surely they left a forwarding address for mail and things?"

He grudgingly informed her that the young ladies had received no mail. The New York address given when they registered would have been located, the schoolteacher realized, somewhere in the midst of the Central Park Zoo.

"Perhaps Miss Jones and her companion will return here," she said. "Meanwhile the room they left must be vacant, is it not? May I see it, please?"

The objections were almost interminable. The rent of the suite had been paid for the rest of the week, and really it should stand vacant. Moreover, the rooms were no doubt in great disorder. They would have to be set to rights, and the maids would not return until tomorrow. The clerk was a thousand times sorry, but he himself could not leave his desk to do the work of the housekeeper.

Miss Withers played her ace in the form of another five-dollar bill, and a moment later was headed up the stairs with a key in her hand. Three-A was at the end of the second-floor hall, in the front. Her heart beating high, the schoolteacher entered and turned on the light. She found herself in a surprisingly comfortable living room, furnished in ranchero style with hand-made leather chairs and couch, and even a venerable radio in one corner. The place, however, had the appearance of having been tossed like a mixed green salad. Whoever had lived here had decamped as if all the devils of hell were after them, instead of one lone spinster.

The dust of their departure was only just beginning to settle, and, old Indian tracker that she was, Miss Withers decided that half an hour sooner and she would have bumped into the girls head-on. So near and yet so far; she felt like the farm boy who almost heard the cow bell. Yet just possibly there were things still to be learned here. She closed her eyes and sniffed, noting a heavy, exotic perfume and a lighter one, probably gardenia; bath salts, cigarettes, leather, and fingernail polish.

Pari-mutuel tickets from this very afternoon's improvement of the breed at Caliente were scattered on the floor, mostly ten-and fifty-dollar win tickets. There was a marked program, much thumbed and twisted. Somebody had made neat checkmarks against the names of the lighter-weighted horses. Somebody had also, if one could judge by the remaining tickets, lost well over eight hundred dollars today. Other flotsam and jetsam included a spool of No. 50 white thread, a sheer nylon stocking (size 7) without a visible snag or run, an almost new Canasta deck, a dozen tickets on next

Wednesday's drawing of the Lotería Nacional at Mexico City, a bitten apple and an empty aspirin bottle.

The bathroom was equally unrevealing, except that forgotten in the tub was an almost new cake of scented soap which the schoolteacher estimated would have cost two or three dollars back home. In the trash basket were used facial tissue, the shell of a carmine lipstick, half-a-dozen empty beer cans and a quart bottle that had once held prefabricated Manhattan cocktails.

There was still the small bedroom with its twin beds, both neatly made up but bearing on their spreads the mark of suitcases flung open for packing. The closets were bare except for dangling wire hangers, the bureau drawers all half-open and askew. In one of them Miss Withers noticed several bronze hairpins, a pair of tiny green dice, some spilled face powder, and a sales slip from Anton's on the Avenida for a fifty-dollar alligator handbag. She began to have a growing feeling of frustration. No letters, no lost little address book, no diary or telephone numbers hastily scribbled on a wall somewhere.

Back in the living room the schoolteacher riffled through the piles of American magazines on the table, *Vogue* and *Flair* and *The New Yorker, Harper's* and *Holiday* and *True Romances*; all the current movie fan magazines, enough of them indeed to stock the periodical room of a fair-sized public library. As a last resort she probed beneath the cushions of the couch and chairs, coming up with eighty cents in change, a twenty-five-centavo piece, a smashed liqueur chocolate and a single copper-jacketed cartridge which she fancied must fit a small-caliber gun, such as a .28. This, as everything, she left as it was.

The birds had flown, and there seemed nothing in the abandoned nest to suggest the probable direction of flight. Yet perhaps the simple fact that they had decamped at the first hint of an inquiry being made about them was significant. Why leave a comfortable haven like this? They were safe here on Mexican soil; they could laugh and snub their pretty noses at amateur detectives and, for that matter, at police and process servers, too.

Unless Dallas Trempleau was afraid that little Ina would weaken under pressure. She must be determined, of course, to keep the younger girl down here until after Junior Gault's trial, which couldn't be postponed forever. There might be some point, Miss Withers decided, in getting Ina alone sometime and pointing out to her a few of the facts of life about murder— and murderers.

The schoolteacher realized that from the point of view of the room clerk she must be taking a rather long time to decide about whether or not she wanted the place. She snapped out of her musings and went hastily back to turn off the bedroom light. Standing in the middle of the room to have one last look around, suddenly she heard a brisk tattoo at the front door and the sound of its being thrown open. "Comes trouble," murmured Miss Withers under her breath. Her five dollars' worth was evidently up. "Yes?" she called out.

"Come out, my beautifuls, wherever you are!" It was a man's voice, young and strong and musical. "Look, my ball-and-chain-to-be had to start back to Hollywood because she has a story conference early tomorrow morning, and see what she has left behind!" He was a tall, beautiful, lightly-bronzed young man, wearing a frantic Hawaiian shirt, English flannel slacks, and red sandals. In each hand he carried a large green bottle. The smile on his classic features froze there as Miss Withers suddenly appeared in the doorway. "Who're you?" he demanded suspiciously. "And where are the girls?"

"I am all the girls there are," Miss Withers said crisply. Then she noticed that there was another man behind the first intruder, an older, less beautiful character in a sober blue-serge suit. He was obviously Mexican, with In-dian cheekbones and an old-world beak of a nose.

"Sorry," said the young man in the fancy shirt. "Wrong room. We were looking for Dallas and Ina. ..."

"It happens to be the right room," said Miss Withers. "But no girls. My—my nieces seem to have suddenly moved out. But don't be in a hurry, young man. If you're a friend of theirs, perhaps you can suggest where to find them?"

The colorful youth, it developed, was not only a bosom friend but a next-door neighbor. He introduced himself, with professionally charming manners, as one Nikki Braggioli. His companion was Ramon something-or-other. ...

"Ramon Julio Guzman y Villalobos, Lic., Investigationes Privados," was the legend on his card, with an address on the Calle Augustin Melgar. He was charmed to make the acquaintance of the Señora—sorry, *Señorita* Withers—and after a quick but searching glance around the room he sat down on the edge of a leather chair, obviously alert and ready to rise again at any moment.

But Miss Withers had set about cultivating them both shamelessly. It was not too difficult to pump Nikki—he was friendly as a puppy. Or per-haps a kitten would have been more apt as a comparison, for he was filled with an innocent selfishness. In ten minutes the schoolteacher learned that he was the son of an Italian father and an English mother, educated at a public school in Surrey but caught by the war in his native land. He had managed to avoid active participation in Mussolini's youth movements, but after the war and the invasion of Italy by American motion-picture companies he had been chosen to play a bit part in Paradox's mammoth "Hannibal at the Gates," the eight-million-dollar epic they had recently shot on location in Rome. There he had met and wooed or been wooed by the coauthor of the screenplay, Mary May Dee, who had had to return to Hollywood when the picture was in the can, but who had arranged for his flying across the Atlantic and who now drove down every week end to be with him. He himself would have to remain here until his number came up on the quota, after which would ring out the wedding bells. Too bad he had missed a chance to try out for the part of Valentino in the screen biography, but there would be other parts, and with his future wife's influence. "You have heard of her, of course?"

"Of course," admitted Miss Withers, trying hard. She never noticed the names of writers on the screen. There had been her own brief whirl in Hollywood, as technical adviser on the life of Lizzie Borden, but that had been many years ago. Since then Paradox Studios had probably changed ownership, management, all of its writers and everything except its inge-nues and the plots of its pictures.

With an effort the schoolteacher managed to get the conversation back on the track, but Nikki's mind seemed to be a perfect blank on the question of where the missing girls might be. They had, he implied, been simply delightful neighbors and companions for going places. On the Trempleau pocketbook, Miss Withers presumed; this orchid man was purely a decora-tive, parasitic growth. "We had much fun," Nikki admitted wistfully. "They love to gamble."

That much Miss Withers would readily concede. One of them at least was gambling for high and dangerous stakes.

"What else would *Norteamericanas* come down here for?" put in the older man suddenly. His jet eyes sparkled, his sardonic mouth tightened into a wry smile. "They come here only to gamble, to marry or divorce or get drunk."

A brief silence, tactfully covered by Nikki's saying, "Perhaps then the young ladies go home? Why not? To me—to most Europeans today at least, it seems strange why people who can live in the United States ever go anywhere else."

"There are other good places to live besides in the Colossus of the North," pronounced Señor Guzman sententiously. "And speaking of going home—" He rose.

"An excellent idea," agreed Miss Withers. She ushered her callers gen-tly but firmly out of the place and locked the door carefully. After pausing at the desk in the lobby to return the key and to explain that she would like to think it over and make up her mind about the suite, she hurried out to the rented coupé and Talley. On the sidewalk was Señor Guzman, looking vainly for a taxicab.

"May I give you a lift?" she wanted to know. "I'm going right through town. ..."

He bowed stiffly, and consented to embark. Talleyrand had awakened and greeted the stranger as he greeted all strangers, with great enthusiasm. He was rebuffed. "In my country," said Guzman by way of apology, "we do not sentimentalize over dogs."

"Nor over any animals, especially bulls," said Miss Withers, but to her-self. "Tell me," she said casually. "How long has Mary May Dee been paying you to keep an eye on her handsome young fiancé?"

He said, "But I do not understand."

"Aren't you, according to your business card, a private detective?"

Guzman produced another card, with slightly different lettering. "I am also a licensed *abogado*, a member of the bar."

"I knew it! There is *something* distinguished about you lawyers—"

It was laid on with a trowel, but he softened perceptibly. "Mary May Dee is a client of mine," he said. "I have secured several divorces for her, but she has not hired me to watch over her intended. As a matter of fact—"

Miss Withers had long held a private opinion that "as a matter of fact," like "really and truly," usually meant the exact opposite, but she did not say so. He went on, "I was only introduced to Nikki Braggioli yesterday, when we met in a bar. Miss Dee introduced us, and he seized the opportunity, when she was out of the room, to tell me that he had American friends, beautiful neighbors, who were in some sort of difficulties and who had asked him if he knew someone experienced and discreet who knew about criminology and detective work. I explained that I had some slight experience in the field, and he promised to take the first opportunity to introduce me, which happened to be this evening—or so we thought."

Surprised, the schoolteacher cut the throttle a little. If the girls had been looking for a private detective, then they must have been afraid of something. That might even explain the cartridge in the chair cushion. "I don't suppose, Señor Guzman, that you were advised of what it was that my— my nieces were worried about?"

Inside the dark and moving car she could not clearly see his face, and his voice was without expression. "I was not, señorita. I have no idea what they wanted. Now they have gone, and I have wasted an evening."

They were now coming back into the business section of the town. "You are so busy, then?"

"Señorita," he told her soberly, "on a good night sometimes I marry and divorce half a dozen couples, at a very comfortable fee."

She jammed the brakes. "Don't tell me you are a judge *too?*"

"No, no judge. You do not understand. If anybody really wants to get married here, they must wait three days and go through the usual formalities. If they want a divorce they have to have witnesses and appear in court. But for Americans we have a special deal. They merely sign a marriage or divorce paper, which later I mail to Chihuahua, where maybe later the paid proxies appear in court and complete the proceedings—if my esteemed fellow-counselors do not forget about the whole thing or mislay the papers. In any case the *Yanquis* think they are legally married or divorced as the case may be, which is the important thing, no?"

"No," said Miss Withers firmly. "A thing is either true or it isn't. You sound very bitter, Mr. Guzman."

"Who would not be?" The lawyer-detective waved his hand at the Avenida before them. "Thousands of your countrymen pour across the border every day. They laugh at our quaint customs, our funny accents. They pay too much for our poorest liquor and our cheapest curios, and too little for our unfortunate girls. The great city of San Diego, of which we are a suburb, a convenient outhouse, boasts with literal truth that it has no slums, no gambling hells, no red-light district. We here in Tijuana fill that place. ..." He caught himself. "But you must excuse the sermon. I sincerely hope, señorita, that you locate your missing *nieces* and take them back with you where they belong before they get into trouble down here."

"Perhaps," admitted Miss Withers, "it is already a little late for that. I may eventually have to avail myself of your professional services. You will be in your office tomorrow?" Stopping at his direction outside a garishly illuminated little office building just off the avenue, she accepted dry, waspish thanks and watched him disappear inside.

"Dear me!" murmured the schoolteacher. Thoughtfully she wound the little rented car through the still-rushing traffic. The flood of American cars had turned, and soon Miss Withers found herself caught in a sort of riptide, almost fender to fender and bumper to bumper with three lanes of homeward-bound autos, whose drivers seemed weary and nervous and apt to lean on their horns. She inched slowly across the bridge and eventually up to the wide gates. Ahead of her the customs and immigration officials were stopping each car. One in every five or six had to open its luggage compartment for cursory inspection. About every tenth car was thoroughly, meticulously searched. Glad that she had no contraband aboard, she moved up when her turn finally came. A patient man in the uniform of the immigration service wanted to know where she was born.

"Dubuque, Iowa—I have my passport right here, though of course the picture was taken some years ago and never was what one would call flattering—"

"Drive on, lady," he said hastily. But it was Miss Withers' turn to ask a question. The man admitted that he had been on duty here since six this evening, that he had not seen a blue Cadillac with two pretty girls in it; if he had seen anything like that he would remember it; although he was past being interested in pretty girls he still had a soft spot in his heart for Cadillacs.

Relieved but hardly surprised, Miss Withers drove on for a dozen feet or so, still in the no man's land between the two sister republics, and then was halted again. This time it was by a big, burly man, a lobster-visaged character in a uniform that fitted a bit too soon everywhere. "And what did you buy in Mexico?" he demanded.

"Nothing, officer, absolutely nothing."

"So?" he peered with casual disinterest into the little car and then stiffened as he saw Talleyrand, who was now curled up asleep on the back seat. "What's *that?*"

"A standard French poodle."

"It is, eh? Well, lady, you can't bring it into the United States, whatever you claim it is. No animals without a veterinary's certificate."

"Officer, don't be silly!" Miss Withers was suddenly, incredibly weary.

Thoughts of that comfortable bed awaiting her in the room up at the Grant Hotel made her a bit less politic than she might have been. "After all, if you have eyes in your head, you must see that he's not a Mexican dog. I didn't buy him down there, I've owned him for nearly two years. If you don't believe me try him on some Spanish—Talley doesn't speak a word of it."

"Now, lady—"

"I mean, he doesn't *understand* a word. And he hasn't been out of the car, not to speak of, all the time we've been in Tijuana."

Lobster-face stiffened a little. "Well, lady, if you have eyes to see, you can read that sign on the other side, just where you approached the Mexican entry gate, warning people going across not to take their pets. I didn't make the rules."

"But this is perfectly ridiculous! He has a license tag on his collar—a New York tag. That is still, I believe, part of the U.S.A. Officer, I insist—"

Insisting is the wrong way to handle officers, of whatever stripe. This one was obviously at the end of his patience. "You can go through, lady. But we hold the dog. After all, there's a lot of hoof-and-mouth disease down in Mexico, and rabies, too." He jerked his thumb. "If you don't want to leave the dog, I suggest you just turn around and go back to Tijuana and hunt up a vet. There's one on the corner of 7th and Bravo, and he'll only charge you two bucks."

There was nothing else for it. Miss Withers turned around and drove disconsolately back into Tijuana again, finding the town much quieter now because most of the remaining tourists were safely settled down inside the honky-tonks. The veterinary's office at 7th and Bravo was closed and padlocked, with a card on the door saying that in emergencies Dr. Doxa could be reached at such and such a number. She finally found a pay phone, but after fifteen minutes of wrestling with the Teléfono Municipal the harried schoolteacher gave it up as a bad job and drove wearily back along the Avenida to the Primero Hotel.

"Having thought it all over," she told the heavy-lidded young man at the desk, "I have decided to take that suite after all. May I register, please?"

"*Madre!*" he whispered fervently. "At this hour."

Quickly she explained that clean linens could wait until the morrow and cashed a traveler's check for enough to cover advance payment in lieu of having baggage. Eventually she received a receipt and a key and at last led the weary poodle up the stairs and into the little hotel suite she had thought never to see again.

After the plane trip across country and the evening's misadventures, the schoolteacher was wearier than she had ever been in her life. She thought only of bed—and then discovered that under one of the pillows was the little pistol to fit the cartridge, and that under the other had been neatly folded a clean nightgown—a fantastic, black-lace nightgown right out of a Petty drawing. "I would sooner be found dead than wear a thing like that," said Miss Withers to herself. "Or would I?" It must of course have been

Dallas Trempleau's, forgotten in the mad exodus. She held it up to the light, admiring the handiwork. There was a Paris label.

Five minutes later the schoolteacher was asleep in one of the twin beds, with Talley curled up on the other. Both were *hors de combat*, dead to the world. It was not surprising that when an hour or so later a key turned in the lock of the hall door, neither of them heard it or even stirred.

"Each chasing each through all the weary hours,
And meeting strangely at one sudden goal."
—SIR EDWIN ARNOLD

11

The sudden blaze of the bedroom light was the signal for pandemonium. Talley, startled out of doggish dreams, burst into a frenzy of excited barking. Miss Withers popped up in bed, took stock of the situation, and grabbed the dog's collar. "Stay where you are!" she advised the intruder. "He's a killer, and if you move so much as a finger—"

Standing in the doorway was a tallish girl in tailored flannel slacks, a mannish but well-filled white shirt, and a beaver cape. Brown hair cut in a conservative short bob, pale handsome features; a head for a helmet. In a voice that carried polite overtones of Vassar or perhaps Sarah Lawrence she said quietly, "And just what are you doing here?" Obviously this young woman felt able to deal with anything, even a plain middle-aged spinster and a noisy poodle. Yet there was the scent of fear about her, an old fear that she had learned to ignore as one does a limp.

"I'm looking for you." Miss Withers could deal too, sometimes from the bottom of the deck. "And don't deny your identity, Dallas Trempleau, because I trailed you here from New York. Never mind how, either; even we amateur detectives have our professional secrets." She introduced herself, with flattering results.

"You're *that* Miss Withers, the murder lady? But, why—why in the world are you looking for *me*?"

"I imagine you know why, or can guess." The schoolteacher let go her hold on Talleyrand, who had ceased to make even token threats and was now wagging his tail and yawning. "Sit down, my dear, while we have a heart-to-heart talk," Miss Withers commanded. Being commanding (dressed as she was and with her hair in braids) wasn't easy, but she did her best. "Not that you have much choice. The party, Dallas, is over. It's time to go home."

The girl hesitated. "That's a threat, isn't it?"

"If you like. But you must admit that it was a mad idea from the first, this trying to hide an important witness for the prosecution in order to save your fiancé. Do you actually want to marry a man with the mark of Cain on his brow?"

"*Really!*" said Dallas, looking both exasperated and amused.

"Don't you know that murderers who get away with it once usually repeat?"

The girl sighed. "Nothing is ever that simple. You don't really know much about this case, do you? Tony Fagan was a prize stinker. Only Winston didn't kill him, I know it!"

"You dare say that in the face of his confession, and the lie-detector tests?"

"Yes! Winston may have beaten Fagan up, but somebody else killed him!"

"Fiddlesticks! But if you honestly believe that, why are you going to such fantastic lengths to tamper with a witness? Why not just let the defense attorney try to sell the idea to a jury?"

Dallas Trempleau tensed, and for a moment Miss Withers thought that she was about to turn and stride out of the door. But obviously the girl was all pent-up inside, and dying to talk to somebody, to justify herself. "You've met Bordin?"

"Yes. A very capable attorney, I gather."

"So they say. But—" She bit it off. "I don't altogether trust him," Dallas said. "I'm afraid he's defended so many guilty men that he doesn't know innocence when he sees it."

"So he thinks Junior Gault is guilty? It's a rather widely held opinion. The police, the district attorney's office—even I, after an interview with the accused, was reluctantly forced to chime in, for once, with the majority."

Dallas made a rite out of setting fire to a cigarette, and then said, as if it didn't matter in the least, "Oh, you saw him? How's he doing?"

"Not too well," said the schoolteacher. "He struck me as sulky, uncooperative, and guilty as—as anything."

"Some people," Dallas Trempleau admitted, "make a bad impression. Winston may be a little bitter. But he has his points."

"I didn't notice any."

"He made me break the engagement. And he wouldn't even let me come and see him in that place."

"So you took other measures?" The girl said nothing, and Miss Withers pressed, "Did Sam Bordin put you up to the idea of digging up the key witness for the prosecution and spiriting her away?"

"*I* dig her up?"

"Don't fence with me, child. You or Bordin, it makes no difference. Do you happen to know the legal penalty for tampering with witnesses?"

"Something unpleasant, no doubt. But what has that to do with me? If I want to spend some time traveling in Mexico—"

"That's enough of that. I know something about the country, having lived for a time in Mexico City, a very lovely and civilized metropolis. People who travel for pleasure in the Republica don't pass through Tijuana, because it's purely and simply a dead end. It has few charms and less advantages, except to hide out a witness—"

"*Who's* a witness?" Dallas cried. "She was never subpoenaed or anything!"

"At last we are getting around to talking about Ina Kell," said Miss Withers. "Your point is legal sophistry, and I think I recognize the source. You're in trouble, my dear. And don't depend upon Sam Bordin to get you out, because unless I miss my guess he's going to get himself disbarred for this little caper."

"I could hardly be less interested," admitted Miss Trempleau. "Though as far as I know, Mr. Bordin knows nothing whatever about it."

"About what? Never mind. That's your story and you'll stick to it. Where, by the way, is Ina now?" Dallas shrugged, and Miss Withers unlimbered some of her guns. "I know it isn't supposed to be any of my business, but I've made it my business. You're in trouble enough as it is, but I think that if necessary I can make you some more. Where's Ina?"

"I—I don't really know."

"Why did you come back here, after once checking out of the hotel?"

"Why not? The rent was paid in advance, and I didn't think they'd rent the suite. I still had a spare key, and I wanted to see if we'd forgotten anything—"

"Such as a little .28 pistol under that other pillow? And this nightgown?" Miss Withers flushed, and hastily began to explain how her own luggage had been stranded over in San Diego, and about how on finding the nightie here she just couldn't resist seeing what it would be like, for once in her life, to wear such a dashing garment. ...

If the confession had been calculated to disarm the girl it failed. "Oh, keep it by all means," she said. "Ina won't mind; she has lots more."

"Then at least you admit that Ina Kell is here in town with you! Where is she now? I don't suppose that, by any chance, she's right next door at the moment, in Mr. Braggioli's rooms?"

"No," said Dallas calmly. "Nikki is out on the town. It was only because I ran into him up the street just now, and learned that you'd been snooping here and gone, that I ventured to come back at all. The coast was supposed to be clear."

"But Ina shouldn't be alone—suppose something should happen to her?"

"*Suppose?*" Dallas Trempleau whispered. Suddenly the girl's face lighted with triumph. "Then you *are* on my side, after all! Because if Ina were in any danger, then that would mean that the real murderer is still at large, so it couldn't be Winston—"

"Not necessarily," cut in Miss Withers quickly, a little flustered. She hadn't meant that at all. "There could be two murderers. And if anything happened to that girl, it would seemingly prove Junior Gault's innocence. Without the possibility of her ever testifying, the case against him would certainly have to be dropped, you know that as well as I do. And there might be somebody who would go to those lengths to save him."

"Uh-*uh*," said Dallas. "I love the guy, but even I wouldn't."

"Or, with the Gault bankroll in the picture, some third party could easily be hired—"

The girl shook her head. "Not since Repeal. Besides, nobody knows we're here."

"I found you, so it's not impossible that someone else could."

Dallas leaned closer. "But not many people are as infernally clever as you are, Miss Withers. Listen to me, please. I've heard all about you. When Winston was first arrested, some friends of mine suggested that I ought to try to get you interested in the case, only I found you were out of town. But they said that you are a person who likes to interfere when you think there's some injustice done. I wish—I wish with all my heart that you'd start all over, and try to find out who really murdered Tony Fagan. He was a man who must have made many enemies, people who'd realize that anything that happened to him after that awful broadcast would automatically be blamed on poor Winston. It was a perfect setup, can't you see? If I could only convince you—"

"No use buttering me, child," said the schoolteacher firmly. "Sometimes I can believe as many as five impossible things before breakfast, but not now. This time I'm afraid I must string along with the police, who aren't always wrong except in old Hollywood B-pictures. There may have been others besides Junior Gault who had a motive to kill Fagan—"

"Of course there were! Even me, for instance!"

"You?"

"Certainly. Didn't Tony Fagan, on that final broadcast, say some nasty things about me and my voice?"

"He did, at that," admitted the schoolteacher cautiously.

"But did the police ever look into it, did they ever really suspect anybody but Winston? No—they had a ready-made suspect! Of course, I was home and in bed when the murder took place—"

"Of course," said Miss Withers. "And no doubt surrounded by old family retainers who've been devoted to you since your pigtail days, and who would gladly swear to anything you asked them?"

Dallas smiled. "It's obvious that you haven't had much experience with the usual run of servants lately. If it matters, I was at home—though I don't know if the couple who run the place heard me come in or not. What does matter is that the police hardly bothered to ask any questions, they were so sure of Winston. It could have been me—"

"Yes," said the schoolteacher. "That might explain why you're going to such lengths to see that Junior Gault gets off scot-free. And why you insist that you know he is innocent; a fact that could only be known to himself and to the real murderer. But I get your point, and I think we understand each other. Where's Ina, and what is to be done?"

"Must anything?"

"Certainly. You must face the music. Don't you see how much worse it will look for Junior if the news gets out that his fiancée is hiding the chief witness against him?"

"Does it have to get out?"

Miss Withers nodded. "I told you the party was over."

An odd look came into the girl's eyes. "But you have no proof," she said. "You've only guessed—" And then suddenly the starch went out of her. "Yes!" she admitted. "I brought Ina down here—"

Then there was the sound of a door being opened, and a clear young voice in the other room crying, "Hey, Dallas! What in the world is keeping you. It's cold out in the car!"

"In here," said Miss Withers dryly, "It's getting just a bit warmer. Hello, Ina Kell. Won't you come in, and join the party?"

The new arrival, poking her bright head uncertainly through the door-way, was very slight, very young, and very pretty in a nebulous, unformed sort of way. She wore a scanty white playsuit underneath a northern mink jacket, a multicolored bandanna around her sunset-shaded hair, and a pair of cork wedgies. Long-legged, dreamy-eyed, and scared—perhaps also just a bit thrilled with it all. There were brief introductions, marred somewhat by Talley's waking up, since the dog immediately tried to shake hands with the newcomer and lick her face at the same time.

"At last!" breathed Miss Withers, looking hard at the Kell girl. "You might as well relax," she said pleasantly. "It's all among friends. I was just telling Dallas that I am ringing down the curtain on your amateur theatri-cals. I've come to take you back home."

Ina seemed to shrink. She flashed an appeal at Dallas Trempleau, who nodded and said, "Ina, it actually seems to be the thing to do."

"But—but we don't *have* to go! Nobody can make us!"

"Perhaps not. But Miss Withers has pointed out that our staying here any longer may hurt Winston's chances."

"And besides," said the schoolteacher, "now that I've found you I haven't the slightest intention of letting either of you out of my sight, so what's the use?"

Ina shook her bright head wildly, like a spaniel coming out of the water. "You mean, I actually do have to go back there and testify in court?" She sounded desperate, and confused.

"Tell the truth, child," said Miss Withers. "And shame the devil."

"But—but if I testify, they'll find him guilty and hang him! And it'll be all my fault!"

"If Gault murdered a man, then he must be punished," the schoolteacher said.

"But he *didn't!*" Ina's normally gentle chin was defiant. "If I testify I'll have to tell the truth and back up what I said before, only it won't be the whole truth and it's not *fair!*"

"You too?" Miss Withers shook her head. "You maintain that in spite of everything the man is innocent when you yourself caught him practically red-handed? What, I wonder, is this strange power that Junior Gault wields over women, I mean young women?"

"It isn't that." Ina was trembling. "Honestly, I'm not hypnotized or anything. B-b-but honestly, you don't understand. ..."

"Then tell her, Ina," Dallas said coolly.

"D-d-do I have to?" Ina shrunk in upon herself.

"Your teeth are chattering," observed the schoolteacher critically. "What are you afraid of, child? Nobody is accusing you of anything. Is there anything you'd like to tell me—alone?"

Dallas Trempleau shrugged and half-rose to her feet as if to leave the bedroom, but the younger girl said quickly, "Oh, no, of course not! I mean—I guess I just took a chill sitting out there in the car, with the sea fog rolling in and everything. I wish—Dallas, is there any brandy?"

"Why, yes, down in the car. I'll run get it; we could all use a snort."

"Coffee might be more to the point," put in Miss Withers hopefully.

"I'll get the thermos filled," Dallas said agreeably. But as she rose and moved toward the door, Ina was quicker.

"I'll run down and get it," the red-haired girl cried breathlessly. "I should, shouldn't I? If I'm your companion then it's my job to run errands, isn't it?" The door slammed behind her.

Dallas Trempleau looked dazed. "You don't suppose she's running away, do you?" demanded Miss Withers.

"I don't think so. But little Ina is on the unpredictable side sometimes. Anyway, she couldn't run very far—she had a bad run of luck at the *jai-alai* games tonight and I don't think she has more than a few dollars left." Dallas frowned. "Perhaps I'd better run down and see what she's really up to—"

"No, you don't!" The schoolteacher fumbled beneath the other pillow, and came up with the little .28 pistol. "You're not going anywhere!"

"Okay," said the girl, and sat down and calmly lighted another cigarette. "Though I can see that you couldn't hit a barn door with that gun. You don't trust me, do you, Miss Withers?"

"I don't trust anybody." And there was a strained silence until at long last the outer door burst open and back came Ina Kell loaded down with a bottle, a thermos and a bulging paper bag. She had, she explained, had to walk blocks to find a clean-looking all-night lunchroom.

Even so it turned into quite a feast, with coffee drunk out of bathroom glasses and Talley the poodle gratefully finishing off the remains of the chicken enchiladas. The coffee was strong enough to float a spoon, but it was comfortingly hot. Miss Withers had a refill or two, but refused the brandy with which both the girls laced their own. After all, it was their tongues she wanted loosed, not hers.

In the somewhat more relaxed and cozier atmosphere, the schoolteacher plumped two pillows together behind her back and took the floor. "Now!" she said firmly. "Let's get down to cases. All I know about this business is what the inspector and Mr. Hardesty chose to tell me—the latter, Ina, being very disappointed in you."

Ina said quickly, "But if he knew *why* I ran away, he'd understand."

"Perhaps he would, but I most certainly do not. Of course, it's only by hearsay several times removed that I know anything about what happened in Tony Fagan's apartment that morning last December. Young woman, just what do you mean when you say that Winston Gault, Jr., is innocent but that if you tell the truth in your testimony you'll convict him?"

It was a moot point. Ina hesitated, looking at Dallas Trempleau, who nodded encouragingly. "Go on," Dallas said. "She's supposed to be an expert."

"Well—" Ina studied her long, pale fingernails. "I'll have to start at the beginning."

"Of course." Miss Withers smiled. " ' Go on until you come to the end and then stop.' That's from *Alice*."

"I hadn't slept a wink all night," Ina said. "I was *charged*. My first night in the city and all that, I just couldn't sleep. So I lay there and listened. The city at night is full of noises, you know, and I amused myself by making up stories about everything I heard—the foghorns and steamship whistles and taxis and sirens and the voices and the tinkle of the milkmen's carts. It was childish, I guess."

"Go on," said the schoolteacher. "Believe it or not, I spent my first night in New York City once, when I was young and full of fancies."

Ina smile gratefully. "Well, I heard the fight next door, in the same apartment where there'd been the party earlier. So I peeked out of the door and heard the loud final crash, and then I saw Mr. Gault come out after a few minutes and go on down the hall. But—but I didn't go right out then and there and find the body, the way the police think. I—I—"

"What did you do, child?"

"I closed the door and went back inside. It was five or maybe ten minutes later that I began to think about how quiet the next apartment was, nobody moving around or anything. Then I remembered that I hadn't heard the door close when Mr. Gault—I mean when the man I know now was Mr. Gault came out. Whoever was inside, the other man in the fight, should have closed the door and I should have heard him moving around and cleaning up or having a drink or going to bed. It was just like waiting for a clock to strike."

"Or for the man in the hotel room overhead to drop his other shoe," said the schoolteacher. "I know exactly."

"So then I guess I got curious," Ina confessed. "I got to imagining I did hear things out in the hall. So I couldn't stand it any longer and so I went out and down the hall and found the body. But don't you see? There had been time for someone else to come and find the door open and Mr. Fagan lying there unconscious, and kill him."

Miss Withers sniffed a dubious sniff. "But after all, you seem to have heard everything else that went on that morning. You'd certainly have heard anybody going down that hallway and back again!"

Ina shook her head stubbornly, and Dallas Trempleau spoke, a weary smile on her face. "No, she wouldn't. Because she was otherwise occupied."

"What?" Miss Withers looked from one to the other, forehead wrinkling into a frown. Then her eyes lighted with amused wonderment. "Ina Kell! Do you mean to tell me that when the police questioned you, you were actually too modest to say that you'd had to go to the *bathroom?*"

"Yes." With one finger Ina drew an imaginary picture on the coverlet. "Oh, I know it was silly. But when they were questioning me ... all those men around with their notebooks." She looked a little sheepish. "And later I didn't dare to say anything, I didn't even dare to say that I heard—I *think* I *did* hear somebody out in the hall just when I was coming out of the bathroom, because Mr. Hardesty warned me that I mustn't change my testimony for anything. If I didn't stick to my statement I'd get into serious trouble, and put him into a very embarrassing position in court. And he's such a nice man—"

"He's a fool," said Miss Withers sharply. "Not that that makes him unique."

"So now perhaps you understand," spoke up Dallas quietly, "why I thought it would be a good idea to bring Ina down here, where she could think things over and where at least she wouldn't have to go into court right away and help convict Winston."

"Come, come!" put in the schoolteacher. "She could have gone on the stand—"

"Yes. And even if she could have brought herself to conquer her modesty and blurt out the whole story, wouldn't it look only as if the defense had got to her somehow? Hardesty would have brought out her original statement and with it torn her to pieces. And can't you see, Miss Withers, that even if this trip of ours only postponed the trial for a while I hoped that something would turn up—some new evidence—"

"Or perhaps you hoped you could convince the child that she'd heard dozens of murderers prancing up and down that hallway?" The Withers sniff was almost a snort. "If anybody else did go down that hall it was probably only the milkman."

"No," Dallas put in. "The milkman would have found the body, then."

Ina was pressing both hands to her forehead. "Oh," she cried, "it's so hard to remember everything. I was scared and excited—but it somehow seems to me that the door was different when I looked out into the hall again!" She shivered.

Dallas brought out the brandy bottle. "Give her a double dose," suggested Miss Withers wickedly. "*In vino veritas*—perhaps it will help her to remember."

The girl took a big sip, made a wry face, and gagged. "I'm doing my best," she told them. "Honest I am."

"Very well." Miss Withers patted her shoulder. "You said just now that the door was different. Different how? Speak up, child."

"Well," Ina said meekly, her eyes faraway, "when Mr. Gault went out the door looked as if it was shut, only I didn't hear it click behind him. But later—the time I found the body—the door was quite a way open. Somebody could have—" She stopped, and shook her head. "Oh, I don't *know!*"

"A draft, probably," Miss Withers sensibly pointed out. "There was an open window somewhere in the Fagan apartment."

"Maybe," the girl agreed doubtfully. "But anyway, it wasn't the milkman, no matter how open the door was or wasn't. I *know!*"

"But how can you say you *know* a thing like that? Unless ... Of course! I forgot that you said you'd heard the milkman earlier, even before the fight. That was one of the night noises of Manhattan about which you were romancing, wasn't it?"

Ina nodded. "I—I guess so."

"And you told the police that when Junior Gault came out of the Fagan apartment he almost stumbled over the bottles of milk outside the door, didn't you?"

"Yes," said Ina.

"How many, and what color were they?"

"I don't remember ... Two or three, I think. White ones."

"Bluish-white, if I remember our New York milk. Very well. So if anybody did go down the hall at the crucial time we've settled who it wasn't, if that's any help." The schoolteacher sighed. "All this is a little disappointing, but pertinent to the inquiry, and I think the authorities will have to know about it."

Ina nodded. "Then I—I really have got to go back to New York right away?"

"Of course you have," prodded the schoolteacher crisply. "Luckily there's still time to get your whole story on the record, for what it's worth. Though it boils down to just this—that there's a *faint* possibility that while you were in the bathroom some hitherto unsuspected enemy of Tony Fagan's came in and killed him and got away again, unseen and practically unheard. That's a frail straw at which to clutch—"

"But it is something," Dallas put in stoutly. "And whoever it was wouldn't necessarily have gone both ways, not right then. He could have been in the apartment, perhaps hiding somewhere, and on his way out paused to finish Tony. Or he could have come in after the fight, found Fagan unconscious and killed him, and been waiting inside—maybe washing his hands or something—when Ina found the body, and left afterwards."

Miss Withers looked doubtful. "Too complicated, I'd say." She turned to Ina. "Are you sure that Fagan was actually dead when you found him?"

"*Wha-a-at?*"

"It's not easy for a layman to tell. Did you feel his pulse, or hold a mirror to his lips, or anything?"

"I—I touched him. He was dead." Ina barely whispered it.

"Even so, not everyone knows where a pulse is located. He was unconscious and covered with blood, and you leaped to the obvious conclusion that he was dead so you ran back to your own apartment—"

"Yes, to call the police!"

"Fiddlesticks. There your story falls to pieces. You couldn't possibly have held a dead phone for ten or fifteen minutes; everyone who has ever attended the movies knows about dial tones. We know what you were actually up to."

Ina looked scared, confused, bewildered and guilty, all at once.

"Relax, child. What you were actually doing was getting yourself into a more becoming negligee and brushing out your hair and fixing yourself up to be the belle of the ball; it's nothing to be so ashamed of. Only you took so long primping that the boy delivering papers came along and found the body before you were ready, so you missed your big scene. Isn't that the truth?"

"Yes." Ina swallowed.

"And if Fagan wasn't dead but only unconscious when you found him, then the actual murderer—always conceding for the sake of argument that it wasn't Gault—could have done his nefarious work after you went back to your apartment to get yourself all prettied up for the police and the photographers?"

"No!" said Ina. Then she nodded. "Well, just maybe."

"Exactly!" Miss Withers nodded triumphantly. "That settles that. Your secret is out, and not much of a secret at that—though perhaps Sam Bordin can use it to plant a seed of doubt in some juryman's mind. You say that at the moment he knows nothing of it?"

Both girls shook their heads, but Ina said, "I did try to phone him once. But he wasn't in."

"Perhaps not *that* time," said Miss Withers to herself. Yet this was no time to ask too many of the wrong kind of questions, not with these wild creatures eating almost out of her hand. Abruptly she changed the subject. "By the way, why on earth did you girls want to get in touch with a private detective here in Tijuana?"

Ina looked blank and bewildered, but Dallas Trempleau said calmly, "Oh, yes. The man Nikki was going to find one for me."

"A bodyguard, eh?" said the schoolteacher.

"Yes. A bodyguard." Dallas turned quickly to the younger girl. "I didn't want to alarm you, dear. It was just a wild hunch of mine."

"But whatever for?" Ina whispered.

"She was undoubtedly thinking," put in the schoolteacher, "that you girls might be in some danger here. Which explains the pistol she left under the pillow."

Dallas said nothing, but there was an odd expression on her face, as if she had swallowed something lumpy. "You've both been taking certain risks," went on Miss Withers. "But running away is never the answer to anything. I know what I'd do if I were as sure of Junior Gault's innocence as you both claim to be. Suppose for the sake of argument that Junior was guilty only of assault and that somebody else found Fagan unconscious and killed him. That somebody is still at large, confident that he is getting away with it. But deep within him he must carry a weight of apprehension. Suppose we could prevail upon the inspector and Mr. Hardesty to cooperate with us to the extent of playing a little game? It is no secret back in New York that there's a surprise witness; that somebody was eavesdropping in the apartment house hallway that morning. Suppose that accidentally on purpose it leaked out that she had caught a glimpse of somebody else in the hall, and had kept silent up to now because of fear? The real murderer, if any, would then have to come out of his silence and make an attempt at erasing Ina, wouldn't he?"

Both girls were wide-eyed as she explained. "It's the old East India trick for shooting tigers. You tie a calf or goat to a tree in the jungle, and then wait. There'd be some risk, of course, but perhaps less than you're running now. Back in New York the authorities could see to it that you're surrounded by stalwart detectives night and day."

"Wow!" breathed Ina softly, eyes shining. "It would be the thrillingest thing!"

"Thrilling to have all those handsome young detectives around?" Dallas smiled.

But Ina didn't hear. "I bet I could do it," she said, in a voice that would have done credit to her favorite movie star in the role of Joan of Arc. Then she added, "Do you suppose that if I agreed to a stunt like that maybe John Hardesty would forgive me for running away?"

The schoolteacher thought privately that the assistant D.A. would forgive Ina for any misdemeanor and most felonies. "He would certainly forgive you if it worked," she admitted cautiously. "Neither he nor the inspector would relish pinning a murder on the wrong man."

"I'd be a sort of heroine, huh?"

"You might be a dead heroine," Dallas put in. "I've read about how they hunt tigers in India, and I never heard of the calf or goat winning the decision."

"I'm not worried in the least," said Ina stoutly. "I mean, not very." She smiled, a brave, secret smile; one that probably had been practiced in front of a mirror.

Miss Withers found herself yawning, and remembered that it was after two-thirty. " 'Sufficient to the day is the evil thereof. ...' " she said. "I suggest we let the final details go until morning."

For reasons of her own the schoolteacher insisted that the girls take the bedroom and leave her the couch in the living room. After the lights were out she heard low voices in the other room, then whispering which died away to absolute silence. She was incredibly weary, but somehow she spurred herself into getting up again and composing a telegram. Sketchily attired, she slipped silently out and down the stair, where she found a night *portero* who promised to send it for her.

Five minutes later she was back on the couch again. "If I do close an eye tonight," she told herself, "I'll undoubtedly have something special in the line of nightmares."

But the nightmare was waiting for her when she awoke shortly before noon. She was stiff as a board from the cramped bed, and her mouth tasted as if the whole Russian Army had marched through barefoot. Someone was hammering on the door and she tottered over to open it, intending to ask the maid to come back and clean up later. But it was the desk clerk, with a telegram. His eyes bugged out at the sight of the borrowed nightgown, but she snatched the message and slammed the door in his face. She read:

> WONDERFUL WORK. I TAKE MY HAT OFF TO YOU. YOU ARE A BETTER SLEUTH THAN HARDESTY AND I PUT TOGETHER. HANG ON TIGHT TO YOUR SEA SHELLS, I AM TAKING FIRST PLANE AND BRINGING A BIG SURPRISE FOR BABY. LOVE.
>
> > OSCAR

"Bless his heart!" she whispered. It was quite the warmest and most enthusiastic message she had ever received from the man.

She folded the telegram up tenderly and put it safely away in her purse. Talley was dancing around her, whining softly and indicating *out*, but she patted him absently and then knocked on the bedroom door, singing cheerfully, "Come, girls, time to rise and shine."

They had already risen and shone, as she found out a moment later. The bedroom window was open, and outside on the dusty balcony were marks of small feminine feet.

"If I were not every inch a lady," said Miss Withers, "I would say *damn!*"

"The next day is never so good as the day before."
—PUBLILIUS SYRUS

12

Nikki Braggioli awakened from pleasant dreams of signing millions of autograph books for worshiping fans. He sat up in bed, gave a shrill yelp, and clutched the sheet around him. In through his bedroom window was coming a great brownish beast which resembled nothing so much as a bear on whose fur some madman had run riot with a pair of clippers, followed by the apparition of a gaunt and graying female wearing only a black lace nightgown and a blanket, Indian style.

"*Madonna mia!*" he whispered. It had been an evening, but not *that* much of an evening. He shook his head hard, as if to clear it, and then fervently wished that he hadn't. But perhaps if he took an aspirin they'd go away.

"*You!*" cried Miss Withers accusingly. "I might have known it! Where are they, where have you hidden them?"

Nikki slid cautiously over to the far side of the bed, and denied everything. It all took considerable explaining, and the schoolteacher even looked into the living room, the bathroom, and both closets before she gave up. He had an ancient, well-used portable phonograph, a new television set, riding boots and fishing rods and piles of old magazines (mostly *Punch*, photo publications featuring nudes, and hot-rod racing magazines) but he most certainly was not concealing any young ladies in the suite. The closest thing to it was a cabinet photograph of a not-too-young woman hung with costume jewelry, who appeared to have a most determined jaw. That, the schoolteacher decided, would be Mary May Dee, and it served him right.

Nikki was insisting that if anybody had come in his window and gone out through his door he knew nothing about it, nothing whatsoever. Besides, he hadn't come home until broad daylight. …

Miss Withers murmured hasty apologies, and then—remembering her dishabille—dashed for the hall. A moment later she also remembered that her own door was locked and bolted on the inside, and came back through his bedroom again. There was nothing for it but that she and Talley would have to return via the balcony. She half-expected to see a crowd gathered below in the street, but no. Tijuana, on a Monday noon after a hard week

90

end, was as deserted as Coventry during Lady Godiva's ride. "Thank heaven," she said to herself. It was the only thing she had to thank heaven for that day.

Half an hour later, fully clothed and in her right mind, she held open the door of the little rented coupé and said, "Come, Talley, the game is afoot." But as the poodle scrambled in she added, "Only those vixens *aren't* afoot at all, they're in a big fast car. We've lost them, and a fine pair of detectives we are."

Talley wagged his tail apologetically. "You have even less excuse than I," she said severely. "Because you didn't drink any of that odd-tasting coffee last night." She started the motor, and then killed it. There was no use leaping into the car and driving off in all directions; even if she were to catch up with her quarry again, what else remained to be said?

The sensible thing, of course, would be to wash her hands of it all. She had done her duty and more than her duty in just locating the missing witness that was going to hang—or electrocute, if you must be fussy—a certain ill-favored young man who had shouted obscenities after her in a Manhattan jail. It would serve Oscar Piper right if she left him to pull his own chestnuts out of the fire.

And would there be, the schoolteacher asked herself, any great miscarriage of justice even if the case against Junior Gault had to be dropped, and that unpleasant young man went free? He had certainly had extreme provocation; there was no real proof that the murder had been premeditated. Junior had already rotted in jail for eight months, and in one sense at least he would keep on paying for the rest of his life.

But even as Miss Withers told herself all this, she realized that she simply had to go on, if for no other reason than that the faint shadow of a doubt had been planted in her mind. Those sounds that Ina Kell had heard, or fancied she heard, in the hall that night—after Junior staggered out of the place and before the girl found the body—might have been the real murderer.

It would have to have been someone who knew of the feud between Junior Gault and Fagan, somebody who had been hanging around or perhaps even following Junior, and waiting for this golden opportunity; who had seen him come out of the place nursing his bruised knuckles.

And, having once set her shoulder to the plow, how could the schoolma'am stop now—with Oscar Piper winging his way out here, confident in that smug way men had that she had solved his immediate problem?

"I think," Miss Withers told the poodle, "that it's time to go back to San Diego and start sending wires."

Talley intimated that it was also time for breakfast and whined hopefully as she drove up into town. It was a different place now, sun-bleached and empty. Like vampires, Miss Withers decided, the people of Tijuana slept by day and prowled by night. She stopped the car outside a little lunch counter with the intention of picking up a raw hamburger for the dog, and then suddenly a smallish brown ghost re-materialized beside her, obviously out of breath from running. "Watch your car, Miss Withers?"

"Vito!" she cried accusingly. "You little imp of Satan!"

But when the boy found out what it was all about, he almost tearfully denied, in a torrent of two languages, that he had betrayed the confidence of a client. "It was my cousin Carlos, the busboy, I think," Vito insisted. "Sure, that's it. He takes your good money and then sends us off on a goose chase to the greyhound races. And all the time, I think maybe, he knows the gorls are across the street at the *jai-alai*. So he slips across and warns them, for the big tip. I disown him, he is no longer a relative of mine."

"You'll have plenty left," she said. "But never mind." Somewhat mollified, she went on to explain that she had found the two young ladies anyway—or rather been found by them only to lose them later. "They may have left town; they may even have crossed the border though I somehow doubt it. But now it is more important than ever that I locate them, and at once!"

Vito's face lighted up like a lantern. "If they're here, I'll find."

"It won't be so easy this time, now that they've got the wind up. Probably they've hidden the car in some garage and then holed up in an apartment or motel. Perhaps now they'll even go to the extremes of doing their own cooking."

The boy grinned. "Nobody hides a big blue Cadillac where I can't find."

"Very good. And remember, this time they mustn't guess that we're on the trail, or everything is ruined." She reached in her handbag for the inevitable five-dollar bill, but Vito informed her that on a slack day like Monday, and especially for such an old and valued customer, he would accept a retainer of only two dollars. As he tucked the money away she added, "If you do get any clues, leave a message for me at the Primero."

He nodded and was gone. The schoolteacher went on inside the lunchroom, feeling just a shade more hopeful now that she had set her little brown bloodhound on the scent again. She sat down at the counter to wait while the chef made up Talley's snack, and a moment later was surprised to see a familiar face in the doorway. It was Nikki Braggioli again, now dressed—or undressed—in red shorts and a brownish-yellow flowered Hawaiian shirt, quite unbuttoned.

"Looking for me?" she sang out.

Obviously he hadn't been; his face fell and for a moment it seemed that Nikki would turn and bolt. But he recovered himself and graciously accepted her apologies for the surprise visit earlier and an invitation to sit down. "I was looking for some *huevos rancheros*," he confessed. "Wonderful for hangover, and have I got one! You too?"

"Certainly not—" Miss Withers began. Then, "Yes, perhaps in a way I have."

"Two on the *huevos*," Nikki sang out to the man at the grill. "*Muy calor.*"

He lowered his voice. "I had a good time last night, they tell me. Last thing I remember, I was dancing the cancan at the end of the chorus line at the Bali Hai."

The schoolteacher said she was sorry to have missed it.

"I am sorry not to have stayed home." He sighed. "Not one but *two* pretty girls in my bedroom, and I have to be out!"

Miss Withers sniffed. "Perhaps it is just as well. Though if you'd been at home they might have at least dropped a hint about where they were running off to."

"Then you're still set on making them go home? Why must you drive away my playmates?"

"You can find other playmates," she said tartly. "I haven't noticed any shortage of young women hereabouts."

"Ah, but none so pretty, so gay—and so rich!"

"You are really fond of them, young man?"

He held up three fingers close together. "We're like this. On weekends, of course, I'm in love with my fiancée, but weekdays I take turns being in love with those girls. Though I think perhaps the turn of one comes oftener than the other."

"Naturally," agreed the schoolteacher. The *huevos* had been set down before her, and turned out to be eggs fried in liquid brimstone. As she gulped down a bit of the fiery concoction she brushed away a tear and said, "It would be too bad if something unpleasant happened to her, wouldn't it?"

"I beg your pardon?"

"She is in grave danger here, unless I miss my guess."

Nikki considered that. "Because of all that money?"

"Money enters into it, but—"

"You think somebody wants to kidnap her?"

Thinking of John Hardesty and the inspector, Miss Withers smiled wryly and nodded. "I know it. Those girls shouldn't be cruising around down here alone. They need more protection than a little pistol can give them. They weren't joking when they wanted you to find them a good private detective for a bodyguard, you know."

"A strong right arm, you think, is indicated?" A very, very thoughtful look came into Nikki's eyes.

"Exactly. I think they'd both be very grateful, and appreciative—" She rose suddenly. "Well, I must be getting back to San Diego. Thanks very much for the eggs." Miss Withers marched out to her car and drove away— but instead of heading toward the border she simply drove around the block. Sure enough, as she came down the Avenida again she saw Nikki, easily spotted in his flaming red shorts, coming out of the lunchroom. He hurried off down the street in the opposite direction, and she cruised slowly along at a very respectful distance. This was almost too good to be true.

It was. Down at the far end of the block Nikki Braggioli suddenly stepped off the sidewalk and slid in behind the wheel of a battered, but serviceable looking British MG roadster, whipped it out into the street and took off with a tremendous roar. A moment later, in spite of all she could do, he was out of sight. All that Miss Withers had discovered was that Nikki knew, or thought he knew, where Ina and Dallas had gone.

There was nothing more to be done here at the moment, the schoolteacher realized. But she suddenly remembered that certain formalities were in order before she could cross the line. She drove back to the veterinary's office, and this time found Dr. Doxa in, a smiling, beady-eyed beanpole of a man in last week's white jacket.

Breathlessly she stated her business, adding that she was in a great hurry. And anyone with half an eye could see at a glance that her dog was free of rabies or hoof-and-mouth disease or anything else. She put down two one-dollar bills on the desk.

"But, señora—beg pardon, señorita—if the animal has been bitten—"

"Talley hasn't been bitten by anything, unless possibly a local flea, since I made the fatal mistake of bringing him down across the border with me yesterday!"

"As you say." Dr. Doxa nodded, then hunted through the drawers of his desk and came up with a printed form. He picked up a fountain pen, and then put it down again. "First, may I see the bill of sale for the dog, please?"

"I am not in the habit of carrying it about with me!"

"You can then show me the registration papers?"

"They're at home, not here. But you can see the tag on his collar. ..."

The man sighed and shook his head, but his eyes shone with the innocent delight of a child beginning a favorite game. "Señorita Weethers, what can I do? There is nothing to show that the dog, he is your property."

Even then a five-dollar bill tactfully slipped across the desk would probably have sufficed. But Miss Withers had got up on the wrong side of the wrong bed that morning, she was suffering from incipient indigestion and what was very possibly sleeping-pill hangover—remembering that coffee last night. "Is this a racket?" she demanded. "How much are you trying to squeeze out of me?"

There was a short, stiff silence. Dr. Doxa's dark eyes clouded, and his face set like concrete. "I can do *nada* for you," he said, with a formal little bow that pushed her miles away. "Perhaps at the *Ayunamiento* ...?"

The schoolteacher retired, in some confusion. But she gathered herself together. After several false starts she found the city hall; she stood in line at five separate windows before finding the right one, and finally located a clerk who thought he remembered an ancient ordinance about dog licenses. Yes, here it was. Dogs owned by foreigners visiting or traveling in the Territory must be registered and licensed, at a fee of innumerable pesos per annum, under a law passed at the time the first greyhound track had opened.

"But my dog isn't—" she began, and then realized that the less said about Talley and greyhounds the better. It came to a little less than five dollars, American, and she reached into her purse. But it was not to be that easy. Before the license could be issued she must show a certificate from the *Jefe de Policía* showing that no animal of Talleyrand's description had been reported during the last six months as lost, or strayed, or stolen.

The policeman at the *Jefatura*, after she had cooled her heels outside his office for over an hour, bit his pencil and smiled and said that all her troubles were over. He would be most happy to make an immediate search of the records, and if she would come back tomorrow at this very same hour, or perhaps the day after—of course, bringing with her a veterinary's certificate that the animal was in good health.

So passed the afternoon. Miss Withers was caught in a complex Rube Goldberg machine of Latin bureaucracy; she was the unhappy sparrow in the old story who flew over Beverly Hills and somehow got into the goddamndest badminton game!

So this was what they meant when they talked about "a Mexican standoff"! But, she finally remembered, there were more ways than one to skin a cat.

Finally she drove up across the long bridge to the port of entry, at the last minute drawing out of the line of traffic and pretending to inspect a tire until she saw one of the northbound cars ahead of her getting its spot check. That should mean, if her deductions were correct, that the next two or three vehicles would pass through Customs with a minimum of formality. And at this hour it was unlikely that her particular red-faced Nemesis of yesterday's night shift would be on duty.

She pulled back into line, and when her turn came she told the first inspector that she was born in Iowa, and the second that she had purchased nothing in Tijuana. She was waved on, and her heart leaped within her. The coupé leaped too as she hastily let out the clutch, only somehow she had put it into reverse instead of first, and the car slammed smartly backward against the next in line. The collision was noisy, but not hard enough to damage the bumpers. And then suddenly from the rear of her rented vehicle came fearful though muffled howls, and the frantic scrabbling of paws trying to dig their way out.

"*Just* a minute, sister!" barked the customs inspector. "Open it up, please."

So, for the lack of a piece of paper, they turned back to Tijuana. "Exiled!" cried Miss Withers in deep vexation of spirit. "And all because you couldn't keep quiet for another little minute!" Talleyrand, who had been talked into the luggage compartment deal much against his better judgment, sulked alone in the back seat.

There was nothing for it but to stop and pick up some of the immediate necessities of life in the shopping section of the town; one couldn't go on indefinitely without dog food, a toothbrush, and certain articles of wearing apparel. There was no telling how long she would have to stay down in Mexico—unless she disposed somehow of Talley, which was unthinkable.

Perhaps someday another veterinary would open up an office.

Miss Withers came back into the lobby of the Hotel Primero, loaded down with parcels and dragging or rather dragged by the poodle, and then was surprised by a hail from the desk clerk, who even managed a toothy smile. It seemed that a phone call had come in for her but one *momentito* ago. ...

"Vito, already?" she gasped. "What was the message?"

No message. Considerably disappointed, the schoolteacher climbed the stair, opened a can of dog food for Talley, and then proceeded to bathe and change into her new garments. They were, perhaps, a bit on the gay side. But she had certain plans, and in this town the only way to be inconspicuous was to be as conspicuous as possible. She left the poodle polishing the bottom of his dish and was just starting out again when here came Vito up the stairs under full steam, obviously bursting with excitement. "No!" she cried. "You haven't located—"

His finger was to his lips, and with a wary glance behind him he motioned toward her door. Once inside, the boy said in a most conspiratorial air, "Careful! Somebody is snooping, I think."

"*What?*"

"I just come in and ask for you at the desk. And suddenly a man comes up and offers me a dollar to tell him what it's all about and what errands I run for you."

Miss Withers gasped. "Why, the nerve of that clerk!"

Vito shook his head. "Not the clerk, another man. A curly-haired, good-looking foreigner in a fancy shirt. I took the dollar—"

"You accepted a dollar bribe from Nikki Braggioli? Why, Vito!"

"Sure. More better this way. I tell him you send me to find out where you can see dorty movies from Havana."

The schoolteacher sat down suddenly in a chair, spluttering. Finally she said, "Very well, Vito. What's done is done. Come tell me, what did you find?"

In a stage whisper, he told. This time it hadn't been so easy. The girls hadn't taken a train out of town, because there was none to take. They had not chartered a plane at the little local airport. Nor had they gone back across the line into the United States, because Vito had a wide acquaintance among the peddlers who hawked pottery pigs and bulls and horses on the bridge twenty-four hours a day, and would certainly have noticed two little girls in a big Cadillac. ...

"Young man, will you please come to the point? I don't want to know where they're *not!*"

He nodded. "Finally I check the filling stations. The gorls stop at the gas station on the corner by the Foreign Club very, very early this morning, and fill up their car with much gas and oil, also extra cans of gas and water."

"But where could they drive to?" she demanded. "I know they couldn't have set out for Mexico City or anywhere, because the only motor roads in

Baja California peter off in the desert, leading nowhere."

"Yes, ma'am. But they also ask for a road map, and want to know about the new highway that runs just south of the border all the way to Mexicali and San Luis. The cousin of a friend of mine wipes their windshield."

"Mexicali?" Miss Withers frowned.

"Yes. But the new highway it is to be built soon, it now exists only on paper. The old road is passable for a jeep perhaps, more better for burros. Much sand. I do not think—"

"I see, Vito! Good work. It's obvious that they took a chance, but that they will get stuck in the sand and have to be pulled out. Probably then they'll be heading back here sometime this evening, very worn out and weary and perhaps in a more vulnerable mood." She nodded. "It would hardly be worthwhile setting out after them—"

Vito shook his head emphatically. "It would not! Because—"

But Miss Withers was making new plans. "I must gather reinforcements. Perhaps I'll even have to try to put through a long-distance phone call from here. And speaking of phone calls, why didn't you leave a message when you called me earlier?"

Vito stoutly denied that he had ever called her. He wouldn't take that much chance of someone listening in. "Then it must have been Nikki Braggioli," she said. "Checking up to see if I had actually left town or not." Miss Withers hastily rearranged her plans. "You stay here," she told the youth, "and act as baby-sitter for Talley. When he's alone in a strange place he has a way of howling softly, and I don't want to get thrown out of the hotel."

She set forth again, with a very grim and unpleasant light in her eye. It was now after five o'clock in the afternoon, but the summer sun was high and hot in the sky and she thought it more than likely that Ramon Julio Guzman was still in his office.

The waspish *licenciado* greeted her oddly. "Miss Withers, you have almost made me lose a bet with myself. I thought surely you would come calling on me earlier."

"Really? Why?" The schoolteacher followed him into a small inner office, sparsely furnished but meticulously clean. Photographs of Presidente Alemán and the late Franklin Roosevelt grinned toothfully at each other from opposite walls, and there was also a calendar depicting a buxom brunette, exceedingly nude, quaffing Tecate beer.

Guzman held a chair for her. "I thought," he said wisely, "that you might come to the conclusion that you need assistance."

"Assistance? To find my nieces?"

Smiling, he showed strong gold-crusted teeth. "Your interest in the two young ladies seems hardly that of an aunt."

"Really? I must brush up on my acting. You are quite right. They are not relatives of mine, except to the extent that all women are sisters under the skin. But I am very interested—" She paused. "The girls haven't made another attempt to reach you, by any chance?"

He shook his head. "But I understand that they have left town, no?"

"No. Or maybe yes. If they've gone anywhere I'm sure they'll be back. I want to prevail upon them, or force them if necessary, to return to New York. Is there any way?"

"You mean legal means? There is no treaty of extradition between our countries. Sometimes in the case of a fugitive from justice, it is possible to have him very quietly picked up and deported; turned over to the United States authorities at the border as an undesirable alien. Are the American police interested in these young ladies, perhaps?"

"Perhaps. But—"

"But there are no charges against them?" Guzman nodded wisely. "Then there would have to be a strong request, and even so—" He put out one cigarette and lighted another. "Of course, here as everywhere, money talks. But in this particular case there is the added difficulty that the officials with which we would have to deal are *hombres*, in the gallant Spanish tradition. It is unlikely that they would be hasty in pronouncing either of those young ladies *undesirable*."

"You mean, they are young and pretty?" said Miss Withers a little wistfully.

"They are young, and pretty, and rich. They spend well. To have them deported as you suggest, especially since there are no criminal charges against them, would take a considerable amount of dollars." His voice lingered on the last word.

The schoolteacher thought about that for a moment. Then she said, "Thank you very much, Mr. Guzman. We'll see what is to be done. And what is your fee for this advice?"

"Nothing now, I think," he said with quiet deliberation. "Perhaps later, after you have had an opportunity to contact your principals in New York, shall we say five per cent of the dollars, for handling charges?"

Miss Withers was reminded of the few crumpled currency notes left in her purse, and of the thinness of her book of traveler's checks. This was all getting to be more complicated than ever she had expected when she so merrily dashed off to prove to Oscar Piper that she still had a shot or two left in her locker. And yet it still seemed increasingly important to her that the one who had smashed out Tony Fagan's brains be brought before the bar of justice, and equally important that innocent persons came out unscathed.

Or just perhaps that one little pink-haired girl from the country be just a trifle *scathed*, preferably with a hairbrush in Miss Withers' own firm hand. Because there was really no legitimate excuse for Ina Kell having behaved as she had; Junior Gault was nothing in her young life. Or had the girl somehow been persuaded against her will—perhaps by that nasty little pistol?

Thinking dark thoughts, Miss Withers came back to the hotel again, where she found Vito happily engaged in teaching Talley the poodle to roll over and play dead in Spanish. "I am also keeping one eye out of the window," the boy told her. "No blue Cadillac."

"Do you suppose that somehow they actually managed to get through to Mexicali?" she wondered. "Or perhaps they're still stuck somewhere in the sand."

But Vito shook his head firmly. "That's what I'm trying to tell you before you rush off so fast just now. Those gorls don't go to Mexicali, they don't even start."

"What? Why do you say that?"

"Because they make too much fuss about it at the filling station, where they must be smart enough to know that sooner or later somebody comes asking. I think it is a phony; I think they go any place but."

"Vito!" she cried. "You do have the makings of a detective. But where else could they have gone?"

He shrugged, the all-expressive shrug of the Latin. "Good paved auto road to Rosarito Beach; nice fishing there."

"I doubt that the young ladies are avid anglers."

"That same road, it goes on down to Ensenada. Very beautiful, Ensenada. Right on the Bay, high-class hotel. Then on inland to Real de Castillo, very famous ruins."

But Miss Withers wasn't listening. "That telephone call!" she gasped, and then turned and hurried out of the place and down the stairs. The desk clerk, putting aside his inevitable newspaper, informed her in a hurt tone that he had never said the phone call was from a little boy. As a matter of fact, it had been only the voice of the long-distance operator, and the call had been canceled a moment later—even before he had had a chance to ring her room and find out if she was there or not.

"Long distance!" she whispered. "It wasn't—it wasn't Mexicali?"

"Oh, no, señorita. From Ensenada."

The schoolteacher gave a little shiver. Somehow, one of the girls had managed to slip off alone for a moment and put through a call. An apology, perhaps, or a word of explanation, or even an appeal for help. According to the guide book on the hotel desk, Ensenada was the southernmost and prettiest of the resort towns on the Pacific side of the peninsula, located a little more than sixty miles to the south and boasting one of the finest hotels in all Mexico, a showplace of the West Coast.

Even in headlong flight, Dallas Trempleau would gravitate to something like that, to a haven with the plush-lined service to which she had always been accustomed; a hotel where well-trained flunkies would fend off inconvenient queries if necessary.

Now Miss Withers understood what the phone call had been meant to convey. There had been no intention, no need, of its ever being actually completed. Its only purpose had been to send that one-word message—the name of a town.

13

"So now we go to Ensenada, yes?" spoke up Vito hopefully, his dark eyes alight with the thrill of the chase.

"So now we do nothing of the kind," said Miss Withers. Her birds had luckily alighted in a distant but identified thicket, and she had no intention of flushing them again—not at least until she was better armed.

The inspector, even with the best of plane connections, could hardly be expected to arrive in San Diego until sometime tomorrow morning. She still had time to take certain steps, even though she could not hope to offer him everything tied up neatly in a paper sack. Undoubtedly he would consider what she was about to do as nothing more than flinging monkey wrenches into the machinery.

But this was a somewhat more complex machine than even Oscar Piper realized, a Rube Goldberg machine which a flung wrench couldn't hurt and might help. At any rate, detectives, like criminals tend to repeat their *modus operandi*, and the method had worked rather ,well for her once or twice in the past. She sent Vito out to walk the poodle—a long, long walk was indicated, she said—and over a sketchy meal sent up from the restaurant she settled down to pulling strings. Or rather to the pulling of long-distance telephone wires.

At first everything went like greased clockwork. The switchboards seemed to be as quiet as everything else in Tijuana on a Monday evening, and she was also lucky enough to fall into the hands of a telephone operator who spoke English quite as good as her own. Her first call got through to New York in a record fifteen minutes; then she struck the first snag.

Attorney Sam Bordin was not in his office. That, since it must now be after ten o'clock in Manhattan, was not to be wondered at. But he was not at home either.

Neither Mr. Winston H. Gault, Sr., nor his wife was at home, according to the maid. She would not accept the call or take a message.

Mrs. Ruth Fagan had a private and unlisted number, which could not be given out to anyone.

By now the Tijuana operator's voice was getting noticeably patient and strained, but in desperation Miss Withers remembered that the people who worked in the world of television were strictly nocturnal creatures, so she asked for just one more New York number. And then at last she heard the nervous pseudo-Harvard accents of Art Wingfield, back at Station WKC-TV. He seemed to have some difficulty in remembering just who she was, and why.

"Hildegarde Withers!" she cried, and then spelled it out. "I'm in Tijuana, and it's terribly important that I talk to Ruth Fagan, only she seems to have a private number and the operator won't give it to me. What is it?"

"Her number?"

"Yes, the number of her telephone in the apartment on East Fifty-fifth. I know you have it, because when I went over to see her the other night you had already called her on the phone and warned her. Please cooperate, Mr. Wingfield; you have no idea how important this is."

"Important to who?"

"*Whom*—I mean to her! In fact it's important five thousand dollars' worth to her, which is the amount she offered me to mix into this affair."

He hesitated, and for a moment Miss Withers thought the man had hung up. Then he said, in a rather dubious voice, "Well, really—"

"Oh, stop stalling, young man. I know all about you and her." When necessary the schoolteacher could show her claws. "*Everything!*"

"Huh?" His gulp could be heard across the miles.

"You wouldn't want all that to come out, would you? Well, then!"

"Come out where?" he asked, in a rather dazed voice. "Oh, skip it. Can't you tell me just what this is all about? It wouldn't do you any good if I did give you her number; Ruth's not at home tonight, anyway. But I guess I could take a message, and then she could contact you—"

Miss Withers didn't hesitate at all. "Very well. Tell her that if she still is interested in seeing the murderer of her husband brought to justice, I am now in a position to help her. But it will take money, a great deal of money—perhaps even the whole amount she specified, though I don't want any of it for myself. Only I think I can promise immediate and interesting results. If she's really serious, have her send the money to me at the Hotel Primero here."

"I'll certainly tell her," Wingfield promised, but she sensed that his tone had changed; that he was thinking hard about something else. "What town did you say?"

She told him, and he echoed, "*Tijuana!* I didn't get it at first! Then you're down there on the track of that missing witness?"

Miss Withers had nothing to say.

"It was in the gossip columns!" he went on excitedly. "Is Ina Kell going to give herself up and come back voluntarily to testify? Is it true that she admits she knows something about the murder that might pin it on somebody else besides Gault? Are the authorities actually on their way out there to pick her up?"

"Listen in again tomorrow night for the next chapter of Tony's Other Murderer," said Miss Withers under her breath. "I really can't tell you that at the moment, Mr. Wingfield."

"But it's true? The girl wants dough before she'll surrender, is that it?"

"Not exactly—"

"Wow!" he said. "Think of the angles—"

"Never mind the angles. All I asked you for was a phone number. This call is costing a fortune."

"Sure, sure. I'll give Ruth your message. Sit tight and don't worry about a thing, not a thing." He hung up.

" 'Don't worry about a thing,' he tells me," said the schoolteacher. "Except that I'm running up bills in two hotels at once, not to speak of car rental and all the rest of it, including phone bills for long-distance calls that had come to nothing."

Because she was more than reasonably sure that Mr. Wingfield had no intention of giving her message to Ruth Fagan. "Men!" said Miss Withers.

Which reminded her that the inspector would arrive tomorrow morning, blithely confident that she had landed and had the situation well in hand. When actually, as she would be the first to admit, she was no forrader. Except, of course, for some very nebulous questions and answers that were beginning to take shape in the very bottommost levels of her mind, questions and answers that didn't connect with each other.

Talley and Vito were out on the town, making a night of it. She hoped for Talley's sake that the boy wouldn't stand treat to ice cream or anything else that was bad for dogs. Meanwhile, she was alone with her thoughts—which eventually led her to the realization that telegrams had it all over phone calls. Telegrams got delivered.

Rashly, Miss Withers sat down and composed a wire to Sam Bordin, another to Mrs. Fagan, a third to the elder Gaults, and finally in a burst of reckless abandon she sent one to Junior Gault himself, care of Detention. Probably they wouldn't let him have it, and if they did he probably wouldn't answer it, but if they did and if he did it ought to prove his innocence—or his guilt.

She got the wires off and then leaned weakly back in a chair and took off her shoes. She hadn't meant to fall asleep, not in the least, but suddenly she found herself mixed up in a dream; struggling in a little-girlish, frightening dream. In the past she had liked to think that sometimes her subconscious chose that means of bringing light on a problem, but even as she dreamed she realized that there could be no sense in this melange of nonsense, of great clumping feet that made no sound, of Kermanshah carpets and alabaster vases and milk bottles, of gold cigarette lighters and yammering telephones and what the ancients used to call "bare-head and bones," like a pirate flag.

Miss Withers woke suddenly, to find that by her watch it was half past twelve. The hotel suite was clammy and cold. Another sea fog had rolled in tonight, and she was shivering in the bright sport clothes she had purchased last afternoon. And she shivered a little more as she realized that Vito and her poodle were still out for a walk, and nobody could be walking this long.

"What in the world—" she started to say. But then the phone rang again, and the schoolteacher realized that was what had awakened her. She seized the instrument.

"Allo? Allo, Mees Weethers?"

"Vito?" she cried, a little doubtfully.

"Yess, Vito," came the voice. "Vito García, eet is about heem, and your *perro*—"

"My pair of what?"

"Your *perro grande*, your beeg dog. I am Vito's cousin—"

"Not another one! But never mind, never mind. Where are they? What has happened?"

"Notheeng 'as 'appen," was the answer. "Except, I am sorry to tell you, that your dog and my leetle cousin, they are down at the *Jefatura*, in the *cárcel*—how you say, the jail?"

"What on earth—" began the schoolteacher. "That child, in jail? And the dog? But what for?"

"Is better you come," said Vito's cousin. "And bring some money."

"Immediately," said Miss Hildegarde Withers. Then she hung up, and began to put on her shoes as if they were armor.

"The horrid tale of perjury and strife,
Murder and spoil ..."

—WILLIAM CULLEN BRYANT

14

No beds are provided, even in the female ward, of the detention cells of the Tijuana *cárcel*. Miss Hildegarde Withers had spent most of what was left of the night alternately stalking up and down like some caged, ungainly bird of prey or dozing in a hard wooden chair. Her watch had been taken away, but pale squares of filtered sunlight moved imperceptibly across the worn stone floor of the cell, and she guessed that it must be around nine o'clock in the morning when she heard heavy steps in the corridor and someone rapping sharply on the chilled steel bars.

"Go away," snapped the schoolteacher. "I don't care for any breakfast."

The jailer, a rotund brown man with luxuriant mustaches and a two-day beard, laughed appreciatively, since everyone knew that almost no meals were served here except to such guests as were able to make their own outside arrangements with some nearby restaurant. Then he unlocked the door, with much clattering of an immense iron key, and flung it creakingly open. "*Adelante!*" he said, with a gesture.

"I demand the right to make a phone call!" Miss Withers said. "I want the American ambassador or the consul or somebody ..."

"Is here," announced the jailer with jovial inaccuracy. He moved politely aside, and she looked into the quizzically sardonic face of the last person in the world she had expected, or wanted, to see at the moment. Inspector Oscar Piper had a long greenish-brown cigar cocked in one corner of his mouth; his eyes were distant and disapproving.

"Oscar!" she cried quickly, and then bit her lip. "I—er—words fail me."

"Do they, now?" said the little Hibernian coldly.

"I'm very glad to see you. I meant to meet you at the airport, but—"

He looked her up and down, very critically. "Get yourself arrested at a costume ball, or a Hard Times party?"

Suddenly the schoolteacher realized that she was still wearing the outfit she had purchased in the shops along the market arcade; voluminous greenish-pink wraparound skirt, lavender sweater, wide leather belt studded with bits of colored glass, and even the straw hat with the incredibly extensive brim that ran off into unfinished fringes. "Only protective coloration, Oscar," she said with forced lightness as she marched out into the corridor. "In this town the only way to be inconspicuous is to be as conspicuous as possible."

"Is it, now?" There was no warmth in the man at all; he was all New York cop.

"Yes. How—however did you find me?"

He took her arm, not affectionately. "Went to the hotel, discovered you'd been out all night. Tried the hospital first and the calaboose second."

"Thank heavens. I might have rotted there for weeks."

"You might at that," he said. "It's an idea. But I figured I owed you at least something for old times' sake. Now listen. They say the *magistrado* isn't such a bad guy. All you have to do is to talk soft and plead guilty."

"*Guilty?*" she cried indignantly.

"Well, you did knock a police officer down with your handbag last night, didn't you? With all that stuff you carry around in it, it could be assault with a deadly weapon, only they've been nice enough to reduce the charge to disorderly conduct."

She sniffed. "How was I to know the man was a policeman, in that sport shirt and slacks? I thought all detectives wore blue suits and bump-toed shoes and smoked cigars. And I was so furious when I found out that they'd had the nerve to pick up that nice Mexican boy and my own poor Talley and whisk them off in the black Maria over nothing at all ..."

"Maybe it isn't as nothing at all as you think," the inspector told her.

"This is another country, and they have their own laws down here. But the boy and your dog don't enter into this hearing; I suggest you leave them out of it." He indicated a door, where the broadly smiling jailer was waiting invitingly. "You're on. Remember what I said, and don't make it any worse than it is."

Miss Withers was led into the tiny magistrate's court, where with the help of a bored young interpreter Miss Withers listened to the charge, refused legal assistance, refused a jury trial and quietly pleaded guilty to disorderly conduct. After a long stern lecture in Spanish, which the interpreter boiled down to three sentences, she was fined five dollars. Magistrate, interpreter, and clerk were all very polite to her, and she got the impression that they all thought her queer in the head but harmless on the whole. Finally her watch and handbag were returned to her and she was told that she was free to go.

"Not so fast!" she cried. "What about Talley?"

The inspector nudged her and shook his head. Edging her out the door, he said, "That's what I was trying to tell you. The dog is impounded."

"*Impounded?* Just because he doesn't have a license that I tried all day to get?"

He shook his head, leading her along. "They have a local rule down here. They can impound the property of any Americano who gets mixed up in a lawsuit. I mean, if you bump fenders with a local car, yours is locked up until the case is settled."

"But I didn't bump anybody—"

"Your dog did. You took him to the races, and he jumped the fence and upset one of the greyhound sprints. The complaint was filed yesterday, and the police had orders to pick up the dog on sight. A group of insulted sportsmen who had tickets on the favorite got together and decided to sue."

"So *that's* what they were jabbering about last night! Why, it's perfectly silly. A thing like that would be laughed out of any court."

"I hope you're right," the inspector said. "Anyway, you'll be served with the papers sometime later today. The boys want to be recompensed for whatever they might have won if old Talley hadn't tripped up their picks."

"And I didn't take Talley to the races; I left him in the car! I even have a witness to prove it!"

"Fine, fine," said Piper. "You'll have your day in court. Meanwhile—"

But she pulled at his sleeve. "Oscar, that poor boy—the one who was walking Talley for me last night. Are they still holding him, too?"

The inspector shook his head. "Nope. They grilled him awhile and then had to let him go when he swore that he'd only found the poodle loose on the street, and was trying to locate the owner for a possible reward. The night desk sergeant said that the boy hung around a little while and finally went home."

"Thank goodness! Poor Vito needs his sleep. And where is Talley now?"

"I told you," said Oscar Piper wearily. "He's impounded, and until the case comes up he'll be maintained at public expense somewhere—"

"But you don't understand!" cried Miss Withers. "There's only one *somewhere*, just one veterinarian in the town. Which means Dr. Doxa, a man I've already had difficulties with. We've got to go over there right away, and if that nasty man won't give my dog back at least we must furnish some decent dog food—"

"No," the inspector told her, as they came out of the grim official building into the bright morning sunlight. "Your dog can wait. Have you forgotten that this is a murder case?"

She sniffed eloquently. "I'm certainly having it proved to me, more clearly every day. You may find out before we're through, Oscar Piper, that everything is tied up together. It should be obvious, even to the most limited intelligence, that this trumped-up lawsuit is an attempt at frightening me off, or at least at keeping me from any further sleuthing. These are deep waters, deeper than you think."

"So you're still trying to upset the applecart, eh?"

"You should know by now that it's easier to get me started than to stop me. Can't you see yet that there is a whole lot more to the Fagan murder than meets the eye? I imagine you must think so too, deep down inside, or you wouldn't have come rushing out here to pull John Hardesty's chestnuts out of the fire."

Piper wearily told her why Hardesty had not come out in person, being stuck somewhere off in the Virgin Islands.

"Of course!" the schoolteacher cried. "Virgin Islands ... Mexicali ... both of them are red herrings. I seem to see a pattern emerging."

"Pattern-schmattern," he said. "Where's the Kell girl, Hildegarde?"

"Quite—quite safe."

"Safe where?"

"I'll tell you all about it. But—but first couldn't I have some coffee or something? It was rather a hard night, on the whole."

"Okay," he conceded, grudgingly. She bristled at his tone, and then, womanlike, decided to wait for another time. Something was gnawing at the inspector's vitals, but as she well knew he was not a man to meet head-on.

They wound up in a little lunchroom on the Avenida, the same lunchroom. But today where was no sign of Nikki Braggioli around, and Miss Withers ventured to ask the counterman if she could have her *huevos rancheros* without the *rancheros*. While they ate, and drank innumerable cups of coffee, she brought the inspector up to date on her adventures below the border, or nearly so.

"I'll admit, Oscar, that pride goeth before a fall. When I sent you that telegram early Monday morning I was drunk with success. I had won my point, proved my hunch about Dallas Trempleau being here only for one special reason—to hide the important witness. Through Vito I'd found the girls and I thought I had both of them convinced that they should start back to New York with me next day."

"You should have a guardian," the inspector said. "Or a keeper."

"I'll frankly admit that something went wrong. All the time the girls were obviously pulling my leg, I see it now. I'm more than half-convinced that they even put sleeping pills in my coffee. I've always prided myself on being a judge of people, but I just don't understand Dallas and Ina, I really don't."

Piper, still obviously unmollified, waved his hand. "It's perfectly simple. Take Ina Kell, just a little girl from East Nowhere, Pennsylvania, who always had wondered what it would be like to dwell in marble halls and wear mink underwear. She stumbled into a murder, found herself in the catbird's seat, got tempted by the glories of this world, and fell. She had the world by the tail with a downhill drag when you came waltzing in, and she suddenly realized that the ball was about over and it was almost midnight, and she couldn't face riding home in a pumpkin."

"Oscar, I do wish your reading would progress beyond *Cinderella*."

He didn't smile. "Anyway, the girl rushed off in a panic, just to put off the evil hour of reckoning. As for Dallas Trempleau—"

The schoolteacher nodded complacently. "She's more complicated, eh?"

"Not if you understand the type. You don't think she's doing all this just out of the goodness of her heart, do you?"

"There's such a thing as love, Oscar—"

"What does a spoiled Park Avenue brat know about love? She doesn't really love Junior Gault. She'd probably never go through with the marriage if by some miracle he did beat the rap. But she just doesn't want it said that she was once engaged to a man who got sent to the chair. So when Sam Bordin got this bright idea of luring away the one important witness, she put up the money and her own time. Probably she's getting a big thrill out of it."

Miss Withers frowned. "You're sure, Oscar, that it was Bordin who pulled the strings? Wouldn't he, as a lawyer, have known how dangerous it could be for him?"

"It adds up. Lawyers like him follow a certain tradition—Fallon, Darrow, Steuer. There's more ham actor in them than there is law. They take cases that look hopeless and then somehow get the client off. But they must maintain a reputation for infallibility. Bordin found, after he accepted the Gault case and the publicity involved, that it was red-hot. With that motive, and with Gault pinned on the scene of the crime at the right time, he didn't have any out in court. Yet if a big-name client of his got the chair, he would lose his stock in trade. So he pulled a fast one."

The schoolteacher said, "But both girls deny that it was his idea."

"Then both girls lie like a rug."

"Bordin himself, when I dropped in at his office last week, impressed me with his earnest desire to find Ina Kell and subpoena her as a witness for the defense. He seemed to think that the prosecution had spirited her away." Miss Withers stirred her coffee thoughtfully, first clockwise and then counterclockwise. "I'd have sworn that he didn't know where she was."

"Well, he sure as shooting did know! Because within a few minutes after I started making plans to come out here, he tried to beat us to the punch and whitewash himself by releasing the inside dope on Ina Kell's being in Tijuana to the gossip columns!"

"No, Oscar!"

"Yes. So he knew all the time." The inspector sucked hard on his cigar, which had gone out. "Unless you yourself tipped off your dear old former pupil with another of your cute little coded wires about sea shells?"

"Don't be impertinent."

"Well, we'll take care of Bordin in good time. The situation right now is that you had your hands on Ina and the other girl and let them get away. They took time out to try to leave a false trail that would send pursuit off in the wrong direction, just as Ina had earlier done in New York, and then presumably ducked down to Ensenada or whatever it is."

"Yes, Oscar. But you forget one thing, a very important thing. One of those girls managed to put through a long-distance call tipping me off to the fact that they had actually gone to Ensenada. It must have been one of them—nobody else knew I was at the hotel. And she—whichever it was—paid me a considerable compliment by taking it for granted that I'd know what the call meant." Miss Withers flounced a bit. "Do you see what that means?"

"So the two young ladies are not in complete agreement. Ina is holding out on Dallas or Dallas is holding out on Ina. One of them wants to make sure that you know where they really are, or where they were."

"*Are*, Oscar. There's no place to go from Ensenada but back. Which also proves that only one of those girls wanted to sneak away. If so, I think I know which. I was positive during our talk in the hotel bedroom that evening that I had little Ina convinced that she should go back to New York and face the music. She even seemed to be looking forward to being the heroine of the occasion. But something must have made her change her mind."

"She'll have to change it back," Piper said quietly. "And if she doesn't it'll be changed for her."

The schoolteacher flashed him a glance. "I'm afraid it's rather more complicated than you think, Oscar. If the girl doesn't want to go, it's not going to be easy to compel her. It will take a good deal of money, I'm afraid." She told him about her informative interview with Guzman. "Greasing official palms seems to be a local convention," she explained. "I don't approve of it, but sometimes the end justifies the means. And when one is in Rome, one must burn Roman candles."

"You don't always have to burn them at both ends," said the inspector.

"However," she continued blithely, "I think possibly I have figured out ways and means. I've several irons in the fire, Oscar."

"You have, have you?" He smiled a rather odd smile. "Would those irons in the fire have anything to do with the bushel basketful of telegrams I found sticking under your hotel door when I went up to your room a little while ago?"

She brightened. "Well! They did answer!"

"You can say that again." Piper took a sheaf of familiar-looking envelopes out of his coat pocket. "I suppose I've got to give you the benefit of the doubt. Maybe you've got a good explanation for spilling official secrets to half the people in New York, but—"

"Oscar, surely you didn't open and read my telegrams!"

"Surely I did. I thought they might give me a clue as to where you'd disappeared to. But when I read the first one—what in the name of Judas H. Priest did you say to Winston Gault, Sr., to make him wire you this?" He showed her:

> FORWARD IMMEDIATELY FULL OUTLINE OF ANY INFORMATION YOU HAVE OR THINK YOU CAN OBTAIN RELATIVE TO POSSIBLE NEW EVIDENCE ON MY SON'S CASE. SUCH OUTLINE WILL BE TURNED OVER TO MY ATTORNEYS FOR EVALUATION AND IF SATISFACTORY THEY WILL CONTACT YOU ABOUT YOUR REQUEST FOR MONEY.

"New evidence!" said the inspector bitterly.

"Oscar, I didn't exactly say that—"

"Go on. Read the next. It's signed 'Gracie.' I suppose that's Sam Bordin's big blonde office-wife?"

Miss Withers read:

> MR BORDIN OUT OF TOWN. STRICT ORDERS NOT TO SAY WHERE BUT WHEN YOU SEE HIM TELL HIM TO LEAVE THOSE SENORITAS STRICTLY ALONE.

"I only wanted Sam Bordin to get in touch with Junior Gault—"

"Better and better!" snarled Piper in deep bitterness. "The next one is just a notice that according to Western Union in New York, your telegram to Junior Gault couldn't be delivered."

"They wouldn't let him receive it at the prison? How mean!"

"Of course they wouldn't. Besides, he isn't there."

Miss Withers almost fell off the stool. "You mean, the trial is over and he's already in Sing Sing, all in three days I've been away?"

"No!" He handed her another telegram. "This one's short and sweet."

Attached to a wire remittance form was the message:

> HERE IS $200 RETAINER. BRINGING REST OF MONEY IMMEDIATELY.
> RUTH FAGAN

"I can explain that, Oscar. If only ..."

"If nothing!" he exploded. "Here's one I'd like to hear you explain; this is the payoff." She took the yellow sheet and with trembling fingers read the worst:

DEEPLY INTERESTED IN TELEVISION POSSIBILITIES DRAMATIC EVENT MENTIONED BY YOU ON PHONE LAST NIGHT. IF YOU CAN ARRANGE OUR EXCLUSIVE COVERAGE ACTUAL SURRENDER KEY WITNESS GAULT CASE TO BE RECORDED ON FILM AND USED ON SOONEST VIDEO NEWS BROADCAST WILL GUARANTEE SUM MENTIONED AND REASONABLE EXPENSES. OUR MR WINGFIELD AND CAMERA CREW LEAVING AT ONCE BY CHARTERED PLANE. CONFIRM YOUR ACCEPTANCE THIS OFFER IMMEDIATELY

R L WARRENDER VICE PRES WKC-TV

"Well?" demanded the inspector, much too quietly.

Miss Withers lifted her coffee cup to her lips, found it empty, and set it down with a nervous little clatter. "But, Oscar, I told you—it will take a lot of money to get the authorities here to deport Ina Kell as an undesirable alien since she actually isn't a fugitive from justice or anything. And though she'd given me the slip, perhaps unwillingly, I knew that I had her located down in Ensenada, which is only sixty miles from here and no place to go beyond, so I thought it would be nice and helpful if when you arrived—"

"Helpful! You're as helpful as a boil on my—my neck."

"Ruth Fagan had already once offered me practically a blank check, up to five thousand dollars."

"Five grand? Just to reopen the Fagan investigation?"

"She didn't quite put it that way. She just wanted to make sure that her husband's killer didn't get away with it. She took it for granted Gault was guilty, but I'm sure that she doesn't care who we pin it on as long as the truth comes out."

"The truth *is* out!" roared the inspector. "Judas priest in a cupcake, can't you get it through your head for once and for all that this case at least is all cut and dried?"

Miss Withers stiffened. "There is always the possibility that you cut and dried it too soon. This new evidence ..."

"*What* new evidence?"

She told him about Ina Kell's confession of the other evening; about that possibly all-important five or ten minutes left unaccounted for, when the hallway of the apartment house had been clear for someone to come and go again.

For all his exasperation, Oscar Piper listened carefully. "But *who?*" he demanded at last.

"I don't know, Oscar. Time and time again I've tried to shut my eyes and visualize one of the other suspects in this case coming along that hallway, and it all remains blank."

"*What* suspects?"

"I don't know ... yet."

"Phooey," he said, inelegantly.

"And there's always the chance that Ina is making it all up about going to the bathroom," went on the schoolteacher wickedly. "Perhaps the girl was peeking and listening from her door all the time. Suppose, after Junior left, she actually caught a glimpse of another person in that hallway, leaving or entering the Fagan apartment? Suppose she kept silent for some reason or other—because she recognized him as someone she knew, or because of fear that she would be the next to die if she opened her mouth, or ..."

"As I said once before, you ought to write soap operas."

"But, remember, Oscar, that Ina was oddly reluctant to identify Junior Gault. She still insists that she thinks him innocent, which is unreasonable unless she knows or suspects that someone else is guilty." Miss Withers shrugged. "It certainly is obvious that Ina knows more than you've got out of her, that she somehow holds the key to all this, whether she realizes it or not."

"Oh, brother!" interrupted Oscar Piper. "The witness who knows something but doesn't know she knows it! That went out with the 'If I Had But Known' school."

Very nettled, Miss Withers said, "Nevertheless, it has happened. Will you grant that, as the only person at or near the scene of the crime—besides the murderer and victim—she represents a very real menace to the former?"

"Sure, to Junior. If she tells the truth, she'll convict him."

"Will you admit that only the murderer, or someone protecting him, would want her out of the country?"

"Sure, and that's just what happened. Junior Gault, his lawyer and his girl cooked up a deal to get Ina Kell down here and keep her here."

"I wonder," said Miss Withers. "You're probably right. But I wonder. It occurred to me that perhaps Junior wasn't a party to it at all. Dallas Trempleau could have taken matters in her own hands. And I thought if that by some fantastic coincidence Junior actually wasn't guilty but just the victim of circumstantial evidence, why, then he might leap at the chance to contribute to my slush fund; he might *want* Ina brought back to testify. And if he did cooperate, it would be a definite indication of his innocence!"

The inspector shook his head pityingly. "You must have been smoking these queer cigarettes they have down here." He paid the check, and they went out to the Avenida, deserted as usual at this hour of the morning.

"My car's over this way," she said meekly. "Oscar, now that I've explained, do you see what I meant, even though you may disapprove of my methods? After all, I didn't really let any cats out of the bag when I sent those wires."

"Not much!" he scoffed. "Sealed-lips Hildegarde, they call you."

"Because I'd already learned from talking to Wingfield that it was no longer a secret about Ina Kell being down here."

With chilly politeness he held the car door open for her. "I suppose you've got an explanation for calling in the broadcasting company, too?"

"That, Oscar, was purely an accident. I had to call Wingfield at his office to ask for Ruth Fagan's private phone number. I knew he'd have it—there's something between them, by the way, that will stand looking into."

"Is there, now?" Piper almost forgot himself, and smiled.

"Yes, I feel it in my bones. Anyway, he wouldn't give me the number, though he said he'd deliver a message. He has a quick mind, that young man. I told him as little as possible, but he'd already read the gossip columns, and I guess he put two and two together. He seemed suddenly very excited, but I had no idea he was going to try to make a Roman holiday out of it for his old television program. That last wire was as much of a surprise to me as it was to you." She saw that the inspector was still on the sidewalk. "Aren't you coming, Oscar?"

"Not now. I have business. I have to drop in at the *Jefatura*, and then go back over to San Diego and pay the usual courtesy call on the police there. I may need them later, for all I know."

"Need them, why? Oscar Piper, what have you got up your sleeve?"

He just looked at her cryptically.

"Well then, let me drive you over."

The inspector hastily declined, with thanks. "Don't know how long I'll be," he hedged. But he finally consented to pick up her marooned luggage at the other hotel and bring it back with him.

"You'll be here in time for dinner?"

"Maybe, if you're buying. On that expense account of yours—Ruth Fagan's two hundred bucks."

"Wait, Oscar! We've got so many things to talk about—how to get Ina to surrender, and what to do about this avalanche of people I seem to have brought unwittingly down around our ears, and …"

The inspector turned back and eyed her with a cold eye. "The talking part is over," he said. "I don't know as this is any of your business, Hildegarde, but it's no secret. You may as well know that Junior Gault was released yesterday."

"*What?* But—but I didn't think they ever allowed bail for first-degree homicide. Was the charge reduced?"

"No, to both questions."

"Then the district attorney's office thinks he's innocent, after everything—"

"You don't know what they think, or what I think. Brace yourself, there's more coming. I'm not down here to play polite patty-cake with a missing witness. And there won't be any need to bribe anybody; the local authorities will be tickled pink to cooperate if necessary, though I don't think it will come to that."

"Well, Oscar?" she demanded impatiently. "I'm all ears."

The inspector cocked his head and stared at her thoughtfully. "I wouldn't say that; there's a good deal of nose showing. But if you must know, I came flying out here to pick up your little friend Ina Kell on a murder rap." He waved a cheery good-bye and stalked back up the Avenida.

"Do I contradict myself?
Very well then I contradict myself."

—WALT WHITMAN

15

It was just as well that Tijuana's streets are almost deserted in the forenoon, for on her way back to the hotel Miss Withers' attention was anywhere but on her driving. To her everything had taken on the quality of a walking nightmare, and in the bright shimmering glare of the summer sunlight objects seemed to shift and change their outlines in a sort of living, moving double exposure.

No messages at the desk. Upstairs the rooms were full of Talley's absence, but she put away his tongue-polished dish and his beloved rubber rat. Talley was locked up—and Junior Gault was at liberty. None of it made any immediate sense to her. The world was out of joint. With the best intentions in the world she had alienated her old friend the inspector by sending the innocent messages which had brought almost everyone connected with the Fagan murder heading hellbent toward Tijuana. The monkey wrenches she had flung into the machinery, she wryly admitted to herself, had come home to roost.

When in doubt, wash your hair—it was an ancient feminine maxim, but a good one. After an hour of intense effort spent in trying to cleanse the reek of the Tijuana jail from her person, the schoolteacher finally sat down at the desk, took out a clean sheet of paper and her fountain pen, and then stopped in midair. Her thoughts, her suspicions, were still nebulous.

Somewhere she had read that the super-automatic calculating machine at Harvard, the cybernetic robot, produced now and then, instead of the expected answer, only a code word meaning "Insufficient data."

If Junior Gault had been set free, then the Fagan case was again wide-open. Nor could the schoolteacher take too seriously the murder warrant for Ina Kell's arrest.

Miss Withers found herself idly doodling, drawing doghouses and complicated roses with long thorny stems, involved geometric mazes and bearded snakes and maps of imaginary islands with an X marking the spot where the treasure lay buried. She drew an oversize question mark, and then changed it over into an exclamation point. So much for Ina Kell. The school-teacher tore up that page and started on another. She wrote down the name *Ruth Fagan.*

Some time later there came a diffident, almost apologetic knock at the door. "Come in, Oscar, come in!" she called, much relieved. "It's about time—"

But it wasn't the inspector. A stranger poked his head in the door, an elderly benign-looking stranger with a butternut-colored face and snowy-white hair, his cap held politely in his hand. "La Señorita Hildegarde Weethers?"

"Yes, yes. If it's another telegram just put it there on the table; I'm very busy." She felt in her handbag for a quarter. But instead of taking the coin, the old man placed a thickly folded document in her hand, bowed, and then withdrew. His departure disclosed that there had been still another man behind him, more or less supervising the proceedings; none other than Lic. Ramon Julio Guzman y Villalobos, who was looking very pleased with himself.

"It is not a telegram, Miss Withers," said the lawyer.

"So I see," she murmured, trying to make some sense of the involved legal Spanish, of the interminable list of names which came before the *contra.* But a summons was a summons in any language. "Are you mixed up in this farce?" she demanded acidly.

"I have the honor to represent the plaintiffs in the action," Guzman corrected her gravely. "The eleven gentlemen who had the great misfortune the other evening at the track to lose their wagers and their potential winnings because of the overt act of your dog."

She extended the paper to him. "Go serve it on the dog, then."

The lawyer looked shocked, as if she had moved a pawn sideways in chess. "This is a most serious matter, Miss Withers. You will find that our juries do not take lightly a grave offense by a foreigner against our citizens." He shook his head gravely. "However, it might be worse. My clients are reasonable people. It is sometimes possible to settle these affairs privately, out of court. ..."

She nodded. "For dollars, a great many American dollars?"

"Yes, señorita. But not too many. My clients can show their wasted pari-mutuel tickets, and the total—"

"Good day, Mr. Guzman."

He hesitated, then bowed calmly. "Think it over, señorita. You know where to reach me." The door closed ever so gently behind him.

Miss Withers stalked up and down the room, growing angrier at every step. If only Oscar Piper had been here, to tell the lawyer what his precious clients could do with their pari-mutuel tickets!

But first things first. Finally subsiding after a fashion, she sat herself down at the desk again. After surveying what she had already written, she made a new start under the name *Arthur Wingfield* ... and was lost in deep thought and more doodles when another knock came at her door. Again she brightened, and cried, "Come in, Oscar."

But the watched pot never boils. It was only Vito, looking small, worried and unhappy. Apologies and explanations, in a potpourri of two languages with perhaps a touch of some Indio dialect, poured from his lips. The boy blamed himself for everything. If he had only taken Talley walking on one of the side streets instead of straight down the Avenida last night—

"Heavens, child, it's not your fault."

He brightened a little. "You got out okay, then?"

"I got out, in a manner of speaking." Miss Withers absently tried to scratch her left shoulderblade. "But at the moment Talley's prospects are not so good." She told her young aide about the lawsuit, and even showed him the summons.

"Is not good," Vito said solemnly.

"Is not—I mean, it certainly is not. Someone is obviously laboring under the delusion that I am both gullible and wealthy."

The boy's eyes widened. "But you are not reech, then? You spend much money."

"It is nearly all spent." She sighed. "Vito, it might be interesting to discover just who is trying so hard to put a spoke in my wheel. Do you happen to recognize any of the names of the plaintiffs on this summons? Are there any cousins of yours among them?"

Vito studied the list again and shook his head. "No, lady. Lowlifes, probably."

"Lowlifes most certainly. But you might still make a few discreet inquiries."

"Sure!" said the boy proudly. But then as she reached for her handbag he shook his head. "This one is on the house," he announced.

After the boy had taken himself off, Miss Withers sat down at the desk again and with pen in hand tried to regain the thread of her scattered thoughts. If her suspicions were correct, Oscar Piper was well on the way to the greatest mistake of his professional career. But how at this late hour could she be expected to draw rabbits out of hats—even her own incredible hats? After a little while she wrote down the name *Thallie Gordon*. But she wrote nothing much after it, and finally in spite of herself went back to doodling again. One of the doodles was an engagement ring without any diamond, and another vaguely resembled an eagle with a simpering feminine face, perched high atop a dead pine tree.

Any murder case, she knew, could be broken by only asking the right questions at the right time of the right person. Offhand she could think of three or four—she began to make a list of those.

When finally there was still another knock at her door, the schoolteacher resisted the impulse to say, "Come in, Oscar." She crossed the room and said very cautiously, "I'm not sure I'm home. Who is it?"

"It's me, teacher—Sascha Bordin!" came the surprising answer.

Hastily Miss Withers threw the door open. Bordin today was turned out in lightweight gabardine, sea-green in color, and he held in his manicured hand the sort of Panama hat which is never made in Panama at all, but woven underwater by Peruvian mermaids or something along those lines— the schoolteacher was never sure about men's clothing. But she was sure about English grammar. "You might have said, 'It is *I*,' " she reminded him.

"Okay, so I've backslid," said the lawyer cheerfully. "Things are bad all over, and getting worse. May I come in?"

He already was in. Miss Withers shook hands warily. "Just how did you find me, and what do you want?"

"I happened to phone my office a little while ago, and Gracie gave me your message. I also learned that my client has been turned loose—"

She sniffed. "And did you also learn that Inspector Piper is down here with a first-degree murder warrant for Ina Kell? I suppose that, having lost the chance to defend one client, you're down here looking around for another?"

"You wrong me, Miss Withers," said Bordin easily.

"You mean to say you wouldn't defend Miss Kell?"

"From all I've heard of the girl, I'd gladly defend her for free if only she'd go out to dinner with me afterwards." He sat down, asked for and received permission to light a cigarette, and then patiently explained, "So you don't get the point yet, Miss Withers. The D.A.—and your friend the inspector—don't really want Ina Kell in the dock. But they do want a warrant to hold over her head, a warrant strong enough to force the Mexican authorities to deport her in case the girl still refuses to return willingly. If she surrenders peaceably they'll later reduce the charge to accessory, or even drop it if she testifies just the way they want."

"Sascha, that isn't true!"

"You think not? Those things go on all the time."

"But whom is she supposed to testify against, now that Gault is free?"

He laughed. "My client is released from custody only because the D.A.'s office couldn't very well hold him while they were asking for a murder warrant, even a phony one, against someone else. But the moment they have her tied up tight and scared half to death, they'll rearrest Gault and then off we go to trial."

"Oh," said Miss Withers.

"I'm down here," Bordin continued briskly, "because I'm determined to talk to the Kell girl before anybody else gets their hands on her. I'm asking your help, because I think you believe in justice and fair play. She's left this hotel—but do you know where I can find her?"

The schoolteacher hesitated, and he said quickly, "I see that you do know. Look, all I want is a chance to get a deposition out of her before she's taken into custody. Is that asking too much?"

"Perhaps not," Miss Withers admitted cautiously. "But, Sascha, who are you to ask for fair play when you yourself sent her down here?"

His eyes clouded. "*I* sent her?"

"You knew she was here, or else why did you rush down to Tijuana?"

"If you must know," he said wearily, "it's because last Sunday night—Monday morning, rather—I got yanked out of bed by a long-distance phone call from here. It was Ina Kell—"

"Whose voice you recognized, even though you'd only heard it once or twice?"

If that was a trap, Sam Bordin neatly sidestepped it. "Correction. I was called by a girl who said she was Ina Kell, missing witness in the Fagan murder. I'd never talked to her, though I knew in a general way that she existed, and somebody by that name called my office once when I was out. The girl wanted me to give her some free legal advice about how she could avoid being dragged back to testify against my client. It seemed that somebody—presumably you—was on her trail and getting close. I told her that she was mistaken in thinking the defense wanted her out of the country; that I wanted her brought back as much or more so than the prosecution did. So she gasped and hung up. I thought it over and then next morning I tipped off the press, having a feeling that a little publicity would bust this thing wide-open. Not that I expect your friend the inspector to believe me."

"But tipping off the press was supposed to prove that you'd previously known nothing about Ina's being in Mexico." The schoolteacher sniffed. "What was her voice like, over the phone? Was it a finishing-school voice or a high-school voice?"

"Just a voice. Like most voices over three or four thousand miles of wire; why do you ask?"

"I'm just asking questions at random these days. Sascha, where are you rushing off to?"

The lawyer had risen and was moving toward the door. "Things to do," he told her. "I see now that you're not going to tell me where the Kell girl is. I guess I'll have to start combing the town for her."

"Save your breath, she isn't here."

"Gone? But she's nearby?" he asked quickly, his eyes searching her face. "A few miles away—say, half-an-hour's drive, or an hour, or—"

Miss Withers tried valiantly to immobilize her features, and pressed her lips tight together.

Bordin was smiling. "I'll find her," he promised, his hand on the knob.

"Wait, Sascha. I'm beginning to think that we're not really at cross-purposes, after all. Stay here until the inspector gets back, and perhaps I can convince him—"

He shook his head. "Inspector Oscar Piper wouldn't give me the correct time. You know something? It would serve him and the D.A. right if I got word to Junior Gault advising him to put on a wig and a set of false whiskers and sneak out of town for good. I think I might even be ethical in telling him that; after all, he's technically in the clear for the moment. It might save his neck."

"What?" The schoolteacher gasped. "You're that sure he'll be rearrested? But—but that must mean that you really do think the man is guilty!"

Bordin started to open the door, then turned with a confiding smile. "This is off the record, but strictly between you and me and the fencepost, who doesn't?" He waved his hand. "Thanks for your help, anyway." The dapper lawyer winked at her over his shoulder and then stepped briskly out into the hall, falling over two suitcases and into the arms of Inspector Oscar Piper, who had been standing frozen there with his fist upraised to knock.

"This," murmured Miss Withers helplessly, "just isn't my day."

"These two hated with a hate
Found only on the stage."
                                    —BYRON

16

It was some time before Miss Withers, who hadn't giggled in forty years, could quite contain herself. The picture of the two hereditary enemies struggling to extricate themselves from their accidental embrace outside her door had been a little too much, even for her. Of course it had all been over in a second or two; Sam Bordin had regained his hat and something of his aplomb and taken himself hurriedly off. The inspector brought the suitcases inside, kicked the door shut, and slammed them down before her.

"Oh, dear," murmured the schoolteacher. "Thank you, Oscar. And don't glower so. How long had you been listening outside the door?"

"What makes you think—" he began indignantly. "Only a couple of minutes, why?"

"I just hoped you'd eavesdropped on the entire conversation, so I wouldn't have to repeat it all. But I will." And she did.

Unmollified, Piper said, "I don't believe it. I mean I don't believe it when Bordin says he didn't have any idea Ina Kell was down here until that phone call—if there ever was a phone call."

"There could have been," Miss Withers offered hopefully. "The girls could have put it through when they were hastily packing to get out of here, just after they learned someone had been asking about them. Or Ina could have done it when she was taking so long to get the coffee and sandwiches."

"So what? We have only his word for it as to what was said."

"Yes, Oscar. But when Sascha was a little boy, back in my class at P.S. 38, he never cheated. He argued a lot, but he never cheated."

"You mean you never caught him. Besides, people change with the years."

"Some of them don't change enough. You are overly suspicious, Oscar. If he had known where Ina is, Bordin wouldn't have come here to the hotel asking me. That should be obvious, even to a professional policeman. I'm disappointed in you."

"Disappointed!" he exploded. "You listen to me! I only came back here because I thought it over and decided that for old times' sake I ought to forgive you for making a mess of everything. I was all ready to admit that maybe you meant it for the best even when you inaugurated this fantastic fund-raising campaign to get money to grease the local authorities. That dopey idea was only planted in your gullible mind by this shady lawyer you were telling me about. It wouldn't have worked. He probably would simply have put the dough in his own pocket, and then given you the horse-laugh."

"Perhaps," she admitted meekly, thinking dark thoughts about Lic. Guzman.

"I was going to tell you how everything's fixed up—I made a courtesy call at San Diego police headquarters. The warrant hasn't come yet, but they'll let me know here when it does, and they're willing to give me any cooperation on that side of the line that I need, even to lending me a police-woman to escort the Kell girl back to New York. I was going to tell you about the warm welcome I had from Chief of Police Joe Robles over at the *Jefatura*—"

"Oscar, how splendid!"

He wasn't listening. "And then I have to walk in and find you hand-in-glove with a high-class shyster from our own side of the border who's trying to get Junior Gault off by fair means or foul even though he admits he knows his client is guilty. I suppose you had to go and blab to him about where Ina is?"

"I didn't tell him—at least I hope I didn't! And, Oscar, nobody's hand was in anybody's glove. Was it so wrong to chat with an old pupil of mine?"

"Sealed-lips Hildegarde!" he said bitterly.

"Well," she snapped with some asperity, "there have been too many lips sealed around here; it's high time we had a touch of frankness. Has it ever occurred to you that there are a lot of unanswered questions in this Fagan case?"

"Sure," the inspector said wearily. "There always are. Everybody has an axe to grind, and everybody has something to conceal."

"The truth lies deep down, but sometimes a ruthless stirring will bring it to the surface. Worse even than unanswered questions are the ones nobody remembered to ask. Oscar, while you were gone I've been doing a little ratiocination of my own, and I've made a sort of list. Sit down, won't you?"

"Oh, lord, here we go again," said Oscar Piper. But he sat down, crossed his legs, and lighted a fresh perfecto.

"Oscar, can't you imagine for a moment that after Junior Gault, with considerable provocation, beat Fagan to within an inch of his life, some other and more subtle enemy came along and completed the job?"

"We don't use imagination in police work; we use facts."

"Perhaps you should use both. Here's another question. Why did Arthur Wingfield turn green that evening when you came up behind him and touched his shoulder and asked if he'd come along quietly?"

"Why ..."

"Wait. What is there between Wingfield and Ruth Fagan?"

Piper laughed. "A big-bosomed thrush named Thallie Gordon, mostly. He's going to marry her."

"Why did Wingfield call Ruth on the phone and warn her that I was likely to come snooping around?"

"And why shouldn't a man be on speaking terms with his ex-wife?"

"*What?* You never told me that Ruth was once Mrs. Wingfield!"

"You never asked me. Sure, we knew all about it. They were married for a year or two, back in the forties. She was his first secretary when he came to New York from WGN in Chicago. They had a friendly split."

"Is there such a thing? Of course, I wouldn't know." The schoolteacher frowned. "Of course, Ruth did admit to me that she'd been to Reno once before. But Oscar, isn't there a possible motive—"

"I don't see it," he objected sensibly. "It proves nothing, especially in show business where a divorce is only a dropped option anyway. I can't go along with you when you suggest that Wingfield might commit murder over a woman he'd lived with and already outgrown. Try again."

Miss Withers sighed and stole a look at her notes. "Well, there's Ruth herself. How do you think a woman would feel, after having got a divorce only because her husband insisted on it, if he called her back—and then when she came, she found instead of the warm reconciliation she had expected, only a gay party? Ruth had never fitted into the bourbon and Benzedrine group; she didn't like any of his friends except possibly Wingfield, so she walked out boiling mad. Couldn't she have come back later after the party was over for one last try, found him unconscious and finished him off?"

"And then went to bed in the spare bedroom, so she'd be handy for us to find next morning?" The inspector blew a large smoke ring, and another smaller one through it. "No dice."

"I'm not through. What was the murder weapon, Oscar?"

He shrugged. "We figure it was one of those heavy vases."

"And yet the walls of the Fagan apartment were hung with better weapons—with primitive battle-axes and krisses and spears. Wouldn't it seem reasonable ..."

"Murderers are never reasonable, or they wouldn't commit murder."

"I wonder, Oscar. It has always seemed to me that they were reasonable, according to an odd, twisted logic of their own. This was an unusual murder, too—with a very unusual victim. A man who drank milk, laced with whisky, even on his television show. Where did that bottle of milk come from?"

"That's easy," said the inspector. "Fagan brought it from home. He had a standing order with his milkman. So what?"

"I'm not through. Why did Thallie Gordon come rushing into the projection room when Wingfield was showing me that film, to warn him that you were snooping around? That would certainly indicate a guilty conscience."

"Or else indicate that she was smart enough to realize that some kinds of publicity are no good for an actress or a singer. Of course, she was afraid that the Fagan case was being reopened—she didn't know that Wingfield was only doing me a favor by running that old film. She and he both had been out of work for months after the murder. They were both reestablished, and she was afraid of new headlines."

"But you will admit that she had been mixed up with Tony Fagan?"

"Sure." For the first time that day the inspector grinned. "Why should she make an exception in his case? Thallie is like the girl in the limerick, the young lady named Gloria, who went out with Sir Gerald du Maurier, and then with some men, then Sir Gerald again, then the band at the Waldorf-Astoria. At least she had that reputation until she started getting serious about Art Wingfield. Fagan was her meal ticket; she had no motive."

Miss Withers eyed him coldly. "Well, then, I know somebody else who *did*. What about the girl who played corespondent in the Fagan divorce case, the one who got surprised by a raid on a certain hotel bedroom and had her picture taken in a nightgown? That's one of my questions—I think I asked you once before to try to find out who it was—"

"Judas priest on a hayride, I did!" Piper confessed. "Forgot to tell you. It was only Thallie, though, doing her boss a slight favor." He told her about the photo Sergeant Smitty had enlarged so that it showed the telltale ring.

"And you sit there with your bare face hanging out and say *that* isn't a possible motive?"

Piper shook his head. "No. Even if Fagan played a dirty trick on her and didn't tell her the detectives were scheduled to break in and take pictures, Thallie wouldn't be really sore. A nightgown is practically working uniform for a girl like her. Her name wouldn't be mentioned, and even if it was—that sort of publicity doesn't hurt a singer."

"I'll thank you to stop talking like a—like a policeman," Miss Withers said. "Anyway, I hope I have made it obvious to you that, apart from Junior Gault, there are four perfectly good suspects—"

"Three," he reminded her. "But who's counting?"

The schoolteacher frowned. "Yes, that's right. Now I wonder, why did I say four? An unconscious slip of the tongue, I suppose."

"Maybe you're trying too hard," the inspector prodded her gently. "You're so intent on proving that Junior Gault is innocent that you've been scraping the bottom of the barrel. Were you thinking of Dallas Trempleau? Maybe she was so mad at having her voice kidded on Fagan's last program that she did him in. Only I doubt it, because we checked with the servants at her family home out on Long Island, and she drove her car into the garage hours before Fagan got killed. Or there's Ina Kell, your favorite suspect as of last week, who had never met Tony Fagan in her life but still—you said—must have killed him out of unrequited love."

"You're *not* especially funny, Oscar." Miss Withers flushed slightly.

"Well, whatever suspects have you got? Do you suppose that teacher's pet Sam Bordin was so hard up for a client that he went out and committed a murder that would be pinned on a guy he knew would have plenty of money for a big fee, knowing that anybody in that income-tax bracket would automatically come to him? Or maybe our friend John Hardesty is a homicidal maniac—"

"Be quiet, or go," the schoolteacher snapped. "I won't say *where* you can go, but you guess."

"Okay, okay," said Oscar Piper, subsiding. He looked at his watch. "Say, can I use your phone? I was supposed to call the Chief's office about now."

He talked, or rather listened, for a few moments, and when he hung up the little Irishman was obviously in a much-improved humor. "You were right about one thing, anyway," he said. "Ina Kell is safe and sound in Ensenada."

"But, Oscar," she said wonderingly, "what fast sleuthing!"

"You can give the credit to Chief Joe Robles. When I walked into his office a while ago he laid out the red carpet, remembering me from the last police chiefs' convention in Chicago. Robles is a sour-bitten, hard-faced character who looks like a retired jockey, but I for one would hate to offer him a dirty dollar or a dirty peso. He's an old-time peace officer, and a good one."

"He is going to cooperate, then?"

"All the way—as soon as that warrant arrives. Meanwhile he offered to check with Ensenada. The girls are holed up in a deluxe bungalow on the grounds of the Hotel Pacifico; they registered there Monday forenoon—under phony names, of course. But the descriptions fit."

"Of course." Miss Withers frowned. "I suppose that your friend Chief Robles has arranged to have a succession of thumb-fingered policemen watching that bungalow twenty-four hours a day? There would be no better way to frighten those girls into further flight."

"Still trying to teach your grandmother to suck eggs, aren't you? No, there's no surveillance, by my request." The inspector kicked the nearest suitcase. "I wouldn't bother to unpack these if I were you," he said. "This case is just about wound up."

"I hope so," said Miss Hildegarde Withers doubtfully. "At any rate it is getting on toward dinnertime." She edged him out into the hall. "Would you mind running along so that I can get clothed and in my right mind, if any? How about picking me up at six-thirty?"

He went, but it was only a minute or two after six when a heavy knock came at the door. "Oscar, I said six-thirty!" she cried.

"Is not Oscar," came the voice outside. "Is me." And Vito came in, swaggering, obviously pleased with himself. "These ones who are suing you with the lawsuit," he announced, "they are not upstanding citizens. They none of them have regular jobs, they don't even guide for a living like me. They are peddlers of junk jewelry and lottery tickets, very much lowlifes."

The schoolteacher nodded. "Then you would say, Vito, that none of them was likely to have been gambling heavily on the greyhound races?"

"Not much."

"But somebody must be behind it all!"

"Sure. I don't know who that somebody is, but—well, one of the hombres whose name is on that paper has a brother who works in the garage down the street where Mr. Braggioli keeps his expensive imported automobile from England."

"Ah *ha!*" cried Miss Withers. "That was one rat I already smelled. Which reminds me that Nikki Braggioli has been conspicuous by his absence of late. Vito, would you please go out in the hall and warn me by rapping three times if you see anybody coming?"

"Sure—on this door?"

She shook her head, and told him what door she meant. A moment or so later the schoolteacher was out on the little iron balcony again, stepping gingerly in through the window into Nikki's bedroom.

There had been, she immediately noticed, some changes made. It was an empty, bare sort of bedroom, the pictures gone from the walls, the closets bare. In the middle of the living room were three big suitcases, packed and waiting. Nikki Braggioli, it appeared, was about to take off. In one wastebasket, torn in bits, was the portrait of his intended bride, Mary May Dee.

Miss Withers was very thoughtful for a moment, and finally withdrew the way she had come. But this was the wrong time of day, she found, for balcony-prowling. In the street below somebody cried a derisive "*Hola!*" and a moment later a group of strolling *mariachis* broke into "*Amor, amor,*" all looking up and grinning at her. Leave it to the Latin temperament to put only one construction on things.

Somewhat flushed, the schoolteacher hustled back into her own suite, to find that somebody was pounding rhythmically on her door. She hastily opened it, all set to remind the inspector that when she said six-thirty she meant six-thirty, but it wasn't Oscar Piper. It wasn't even Vito, though that young man was hovering about in the background, looking vaguely worried and very conspiratorial. She slipped him a quick wink, and then admitted her visitor.

The inspector came jauntily down the hall at exactly six-thirty and rapped sharply on her door. As it opened he said, "Okay, I'm more than ready for that free dinner. Leave us be off—"

Then he stopped short. Miss Withers already had company, in the shape and form of a tall, unhappy-looking young man in rumpled flannels. "Oscar," the schoolteacher said pleasantly, "I believe you know Mr. Wingfield?"

"That I do," said the inspector without warmth.

"He's come all the way out here with a camera crew to take motion pictures of the surrender of Ina. He has two photographers and a sound man and a script girl all waiting; it seems that they are most anxious to make a big production of it all, and to supplement the actual event with background shots of Ina and Dallas at home, at the races, or just lying on the beach in Bikini bathing suits. I have been trying to explain to him—"

"You would," Piper told her bitterly.

"Yes, as I said, I've just finished explaining that there isn't any possibility of all that fanfare. Such publicity is out, because the situation is much too delicate—"

"Maybe we did go off half-cocked," Wingfield admitted. "But it would have been a great story. It wasn't the sort of thing we could wait for confirmation on, if you know what I mean. So we took a chance." He sighed. "Well, I guess we'll have to go back." He sighed again.

The inspector swallowed, and then said, almost sheepishly, "Don't be in too much of a hurry. Maybe we can work something out."

They both stared at him. "Oscar, have you got a touch of the sun?" she asked. "You mean, you actually have no objections?"

"My personal opinion has nothing to do with it," the inspector told them bluntly. "I talked to New York on the phone a little while ago, and some of the higher-ups think it might not be a bad idea to have this put on the air. Look at the Kefauver thing and the splash it made. The Department has had enough bad publicity in the past, with those old bookie scandals and so forth. Not that any of that mud landed on Homicide. But the Commish thinks it might be good publicity for the service."

"Whoops!" said Art Wingfield solemnly. "Let's go!"

"Not so fast, there's a catch to it. We have to let the district attorney's office in on the ceremony, for various reasons of protocol. So the date is Friday afternoon, say two p.m. By that time John Hardesty will be out here with his warrant."

"Don't forget to invite the guests of honor," Miss Withers said gently.

"That'll all be taken care of. Chief Joe Robles, with a motorcycle escort, will walk in on 'em Friday morning and give 'em a few hours to pack and get going. If they still act coy about it, they'll ride up in handcuffs."

"Hope they do," said Wingfield. "Make it all so much more dramatic."

"From what I have seen of Ina Kell, once she hears about the television cameras you couldn't keep her away," pointed out Miss Withers. "Unless—"

"Unless what?" the inspector wanted to know.

"Unless nothing, I guess." But all the same, a little shiver had just gone up her spine; a rabbit must have been running over her grave.

Art Wingfield, looking at his watch, said he'd have to run along. "Thallie hates to be kept waiting."

"*Thallie?*" said the schoolteacher wonderingly.

"Oh sure." He grinned. "She tagged along; I guess she doesn't trust me out of her sight. I told her she'd only be in the way on a mission like this, but there was room on the plane and—you know how it is."

"I can imagine," Miss Withers told him.

Wingfield hesitated. "What are you two doing for dinner? Maybe we could all eat together at one of these dives—romantic foreign atmosphere and all that?"

"Why—" The inspector brightened, but Miss Withers shook her head.

"Some other time," she said, and when the young man had hurried off, "Oscar, never come between a woman and her lawful prey. Thallie Gordon didn't come along on the trip just for the ride, you know."

"Huh? Oh, sure." They went out together, and since Miss Withers was paying the check she guided him away from the hotel dining room and on down the street to a less pretentious spot. A marimba band was playing fast bullfight music, there were candles burning at each table, and a bill of fare scrawled on a blackboard was wheeled around the room. Suddenly reckless, the schoolteacher took a chance and ordered the most exotic-sounding entree on the menu. Much to her horror, *cabeza de cabrito* turned out to be the stewed head of a goat, one boiled and whitish eye staring up at her in mute reproach.

"Oh," she said quickly. "Take it away. I'm going to be …"

"You're not going to be sick?" the inspector chided her.

But Miss Withers steeled herself, and picked up her fork. "I was about to say that I'm going to be very busy tomorrow. I just thought of something."

"Get out of town before it's too late, my dear,
Get out of town …"
—*Popular Song*

17

"I'm fed up with this," remarked Winston H. Gault quietly. He threw down the gin rummy hand.

"Take it easy, Junior," Macklin said. He was a big, solid man with sloping shoulders, his general appearance that of a placid, competent detective attached to the district attorney's office, which he was. "Now like I told you before," he went on reasonably, "you can go anywhere you like and do anything you like, as long as you stay in town. Only Solly and I have to stick with you. If you get cute, you get rearrested."

A faint smile crossed Gault's handsome, sulky face. "What real difference does it make? I'm going to be rearrested in a couple of days anyway."

Macklin said he wouldn't know about that. Across the room Solly, a stubby man with a blue chin, looked up from his Western pulp magazine and shook his head, indicating that he wouldn't be knowing about it either.

"Maybe I'll just drop in down at the Stork," Junior suggested. "You couldn't even get past the doorman; Sherman's very choosy about his customers."

"Our badges can get in," Macklin told him dryly. "Try it and see."

Solly suddenly stood up. "Now, why think along those lines, Junior? You're getting a pretty good break as it is, a sort of vacation. The food and liquor here are a lot better'n downtown in that cell, and there's a nicer view—" He gestured with a pudgy hand toward the front windows, fifty stories above midtown Manhattan. "There's nothing to prevent your having a little fun. Why not call up some party girls, and make a night of it? There's a couple phone numbers I know—with all your dough we could make with the champagne and the ersters—"

There was only one girl on Junior Gault's mind at the moment. "But speaking of dough," he suggested softly, "how about each of you taking a couple of thousand and looking the other way while I step out to take care of some pressing personal business?"

The hotel room was suddenly heavy with silence.

"Or maybe five thousand apiece?" Junior said.

"I'll tell you, son," Macklin finally spoke up. "I could use the money, and so could Solly. But if we made a deal, then he'd always have something on me, and I'd have something on him, and that wouldn't do at all. That's why they put two of us on you. Besides, you might forget to come back."

"It was just an idea," Junior admitted philosophically. "But anyway, I'm not going to spend the evening sitting here and playing gin for a tenth of a cent. I'm going out."

"Sure!" Solly spoke up. "I know a guy, he can get tickets to *Guys and Dolls.* "

Junior shook his head. "I suppose it will sound funny to you gentlemen, but I think I'll go and drop in on my mother. You're both welcome, of course."

They all rode uptown in the same taxicab, up Fifth past the Metropolitan Museum, and then turned right to stop at last before a stiff old brownstone house, an old-fashioned mansion crowded between looming apartments but with its own tiny yard on one side, now given over to the dry and decaying rosebushes. "You're coming in?" Junior asked.

Macklin hesitated, and shook his head. "I guess that won't be necessary, as long as you don't stay too long, and as long as there isn't any rear entrance to the place." Solly went to check, and there wasn't. Both plainclothes men took up positions under the street light, flanking the front door of the Gault house. After a while it began to rain, one of the sudden, chill, blustering rains that presage autumn in Manhattan's late summers. After what was probably an hour, but seemed considerably longer to the two sentinels, the lights went out in the front windows, and a light came on in the third-floor front bedroom.

"Do you suppose the so-and-so's up and gone to bed?" Solly demanded.

"If he has, he can get up again," Macklin said. "Give him ten minutes."

They gave him ten, and ten more, and then suddenly the front door of the Gault house burst open and a middle-aged woman in maid's cap and uniform came out, crying hoarse, unintelligible sounds.

"Help, help!" she mumbled when they got to her. "It's Mr. Winston— oh, dear, oh, dear …"

"What about him?" Macklin demanded, shaking her.

"He's gone and locked himself in his old room, and the whole house smells of gas! Come quick!"

They pounded up the stair after her and beat on the door she indicated. Nobody answered, but the sickish-sweet smell of illuminating gas was everywhere. "We bust it down," Solly suggested. "The both of us."

But the door was of honest, inch-thick oak, which only bruised their shoulders. Finally, with the help of a hall table used as a battering-ram, they burst in a panel. All the lights in Junior Gault's boyhood bedroom were on, and the fake logs in the fireplace were hissing with escaping gas. But Junior himself was absent.

If sometime during the melee the front door of the house softly opened and then closed again, nobody heard it.

"I don't mind spending my money—Tony's money," Ruth Fagan was saying, sitting on the edge of the couch in Miss Withers' hotel suite. "But I want to make sure I get value received, that's all." The woman's oleo-colored hair was in tight braids wound around her head, and her face was drawn and strained.

"Your only investment so far," the schoolteacher quietly reminded her, "is the two hundred dollars you wired me. Nothing further seems to be required from you, and if you insist I can make arrangements even to return that. There was no need, really, for you to come out here at all."

"Wasn't there?" Ruth's rather prominent eyes flickered. "That's for me to decide, isn't it? I want to help—and, besides, I had nothing else to do. My time right now is dedicated to seeing that Junior Gault pays with his life for what he did to my husband."

"To your ex-husband," Miss Withers corrected her sweetly. "Or shall we say the latest of your ex-husbands? At any rate, I assure you that matters are well in hand."

"Are you so sure?"

"Why—yes," said the schoolteacher, and then realized that she wasn't so completely sure after all. "Mrs. Fagan," she went on earnestly, "would you be willing to consider the possibility that Junior Gault may not have been the actual murderer of your ex-husband, and would you be willing to cooperate financially or otherwise in pinning it on the right person?"

"I know who killed Tony and so do you," Ruth Fagan retorted stubbornly. "And I know that the only witness who can pin it on him is down here in Mexico, being treated like a petted pearl by you and the police and everybody. In Ensenada, isn't she?"

"That," murmured the schoolteacher, "is one of the worst-kept secrets in history."

"What I want," said Ruth Fagan, "is for you and me to go down there. Give me ten minutes alone with that Kell girl—"

"Do you think frightening her into hysterics would aid materially in solving the case?"

"It couldn't hurt. And I have a few things to say to Dallas Trempleau, too! It occurs to me now that maybe she's deeper in this thing than anybody suspects. It was only a few weeks after she appeared in that charity thing on my husband's program that he started not showing up for dinner—or breakfast."

"Dear me!" said Miss Withers.

"Yes," Ruth Fagan affirmed stoutly. "Perhaps she thought it amusing, as so many of those bored, high-nosed society girls do, to have a passing affair with a big radio and TV star. Perhaps she has personal reasons for not wanting the whole truth brought out. I'm not saying she was actually a party to the murder, but she might know more than she's admitted. And certainly the Kell girl does. All that is necessary to wind this whole thing up is for her to come back to New York and tell the truth in court."

"I'm rather inclined to agree with you there. But I wonder if Ina can?"

"What?" Ruth Fagan blinked.

"Ina Kell seems to have had a shock, a shattering emotional experience that night last December. Perhaps what we all want to know is locked up tight in the bottom of her mind, forgotten because she wants to forget it or because she can't accept it. If there were only some way to release her—"

"You mean truth drugs, and all that sort of stuff?"

"It might be worth trying, if she'd cooperate. I'm going to suggest it tomorrow."

Ruth rose suddenly. "But you refuse to go down to Ensenada with me tonight, and have a showdown?"

"Frankly, I cannot see that anything would be achieved by it. I myself made the mistake a few days ago of frightening those girls into a headlong flight. I suggest you leave well enough alone. If you went there, or even telephoned, you would simply complicate matters. Truly you would."

Ruth Fagan nodded slowly. "Maybe. But if you want my advice, get in touch with Ina Kell and offer her a wad of dough to let down her hair and tell the whole truth, and then maybe you'll get somewhere. Anyway, my original offer still goes—there's five thousand dollars in it for you the day that Junior Gault goes to the electric chair."

"Guilty or not?" queried the schoolteacher.

"You and I both know who's guilty!" Ruth suddenly thrust a copy of today's San Diego *Union* under Miss Withers' nose. "See that? Junior Gault gave the slip to two New York detectives last night and disappeared into thin air. Would anybody who was innocent do that?"

"Possibly not," admitted Miss Withers calmly. "But I've often found that there are degrees of innocence—and of guilt. Nothing in this world is ever completely black or white."

"Phooey," Ruth said, "if you'll pardon the expression."

"And if you're still of the opinion that Miss Ina Kell is being treated like a petted pearl, I suggest that you try to be on hand at the San Ysidro port of entry at two o'clock tomorrow afternoon, and watch her turned over to the American authorities, perhaps in handcuffs."

"Really?" gasped Ruth Fagan.

"Really and truly."

The blonde woman's face set into a mask. "I'll stick around and see," she announced. "I'll be at the Hotel Angel, up the street, if you want me for anything."

Miss Withers made a mental note of it, though she could think of nothing more unlikely than that she would want Ruth Fagan for anything. After the woman was gone, she sat down and carefully reread the A.P. dispatch in the San Diego paper. Finally a faint smile of amusement crossed her face. Junior Gault had taken advantage of the complicated situation to make himself scarce, and she could hardly blame him.

Inspector Oscar Piper knocked at her door later in the afternoon, in an unwontedly good mood. "Stop looking so pleased with yourself, Oscar," she told him tartly. "There is no reason for you to be grinning like a Cheshire cat. With the chief suspect in your pet murder case now a fugitive from justice—"

Oddly unperturbed, Piper said, "We'll pick up Gault any time we need him."

"Really? Ruth Fagan just dropped in, throwing her weight around like anything. Which means that everyone—and I do mean everyone—who has had anything to do with the Fagan case is for one reason or another out here in our midst. Oscar, I don't like it; it's like seeing vultures gathering."

"Relax," said the inspector easily. "That's just human nature. This is the most dramatic and exciting thing that has ever happened to any of them. And everybody wants to get into the act, as Jimmy Durante used to say. ..."

" 'To get into the act,' " the schoolteacher echoed. "Oscar, I do believe that you have a point. Moreover, I notice that you have a new crease in your trousers, your hat has been reblocked, and I think you are wearing a brand-new polka-dot bow tie. Isn't that in honor of your appearance tomorrow before the television cameras?"

Oscar Piper looked faintly sheepish. "Well," he said, "these things only happen once in a blue moon."

"Yes, Oscar, how true."

"It's been a funny case. But after two o'clock tomorrow everything will be over but the shouting."

"In which I can hardly be expected to join. I'm still not entirely satisfied, Oscar."

"Which doesn't matter," he pointed out, "as long as the jury is satisfied. Stop worrying. What are you doing for dinner?"

The schoolteacher explained that she had thought of just sending out for a sandwich or something in that line.

"Forget it," Piper told her jovially. "You can't spend your life sitting around here waiting for the phone to ring. Better come on over to San Diego with me. I've got to meet John Hardesty at seven at Lindbergh Field, and then we can all have dinner somewhere on his expense account."

"Ah?" she said, interested. "So our bright young district attorney is finally joining us, complete with warrant, no doubt?"

"Sure thing."

"I only hope he finds somebody to serve it on," Miss Withers remarked, half to herself. She hesitated. "It's a very attractive invitation—I'd like a few words with Mr. Hardesty right now, and my social life and my financial condition are neither one in such a state that I can afford to turn down a dinner date. Will you be patient while I make myself a bit more presentable?"

She disappeared into the bedroom, and returned half an hour later resplendent in her best dotted Swiss, beneath a hat which looked—the inspector thought—like disaster in a florist's window.

"You had a caller," the inspector told her. "I sent him on his way."

"Oscar! It wasn't—"

"It was a small Mexican boy with a big bag of groceries, which you will find over there on the table. A very suspicious boy, who wouldn't turn over the package to me until I explained that you were dressing, that I was an old friend, and then I still had to flash my badge."

"Vito is a very bright boy," Miss Withers told him.

"Evidently," Oscar Piper admitted. "I tried to pay him for the delivery, but he said it had already been taken care of. He also said to tell you that he had some confidential information about your lawsuit, but he'd report back on that later in the evening."

She nodded thoughtfully. "I'm glad to hear it. Then—"

"We ended on a friendly but strictly professional note," the inspector went on to explain. "The boy showed me his Dick Tracy Junior Detective Badge and then left, giving me a snappy salute."

"A good boy is a good boy in any language," Miss Withers said. "Oscar, on second thought I believe I'll have to forgo the pleasure of dinner. Some other time—"

He looked blank. "Hey, what's up? Just because you got a grocery delivery—" Suddenly the inspector pointed. "Your groceries are bleeding through the sack."

"Mind your own business!" the schoolteacher told him, and hastily picked up the package. But he had already had time to glimpse that the provisions from which she had ostensibly planned to make a light snack consisted of a bottle of milk and the raw and bloody head of a goat, fresh from the butcher's.

"Okay, okay, I'll see you later maybe," said Inspector Oscar Piper hastily. There were times in the past when he had thought that his old friend was deep in her dotage, but never quite so much as now.

"When you see Mr. Hardesty," she asked, "please try to remember to ask him what make of television set Crystal Joris has in her New York apartment, and whether or not he ever saw one of Tony Fagan's milk bills, because four quarts a day at twenty-two cents a quart runs into money, and—"

"Three!" he corrected savagely. "As if it made any difference. I distinctly remember there were three bottles of milk outside Fagan's door the morning of the murder. They show up in the official pictures, too. But are you insinuating now that he was done to death by poisoned milk or something?"

"Never mind," said Miss Withers wearily. "Run along, Oscar."

Piper hesitated in the doorway. "You're feeling all right? No spots before the eyes, or dizziness or anything?"

The schoolteacher sniffed, and closed the door firmly in his face. Thereupon she became very busy indeed. In fact, she was in the midst of a scientific but somewhat gruesome experiment when the telephone rang.

"Bother!" said Miss Withers. "Hello?"

It was the voice of the clerk downstairs. "It is a long-distance call for you, señorita. From Ensenada."

"I withdraw the word *bother*," she said under her breath. "Go ahead, please!"

"Just a *momentito*." It was a long *momentito*, even longer than most, that Miss Withers had to sit beside the telephone.

"The watched pot," she told herself. "I will read a magazine, I will think of the names of vice-presidents, I will count to a hundred."

Then it happened. "Here is your party," said an operator in Spanish.

There was a faint whispering, far, far away. "Hello," cried Miss Withers. "Hello, Ina?"

The line clicked and buzzed. "Is this Miss Withers?" came in Dallas Trempleau's expensive and cultured accents, muffled by distance.

"Yes, yes!" But the schoolteacher felt an odd sense of disappointment.

"Oh, I'm so glad you're still there at the hotel," the girl continued. "Please listen carefully, it's most frightfully important and I have only a minute. Do you know where I can locate that police inspector from New York?"

"Why—" Miss Withers almost dropped the phone. "What did you say?"

"This Inspector Piper, or whatever his name is. The one who's supposed to take Ina and me into custody tomorrow."

"You *know* about that?"

"Of course. That lawyer of Junior's let it out of the bag when he was here this afternoon, trying to get a statement out of Ina. Will you please …"

"Not so fast, young woman," snapped the schoolteacher. "What's happened? Is Ina there with you now, and is she all right?"

A moment's hesitation. "She's in the next room. I wouldn't say she's all right exactly—she's going to have the worst hangover in Baja California when she wakes up tomorrow, but—"

"I don't understand half of what you're saying, and I'm not sure you do either. Did Bordin trade information with you girls, or what? Did he finally get the truth out of Ina? Is that what you're hinting?"

"Why—no. He got a sort of statement, but he didn't uncover much new except that Ina is sure she heard somebody go along that apartment-house hallway when she was just coming out of the bathroom that morning. But Bordin was very nice about it all, and insisted on buying us champagne cocktails at the hotel bar before he left. Ina hadn't had anything to eat since breakfast, and for some reason or other it hit her—so I remembered something you said the other night when we all sat up so late. That gave me the key!"

"It did, really?" Miss Withers felt a little unreal, as if caught in some puppet show where a mad, invisible Tony Sarg pulled the strings. "The key to what?"

"You remember—*in vino veritas*. After Bordin left I simply plied Ina with champagne spiked with brandy. She got so plastered that all her mental blocks and inhibitions and everything just simply dissolved, and she finally spilled it. I *know*, now!"

"Well, for heaven's sake, tell me!" cried the schoolteacher.

"Not over the phone, where somebody could hear. But if you can locate Inspector Piper and have him meet me somewhere in Tijuana tonight, perhaps at your hotel about midnight—"

"I'll do nothing of the kind. No, no, Dallas. You stay right there and I'll bring him to you."

"Please listen a minute. I know what I'm doing. Before I make any accusation I've simply got to see somebody and ask one important question. That's only fair—"

"See who?"

"I can't—I won't tell you over the phone." The voice was stubborn. "But if you'll find the inspector …"

"Most certainly not!" cried Miss Withers desperately, trying somehow to inject a note a common sense into things. "If by any chance you have got hold of something it's simply insane to try to handle it by yourself. This is a murder case, do you understand? We're dealing with a person who has killed once, and may kill again. You mustn't go putting your head in a noose."

"I'm not afraid." The girl laughed, a light Vassar or Sarah Lawrence laugh, but there was an odd echo of bitterness in it. "What happens to me is most unimportant now."

"Don't be ridiculous. And don't you dare go driving off anywhere alone. You and Ina lock the doors and windows and pull down all the shades and—"

"I'm sorry, but that's quite impossible. And I know what I'm doing. I'm driving up immediately."

"Well, then, for heaven's sake don't leave Ina Kell alone and unguarded for a single moment, do you understand? Don't let her out of your sight; bring her with you if you must come up to town, but—" The schoolteacher suddenly realized that she was talking to a dead phone.

Nettled, she put through a call of her own. But unfortunately she did not know what name the girls had been living under at the Pacifico. The desk clerk was very uncommunicative, but at long last he admitted that the bungalow in question did not answer. "The young ladies, they jus' drive away, I think," was his final word on the subject. "Is there any message?"

The only message that Miss Withers thought would fit the circumstances would be the one word "Goodbye." Dallas and Ina had evidently gone roaring off somewhere in the big blue Cadillac to ask the wrong question of the wrong person.

"Yet, should I murder you,
I might before the world take the excuse
Of madness ..."

—BEAUMONT AND FLETCHER

18

The Avenida tonight was a river at flood, a wide stream of slowly moving automobiles packed bumper to bumper and fender to fender, threatening at any moment to overflow onto the sidewalks. The Camino Nuevo and the Calle Larroque and some other side streets absorbed part of the overflow, but the main tide moved northward to push against the dam of the high iron gates at the port of entry.

It had been a big evening at the Fronton, with *jai-alai* players featured who were advertised to be fresh over from Spain, from the Basque mountain valleys, and thus perhaps a little less likely to win and lose their matches by prearrangement with certain cold-eyed gentlemen in Mexico City. It had been a bigger evening at the *Hipódromo de Lebreles*, the greyhound races, where a $10,000 derby had been run off. Over six thousand automobiles with United States license plates had come down to Tijuana for the two sporting events, and now—with the exception of those driven by members of the armed forces and others who had left their wives at home—were headed back across the border.

From the crowded street arose an almost unbearable cacophony, a dissonant medley of dins. Auto horns shrieked and beeped and honked, sidewalk vendors of leather goods and *dulces* and trinkets and lottery tickets raised their plaintive cries, *mariachis* banged their guitars and wailed their syrupy old songs of unrequited love. From a hundred *cantinas* and honkytonks rose the amplified blare of dance orchestras, or women's singing and men's shouts and raucous laughter. Everything seemed raised in pitch, shrill and strange and a little off-key.

From somewhere far away a burro hitched to one of the street photographers' gaudy prop carts lifted its painted head and brayed a lost, derisive heehaw. The animal might very well have been laughing at Miss Hildegarde Withers, who looked down on the street from the balcony of the suite at the Hotel Primero, feeling less hopeful with every passing moment. She turned back inside, closed the window with a slam, and said for the dozenth time that evening, "If I were only a man, I'd do something!"

"Relax, will you?" Inspector Piper took the long-dead cigar from his lips, continuing not unreasonably, "Now what could anybody do that hasn't been done? Chief Robles is cooperating perfectly, every policeman in this end of the Territory has been instructed to keep an eye out for that blue Cadillac."

"There should have been a road block established on the Ensenada highway, to stop them."

"Hildegarde, be reasonable. By the time you got hold of me and I got hold of Robles it had been over an hour and a half since your phone call from the Trempleau girl. She'd had time enough to get up here long before then."

The schoolteacher looked at him coldly. "If you'd only showed up here at a reasonable time—"

"I was only helping John Hardesty work out final arrangements for tomorrow with the San Diego police. It's a complicated thing, taking two female prisoners back to New York. Somebody has to make plane reservations, and all that. And there has to be a policewoman along for the trip."

"You and your arrangements!" she snapped. "It's my private opinion that you were in some dive, watching the cootch dancers! You smell slightly of stale beer and dime-store perfume."

"All right," the inspector conceded. "Suppose I did drop into one of the places up the street to have a look at the floor show? It's a liberal education, and I'm a big boy now."

"You're a big something, anyway. And ..."

"I even happened to run into some of our friends there," he continued. "Art Wingfield and Thallie were at a ringside table at the Ritz, cozy as two bugs in a rug. Holding hands, too."

"I'm not interested at the moment in alcoholics enamorous."

"They only had a pitcher of *cerveza*. You were right about one thing, though. That romance is about to burst into full flower. Thallie was really giving him the works."

"You joined them, I suppose? But you didn't stay long."

"I did not join them. They didn't have eyes for anybody else. And I didn't stick around after the floor show was over because there was a little too much 'Honey, you like buy me one dreenk?' for my taste."

Miss Withers sniffed. "The B-girls probably picked you for an easy mark because of that bright new necktie. I have a feeling, Oscar, that you can take it off and save it for some other occasion. The television party tomorrow is off, I'm very much afraid."

"Say, you really do have a hunch that something is wrong, don't you?" Piper stared at her curiously. "You figure that Dallas Trempleau somehow actually wormed the name of the murderer out of Ina—or something that led her to guess it—and that now she is being fool enough to walk right up to the guy and admit that she knows all?"

"Something like that, perhaps."

"Playing cagey, huh? What bee is this you've got in your bonnet, anyway?"

Miss Withers gave him a look. "Don't get ahead of yourself, Oscar. But the phone call from Dallas was surprising, to say the least—almost out of character. And it doesn't entirely ring true. Why should she have called me at all?"

"That's easy. Because something that shyster lawyer, that prize pupil of yours, said when he was down there, made her think that you might know where I was. She wanted you to have me here at midnight. It's only a little after eleven now; she'll show up."

"I wonder."

"Well, why wouldn't she come?"

"That isn't quite it." The schoolteacher walked across the room, then turned abruptly. "Oscar, I wonder if she took that nasty little .28 revolver with her on her mysterious excursion? Or, if not, what happened to it?"

"Well!" he said. "You don't really think—"

"I'm afraid you're all too right," Miss Withers interrupted bitterly. "Or if I do, I don't think clearly. Somewhere along the line I've accepted a false premise; I've been misdirected. You know, don't you, that magicians perform their tricks by misdirection? I only hope that tonight some innocent person doesn't get murdered because of my stupidity."

"Horsefeathers. You're worse than John Hardesty."

"What about him?" she asked quickly.

"Oh, just a wild idea." The inspector looked at his watch. "He can tell you when he gets here—he only stopped off to send some telegrams."

Miss Withers winced slightly at the word "telegrams." "All the same," she insisted, "I still think that a murder has been arranged and will take place—will take place just about now, somewhere under our very noses. Meanwhile we only sit here and twiddle our thumbs." The schoolteacher sighed. "Oscar, if we only had an inkling of what was behind Dallas Trempleau's phone call."

He shrugged. "Your guess is as good as mine."

"My guesses are much better than yours, as you very well know. But we've got to do something. Why don't you ring Sascha Bordin's room again and see if he's come in yet?"

"Okay," Piper said wearily. "But, as I told you, a man his age isn't very likely to be back in his hotel room at this hour on his first night in Tijuana." But he tried, and surprisingly enough Bordin answered his phone, and, his hair tousled, even obligingly joined them a moment later in shirt sleeves. "I was just sitting down to type out the notes I made on my interview with the elusive Miss Kell this afternoon," he confessed. Bordin looked at the inspector warily. "I suppose our official friend here thinks I stole a march on him?"

"Not at all," Piper said. "It's the assistant D.A.'s toes you're stepping on, if anybody's. Though I'd be interested in learning how you knew the Kell girl was in Ensenada at all."

"Why—" Bordin began.

Miss Withers remembered the little trap into which she had fallen, and said hastily, "Not an unnatural inference, since the girls weren't here and there was no other place for them to go. Anyway, Sascha, there was no harm done. And ..."

"No harm," said Piper, "except you tipped them off to what was planned for tomorrow."

"I did," the lawyer admitted. "With a purpose. I thought that if anything would shock the Kell girl into telling the whole truth—" But he shook his head. "I got nothing new. You can even read the notes if you want. If the case ever does come to trial, I'll make all I can of the fact that now Ina thinks she heard somebody in the apartment hallway after she saw my client leave; but it's not what I'd hoped for."

"Perhaps," suggested Miss Withers brightly, "you didn't use enough of the right technique—the *in vino veritas* approach." She told him about Dallas' plying the girl with wine and cognac.

Bordin looked completely incredulous. "What? You mean to say that alcohol would work like scopolamine and pentothal to release buried memories?"

"The only answer to that is that it *seems* to have worked, in Ina's case at least," the schoolteacher pointed out. "Only unfortunately we don't have the slightest idea of what it was that Dallas managed to uncover." She told her former prize pupil all or almost all of the phone conversation that had set all this spinning.

"Now," the inspector took over, "what we want to know is this. What was dropped during your interview with those girls down in Ensenada this afternoon that might help us figure out where they've gone?"

Bordin thought, and slowly shook his head.

"No names were mentioned at all?"

"Not in front of me. I found it hard to get anything out of Ina Kell with the Trempleau girl around. It was almost as if—"

"As if Ina were afraid?" the schoolteacher pressed.

Bordin nodded slowly. "Or under some sort of strain. When I bore down on her too hard she burst into tears."

"A woman's refuge. Well, thank you, Sascha."

"I wish I could help you further," the lawyer told them. "Honestly, I can't."

"Thanks," Piper told him. "That's all, I guess. Oh—unless you have some idea of where your client, Junior Gault, might be at the moment?"

Bordin said, "My guess is that he's on his way to Tahiti, or Baffin's Bay or Guatemala, or any place where he might get lost and stay lost. But I have no direct information—I don't even know where to send my bill." He nodded pleasantly and went out.

"I still don't like him," the inspector said.

"At the moment I don't like anybody or anything," Miss Withers snapped back. She stalked up and down the room. It was now more than three hours since the phone call. "Oscar," she said finally, "it's getting on for twelve o'clock. No word from the Mexican police and, what's worse, no word from either of the girls."

"Women," he pointed out sensibly, "are usually late for appointments."

"*I'm* not that sort of woman," the schoolteacher reminded him, "and neither is Dallas Trempleau if I judge her aright. She wouldn't have asked me to have you here at midnight if she hadn't expected to meet us here at midnight. Unless—"

"Unless what?"

"Unless she wanted us both to stay put, where we couldn't possibly get in the way of something she'd planned!" She shook her head. "That's too farfetched, isn't it?"

"Maybe it is and maybe it isn't ..." he began. Then there was a knock at the door.

"Eureka!" cried Miss Withers, and rushed to fling it open. But instead of the girl she had expected she stared into the pleasant, surprised face of John Hardesty, assistant D.A., far off his beat but still clutching his briefcase.

"Just looking for the inspector," he explained. "The hotel is full up, and I thought maybe he'd let me bunk in one of the beds in his room."

"There'll be no sleeping for any of us this night," said Miss Withers grimly, and told him why. "Not until we find out what's happened to the Trempleau girl."

"You think something may have happened to her, then?" Hardesty sat down, and began to ask quiet, probing questions. "You gathered from the phone call that she wanted the inspector here at midnight in his official capacity? You thought that she intended to come here and denounce the actual but hitherto unsuspected murderer of Tony Fagan, or maybe even lure him up here and hand him over for arrest?"

"Why—something like that, I inferred at the time." The schoolteacher was very thoughtful. "Now just what did she say? She said, '*I know, now!*' "

"That could mean several things," the D.A. pointed out. "She could have known something important about the murder, or she could have known that somebody else—somebody other than Ina, presumably—knew. In other words, that the jig was up."

"Yes, maybe she wanted to come here," put in the inspector, "and give herself up!"

"You're not especially funny," snapped Miss Withers.

"Nobody was trying to be," Piper said. "Tell her, John."

Hardesty nodded. "Well, you see, Miss Withers—Junior Gault's escape wasn't exactly a surprise to us."

"What?" she gasped. "You mean it was a put-up job?"

"Not exactly. He was at least technically quite in the clear at the moment, and properly speaking he isn't a fugitive at all. But it was the idea of some of my superiors to let Gault have a taste of freedom, to see what he'd do with it."

"And he certainly did, didn't he?" Piper grinned.

"A guilty man would flee, and an innocent one remain; is it that simple?" Miss Withers looked dubious.

Hardesty looked very wise. "Anyway, don't worry about Gault."

"You mean to say you know where he is now?"

"Just about. He's been watched every step of the way since he walked out of his family's house. We had a report on him from Kansas City, and Albuquerque, and he was recognized getting off a TWA plane around noon today at Los Angeles airport. Not easy for a man to disguise that slight limp he has, you know. He hasn't been reported since noon, but I wouldn't be surprised if he'd be arriving in San Diego on one of this evening's late flights."

"Oh, *no!*" gasped Miss Withers.

Hardesty nodded. "Junior has something on his mind, and we intend to find out what it is. Maybe plant a bug—a concealed microphone—in his room when the time comes." The inspector nodded.

Two little boys playing with gadgets, the schoolteacher thought. Looking for miracles, for the easy way, for the answer in the back of the algebra book. "You mean you think Junior Gault is coming out here to meet somebody?" she demanded.

"Yes," said the assistant D.A. "We think it's very possible. And just in case it's needed, I happen to have brought along a warrant for—" He stopped suddenly, and they all turned their heads toward the hall door. Outside there was unwonted commotion, sounds of heavy footsteps, of gay feminine laughter, and voices raised in singing something about potatoes being cheaper and tomatoes being cheaper and now's the time to fall in love.

"Well!" cried Miss Hildegarde Withers, and rushed to the door just in time to see Nikki Braggioli engaged in carrying a slight, redheaded miss into his suite.

"*Ina!*" gasped the schoolma'am, in a very schoolma'amish tone. "Ina Kell!"

The young couple broke suddenly apart, but their eyes were still shining. "It's all right," Nikki said hastily. "We want you to be the first to know. We're in love."

"How very interesting," said Miss Withers coldly. She pushed through the door after them. "But there is a time and a place for everything."

Nikki gaily picked up the song cue, and in his high tenor rendered something about now being the time for love, honey, because you're near me.

"Now's the time to make some sense!" snapped the schoolteacher. She faced the girl. "Young lady, where have you been? What's been going on? Where is Dallas?"

"Don't know," Ina said. "Don't care."

Miss Withers had had, she felt, just about enough. She grasped the girl firmly by one shell-pink ear, much as she might have taken one of her third-graders down the hall to the principal's office, and led her out.

"Hey!" Nikki cried indignantly. "I mean to say, really!" He followed after, but the schoolteacher pushed him firmly in the brisket with her free hand and shoved him back inside. Then she led the bewildered but unresisting girl into her own suite and slammed the door.

"Oscar!" she cried. "Mr. Hardesty! See what I've found!"

"Bingo!" said Oscar Piper, putting down his cigar.

"Great Godfrey!" said Hardesty. "If it isn't little Ina—"

"Hello," the girl murmured feebly, and then whirled on her captor. "You can't do this ..."

"I can and I am," Miss Withers assured her. "Now you just come clean, young lady. Do you mean to tell us you actually don't know where Dallas Trempleau is?"

Ina nodded, and then shook her head.

"You don't have any idea whom she went rushing off to see?"

"Did she go to see anybody?" Ina looked scared, and bewildered. "She was acting awfully oddly, but—"

The inspector quietly took over. "Ina, you remember me, don't you?"

She nodded. "Yes, I do. You were the policeman who threatened to spank me once."

"And I may still do it, unless you cooperate. Do you ..."

Nikki Braggioli was hammering outside on the door. "Go away!" Piper ordered. "Get lost." He turned back to the girl. "You were living with Dallas Trempleau at a hotel down in Ensenada, weren't you? And this afternoon Sam Bordin, attorney for Junior Gault, came down to see you and asked you a lot of questions?"

"Yes, Inspector."

John Hardesty turned fire-red with anger, but Piper waved him aside. "And after that, Ina?"

"Dallas and I got tight," Ina admitted softly. "At least I did."

"And then she asked you a lot of questions?"

The girl frowned. "I—I guess so. But I don't remember much about it; it's all a blur. I'm not used to drinking."

Miss Withers couldn't hold off any longer. "You certainly must remember what it was she forced you to remember about the morning when Tony Fagan was killed. It was something terribly important, so think hard."

Ina thought. "Honestly, I can't remember. I guess I sort of blacked out. If I told her anything more than I told you, or Mr. Bordin, I just don't recall it. I'm—I'm sorry." She smiled apologetically in the direction of John Hardesty.

There was a moment of silence, broken at last by Miss Withers. "Oscar," she said firmly, "we've got to get to the bottom of this. For a desperate disease, a desperate remedy. Will you please send downstairs for a bottle of champagne and another of brandy?"

"What the ..." he began.

"If it worked once, it may again."

"Oh, *no!*" cried Ina desperately. "I can't go through that again. I don't think I'll ever take another drink as long as I live. And I promised Nikki ..."

"Bother Nikki." Miss Withers was not in one of her gentler moods. "Can't you remember anything you said to Dallas, anything at all? Think carefully; lives may depend upon it."

Ina shook her head, so that the fire-colored curls swung wildly. "Nothing. Except ... But that's silly—"

"Except what?"

The girl looked lost and helpless and rather desperate. "I'm trying to think. I seem to remember something about poetry—Byron and stuff like that. But I can't remember any more."

" 'There was a sound of revelry by night ...'?" prompted Miss Withers hopefully. " 'The Assyrian came down like a wolf on the fold, and his cohorts were gleaming ...'? 'Maid of Athens, ere we part ...'?"

Ina Kell frowned with concentration, and then shook her head again.

"All right, now," John Hardesty said gently, pulling his chair a little closer toward the girl, who was perched on the edge of the couch again as if to take off at any moment. "Never mind that poetry stuff for me. Just tell us everything that happened this evening, in your own way."

"All right, I'll try. I—I finally took a nap, or maybe I passed out. It's not a nice thing to admit, but …"

"Never mind, you weren't the one to blame for it. And when you passed out, was Dallas Trempleau there in the cottage? And did she stay there?"

Ina nodded. "As far as I know. Maybe she went out when I was asleep; neither of us had had anything to eat since brunch. Or maybe she went out to make a phone call; she was always slipping away to make phone calls where I wouldn't hear."

"Very well," Hardesty conceded. "Miss Trempleau might have made or received a phone call other than the one we know about. Maybe that can be traced later, only it may be too late then. And afterwards?"

"I don't know. I don't remember anything until Dallas suddenly woke me up by shaking my shoulder and slapping my face; she said she had to drive up to town right away and I had to come along. She barely gave me time to throw on a coat and get into the car, and off we went. She was driving like a madwoman, I remember that. As if nothing mattered any more, taking the corners on two wheels and like that. I asked her to slow down and she just laughed at me, a wild kind of laugh."

"And then?"

"She had to slow down a little, there where the highway curves coming into Rosarito. I wasn't feeling so well, and I guess I went to sleep. The next thing I remember, we were parked a couple of blocks from here on the Boulevard Agua Caliente, and she was shaking me. 'This is Tijuana, you get off here!' she said."

"But, Ina …" began Miss Withers. The inspector caught her arm, shaking his head warningly.

"And that's all she said?"

"Not quite. She was in a state; out of her mind almost. She told me I could have all the clothes and stuff back at the cottage. She handed me a hundred dollars—here it is right in my coat pocket—and she gave me my return ticket back to New York. Then she almost pushed me out of the car and drove on. …"

"In which direction?" the inspector put in patiently.

"Just—just up the street, the same way we were headed. But I think … Yes, she turned right at the next corner."

Miss Withers was already referring to her map. "There does seem to be a road turning off there, that cuts across the dry riverbed and across to the athletic field and the park, cutting off the town and ending at the port of entry."

The two men looked at her. "So?" Piper said.

"So it would appear that Dallas wasn't bound for Tijuana at all—or else she wouldn't have said to Ina, 'This is Tijuana, you get off here.' That implies that she was going farther."

"A point," admitted John Hardesty judicially.

"She was going to San Diego, or in that direction," put in the inspector.

He faced the girl. "Ina, this is of the greatest importance. Can you tell us just what she was wearing?"

Ina concentrated. "She wasn't fixed up for a party, if that's what you mean. I think … Yes, she had on a slack suit, and she was wearing a red scarf tied around her hair, and she had on her beaver cape and—oh, yes, her sunglasses."

"Sunglasses, in the evening?" questioned Miss Withers.

The girl nodded. "She had a special pair that she said cut out the glare of other headlights or something."

"Excuse me," said Oscar Piper, and picked up the phone. A moment later he was dictating a description of the missing girl, to be broadcast to all San Diego, National City, Chula Vista and San Ysidro prowl cars and to the California Highway Patrol.

Miss Withers came closer to Ina. "Just one thing more, child. You've been fairly helpful. But the phone call was at eight-thirty, and you and Dallas must have left Ensenada shortly thereafter. Allowing an hour or at most an hour and a half to drive the sixty miles, just where have you been since then? Why didn't you come here to me?"

"Dallas told me to, but I'm sick and tired of doing what she says! And I ran into Nikki down in the lobby, and we went out and had something to eat."

"All this time?"

"We sat a long time over coffee!" Ina insisted. "Nikki made me drink a lot of black coffee, and then he walked me up and down the street for a while until I began to feel better. And then one thing led to another, and—well, it does take a little time to get m-m-married!"

"He who asks questions on Thursday dies on Friday."

19

The blue Cadillac had swung off the highway a few miles south of Chula Vista, in that brown and barren no man's land between San Diego and the border. It moved aimlessly east and north and west again along the back roads, past deserted lemon groves and truck farms, coming at last into a raw, new subdivision of half-finished small-down-payment-for-G.I.-homes, boxlike houses all smelling of spilled plaster and paint and sawdust.

The big car slid quietly into the gaping door of a garage, and its light flickered out. There were soft noises, furtive, shuffling sounds, the scratch of a match and then the quick crackling of flames, loud enough to drown out the monotonous sound of heavy drops falling one after the other from the front window of the car to splash on the raw, new concrete of the garage floor. Overhead a flight of Navy planes roared by.

"Married!" repeated John Hardesty foolishly, and sat down suddenly in a chair.

"Married, to *Nikki?*" said Miss Withers.

"Yes!" bubbled the girl. "I know it was awfully sudden, but that's the only way I could ever take the leap. It happened in Mr. Guzman's office, with a ring Nikki bought from a sidewalk peddler. It really isn't a proper wedding ring—" She displayed her finger, graced with a massive silver circlet carved to represent some grinning Aztec deity.

"A wedding ring *is* a wedding ring," admitted the schoolteacher. "But there's a time and a place for everything."

"The time for a wedding ring is when a boy is in the mood," Ina said firmly.

"Speaking of that," spoke up Oscar Piper. He went over to open the hall door and beckon to the bewildered and belligerent young man who was stalking up and down outside. "On second thought," said the inspector dryly, "I guess you can come in after all."

"Darling!" said Nikki Braggioli, not to the inspector. He came into the room like an avalanche. "What have they been doing to you?"

"It's all right," the girl reassured him quickly. "Nobody gave me any third degree or anything." Her voice sounded more confident now, surrounded as she suddenly was by the strong right arm of her new husband. "You see," she carefully went on to explain to the others, "Nikki and I just came back here to pick up his suitcases. Then we're going back down to Ensenada and get my stuff, and head straight for New York in his car. I know I have to testify and get it all over with—" This last was for the benefit of John Hardesty, who still appeared to be in a state of shock.

"Yes," he said.

"But when the trial is over Nikki and I are going to come back to Hollywood, where he has a wonderful starring contract waiting at Metro!"

"A career isn't everything, though," the bridegroom said lightly. "If you want to, dearest, I'll settle for a little penthouse in New York, or a farm in Connecticut."

"Just a minute," interrupted the schoolteacher. "Far be it from me to produce any wet blankets at a moment like this, but isn't there supposed to be an immigration problem in the way?"

"Oh, that!" Nikki grinned engagingly. "That's all fixed. You see, I've had my quota number and entry permit all straightened out for a couple of weeks, only I found I had reasons for not wanting to hurry away from here, and Ina is all of them. I found out that I wasn't in love with her part of the

time, but weekends, too. It wouldn't have been fair for me to marry Miss
Mary May Dee when I was in love with somebody else, would it?"

"Of course not!" The girl suddenly stood on tiptoe and kissed him, very
warmly indeed. "Wow, what a charge!" she breathed dreamily as they broke
apart. "That beats liquor all hollow."

"Okay, fun's fun, but ..." began the inspector, with amused impatience.

But Miss Withers spoke up hopefully. "I have an idea! Why don't our
two lovebirds kiss some more? Perhaps love can further intoxicate Ina to
the point where she'll recall the one essential clue we all want her to remember—something to do with Byron's poetry, wasn't it?"

The girl looked perfectly willing, but Nikki Braggioli stiffened, the English side of his ancestry coming to the fore. "I say!" he said. "It's a bit
public."

John Hardesty cleared his throat, and for a moment the schoolteacher
imagined that he was considering offering himself as a substitute. But he
only ran his hands through his hair, in a baffled and unhappy manner.

"That's enough of fooling around," the inspector decided. "You two
can ..."

"But, Oscar!" cried Miss Withers. "Shouldn't they stick around? After
all, Ina is our only link with Dallas Trempleau, and any minute she may
remember the missing clue. I only wish I could help her by remembering
more Byron. There's 'Death, so called, is a thing which makes men weep,
and yet a third of life is passed in sleep.' Or 'The Devil hath not, in all his
quiver's choice, an arrow for the heart like a sweet voice.' Or 'Childe Harold
to the dark tower came. ...' Don't any of those strike a chord, young lady?"

Ina slowly shook her head.

"As I was about to say," continued the inspector coldly, "you two can
run along. But I suggest you stick around next door. One place is as good as
another for a honeymoon, and we'd rather you didn't try to leave town at
the moment."

"I don't see what authority ..." Nikki Braggioli began.

But Ina touched his arm and shook her head. "We'll be right next door,"
she said. "Until the inspector and Mr. Hardesty say it's all right for us to
go." She turned toward Miss Withers. "And if I should happen to remember anything ..."

The inspector finally shooed them out of the room, and then glared at
Miss Withers. "Hildegarde, sometimes you surprise me. Where's your sense
of—of romance?"

"Where's Dallas Trempleau?" countered the schoolteacher.

"Well, you certainly won't find her by quoting corny poetry!"

John Hardesty said softly, almost to himself, " 'Maidens, like moths, are
ever caught by glare ...' That's from *Childe Harold*, too," he added.

Miss Withers shot him a sympathetic glance, and then faced Oscar Piper.
"Well, Oscar, perhaps this is the time and the place for unorthodox methods. Are you getting anywhere with all your official channels and your

radio broadcasts and dragnets and alerted police? The minutes are ticking away, the clock is running out ..."

Then the phone rang. The schoolteacher seized it eagerly, and then after a moment held out the instrument to the inspector. "Yes, speaking," he said. "Yes. Yes." Then he listened for several minutes, said "Thanks," and hung up. He turned to the two who waited, grinning.

"They've got her," Hardesty said.

"No," Piper admitted. "But for your information, that was the agent in charge at the U.S. port of entry, reporting to me directly at the request of the San Ysidro police. Dallas Trempleau crossed the border sometime around ten-thirty this evening, alone and in a hell of a hurry."

"No, Oscar!" cried Miss Withers.

"Yes, Oscar!" he came back. "At least a girl driving a big blue Cadillac, wearing a scarf around her head and a fur jacket and having—the examiner happened to notice—exceptionally nice legs, came through with the first wave of the crowd from the races and the *jai-alai* games. She said she was born in New York, which matched the license plates on her car, and that she had nothing to declare, and when she got her okay she drove off up Highway 101 as if all the devils in hell were after her."

"I thought so," said John Hardesty, brightening.

"So Dallas is on the other side of the international border," the school-teacher said slowly. "Gone to keep an appointment, and I'm afraid very much I know what sort of appointment it was. Well, what are you waiting for?"

Both men stared at her blankly.

"Obviously," said Miss Withers, "if Dallas went to meet somebody, then somebody went to meet her! Why wait until tomorrow to check alibis, or to see just who is dead or maimed or missing? There are only a few suspects. Why not check on them now, before anyone has a chance to confuse the trail?"

There were times when the inspector was surprising, and this was one of them. "Okay," he said. "Hildegarde, if I had my hat on, I'd take it off to you. Let's go."

But she shook her head. "I'm getting a bit old and creaky for that sort of rushing around. And, besides, somebody ought to stay here." She motioned toward the adjoining suite.

"You mean somebody has to keep an eye on the newlyweds?" Hardesty asked.

She nodded. "It would only pile confusion upon confusion if they got panicky and started to dash off somewhere right in the midst of things. Besides, there is always the possibility that little Ina will have a brain-storm, and let her subconscious loose. I want to be around when and if that happens."

Oscar Piper gave her an odd look. "I think you may be up to something," he said slowly. "Because you know darn well that if those kids tried to go anywhere, we could have them dragged back in a few hours, especially since they'd be driving in that circus wagon of his. And I somehow don't think that you put any more stock in that poetry stuff than I do."

"No, Oscar? You're wrong."

"Maybe," he conceded. "But I still think that you have an idea that Dallas has put her head in a noose because of something she found out from Ina, and that therefore Ina is in danger too."

"In great danger," admitted the schoolteacher. "Whether she knows it or not."

"But ..." he protested.

"Stop butting. You two men go ahead; I'll hold the fort. Round everybody up, and we'll have a showdown. I hope." Miss Withers added the last two words in a whisper. After they were gone, the schoolteacher pulled an easy chair over to the hall door, opened it a scant inch and, with all her lights turned out, settled down to wait. She knew or thought she knew what the eventual outcome must be, but not how or why or when.

She got up once to make an unsuccessful telephone call, and a little later to receive one from Vito, of all people. "Thank you for the information," she said. "But, young man, at this hour you should be at home and in bed!"

"Is not much home since my father die," the boy explained. "Sometimes this guide business is very good late at night, only I would rather work with you on being a detective. Besides, I have to wait for the bed until my cousin gets up early and goes to work. You have something for me to do, no?"

"I have something for you to do, yes." And she told him.

Then the schoolteacher settled down in the easy chair again, her mind going around and around in circles, tying up loose ends, untying them again, and sometimes cutting the Gordian knot and starting over.

Eventually she must have drifted off to sleep, in spite of her good intentions. For minutes or hours later she jerked awake to see John Hardesty standing in the doorway staring at her, his finger on the light switch. The assistant D.A. looked more harried than ever, and his hair was tangled as a haystack. "You all right?" he wanted to know. "I saw your door ajar ..."

"Hush!" said Miss Withers, still trying to cling to the disappearing skirts of her dream. "I want to remember something. It was a very odd dream. There were pretty girls dancing to horrible, off-key music, and singing something about 'Things are not what they seem, skim milk masquerades as cream ...' "

"More poetry," Hardesty said coldly. "And that isn't even Byron, it's Gilbert and Sullivan."

"I know, I know." The schoolteacher was suddenly worried. "Where's Oscar?"

"He stopped off to make a phone call—to see if there's anything new over San Diego way. Be here in a minute."

Miss Withers relaxed. "Well, speak up. You obviously have something on your mind."

"Yes, I have," admitted the assistant D.A. very soberly. "This whole thing has gone to pieces."

"But it's always been in pieces! We only have to put them together the right way, and ..."

"Listen," he said. "With the help of the Mexican police, the inspector and I have located everybody ..."

"Not *everybody!*" Miss Withers gasped.

"Everybody but Dallas Trempleau," he corrected himself. "Ruth Fagan was in the bar and grill of her hotel on the Calle Coahuila. She was learning the samba from a sleek character with long sideburns, who, it seems, hangs around there for the purpose of entertaining lonely lady tourists. She claims to have been there all evening, but no corroboration except from the gigolo, who would swear that she'd been there since Christmas Eve if he saw the chance of a fast buck."

"Not the best alibi," Miss Withers admitted. "Go on, please."

"Thallie Gordon was at Ciro's, surrounded by a crowd of admiring sailors who had recognized her from her appearances on television, and who were almost fighting for the chance to dance with her and get her autograph and the promise of a pinup picture."

"Understandable. And Mr. Wingfield, how was he taking it?"

Hardesty shrugged. "He had already taken it—on the lam. He wasn't around. Thallie said they'd had a fight earlier in the evening and parted company. She said it was because he wanted to get married tonight and she didn't, a fairly unlikely story. Particularly since according to the inspector she'd been trying to get him to make an honest woman out of her for months. As you may know, they have connecting rooms at the hotel over in San Diego, where his group is located."

"I didn't know," admitted Miss Withers. "But nothing surprises me any more. Still, I can see ..." She stopped suddenly. "But you said you'd located everybody."

He nodded. "Wingfield we finally found at the Papillon Bar up the street, feeling no pain whatever and buying phony drinks made of vermouth cut with tea for a flock of the so-called hostesses. I imagine he was also promising them tryouts for television."

"*Men,*" said the schoolteacher. "By the way, you didn't happen to run into my former prize pupil, Sascha Bordin, anywhere on your search of the town, did you?"

"Bordin? We weren't looking for him."

"I was," Miss Withers admitted. "I phoned his room a while ago, and he was out. I wanted to ask him if, on his visit to Ensenada, he had spilled the beans to Dallas and Ina about Junior Gault being out here, or supposedly headed here. But I guess it doesn't matter too much."

Hardesty rubbed both hands through his hair. "This whole case is going to hell in a handbasket. We've even located Junior Gault—he was picked up about an hour ago by the San Diego police, in the Greyhound bus station. Just arriving ...”

“Or possibly leaving?”

“Possibly. Anyway, he’s being held.”

“He’s being held? But aren’t they all?”

The assistant D.A. looked more puzzled than ever. “No, why should they? None of them can be properly considered as suspects.”

“Everyone,” said Miss Withers firmly, “can be considered as a suspect, at this stage.”

But Hardesty wasn’t listening. He wrinkled his nose. “Excuse me,” he said apologetically. “But I keep thinking I smell something.”

“Good heavens!” cried Miss Withers. “You do! It’s exhibit A—look in the wastebasket!”

He looked, and stared down in wonderment at the smashed skull of a smallish mammal, and at a perfectly good bottle of milk, stained on the outside with blood.

“I’m not out of my mind, or much out anyway,” the schoolteacher told him. “That is the skull of a goat. I smashed it with one deft whack, using the milk bottle.”

John Hardesty drew away a little, as if he expected to defend himself.

“The murder of Tony Fagan last December,” she went on, “was a woman’s crime. He was lying there unconscious, having been beaten into insensibility, and a woman came along and did him in—using the weapon nearest at hand, a full milk bottle, just left outside the door by the milkman. Fagan had an exceptionally thin skull, I understand. ...”

Hardesty nodded slowly. “Felonious assault by Junior Gault, topped off with murder by—” He stopped, smiling wryly. “You remember my starting to tell you that I came out here with *two* warrants? The first was for Ina Kell, to make sure she’d come back and tell the truth. The second one was for Dallas Trempleau.”

“Ah!” said Miss Withers.

“I’ve been figuring,” he continued, “that today Dallas learned something, quite possibly from Ina when she had the poor kid practically *non compos mentis* from slugged champagne, which told her that to protect herself she had to commit still another murder. So she took off, dumped the Kell girl en route, and went to meet her next victim somewhere just north of the line.”

“An ingenious idea,” the schoolteacher admitted. “Or do I mean ingenuous?”

“Anyway,” he finished, “it’s no good. Because as far as we can find out, Dallas didn’t go across the border to meet anyone, or at least nobody went to meet her.”

“You mean, all her potential victims are still safe and sound down here in Tijuana?”

He nodded.

“Of course, there is this to be considered—” Miss Withers broke off as there came a ring at the phone. "Oscar?" she cried. "Oh, Vito!" She listened a moment, said, "Thank you, young man," and hung up. "Just my assistant," she explained, "reporting with interesting but not immediately important information. I was hoping it was the inspector. You know, I'm getting a little worried about him."

She looked down the hall, to see Oscar Piper approaching. His shoulders sagged, and he looked very much as if he would have liked to be somewhere else, in some other line of business. "Oscar!" she cried, and rushed out to meet him. "Mr. Hardesty tells me that you've located everybody, even Junior Gault. So his theory has collapsed—"

"All our theories," he said. "I was just on the phone to the San Diego police. Guess what they told me?"

"I've given up guessing," the schoolteacher told him. Then she listened. They came back together into the room.

"Dallas Trempleau's been found ..." Piper began.

"Heading north toward the Canadian border?" Hardesty suggested hopefully.

"No," said the inspector. "She was ..."

"She'd had her skull bashed in," announced Miss Withers quickly. "They found her at the wheel of her car, tucked away in the garage of a half-finished house in a Harborside subdivision, a couple of miles north of the border. Somebody had placed a lot of newspapers under the Cadillac and set them on fire, but the flames were seen by a Navy flyer, on a routine flight headed back for North Island, and he reported it as soon as he landed. The police got there in time to put out the fire—it's harder to burn up a modern car than most people realize."

There was a short silence. "God," said John Hardesty. "Dead?"

"Dying," the inspector admitted. "No hope."

"Any chance," the assistant D.A. pressed, "that she might regain consciousness for a few minutes before the end?"

"None whatever," said Oscar Piper.

"This doesn't look so good, for any of us—" began Hardesty slowly.

"It certainly doesn't look good for Dallas Trempleau," the schoolteacher reminded him. "Well, what are you waiting for? I understand that Junior Gault is already in custody. I suggest that you have him brought over here on the double, and that you have the other three major suspects picked up at once. Not one of them has any sort of alibi—they could have crossed the border, met Dallas and done her in, and still got back here in an hour. Whereupon they'd have tried to build up just the sort of alibis they had."

"That's a point," Hardesty admitted slowly.

"Well, Oscar?" pressed Miss Withers.

He gave her an odd look, and then nodded. "I'll see what I can do. It's a little irregular, at least as far as Junior Gault is concerned. But old Ed Beekman, who runs homicide in San Diego, is a pal of mine. He'll stretch a point. And, besides, they haven't as yet any official connection between

Junior and the Trempleau girl—" He got on the phone, and then they all waited.

"But what I want to know …" Hardesty began suddenly. Then he saw that Miss Withers had her finger to her lips. The room relapsed into silence again, broken finally by the ringing of the telephone.

"For you," said Piper, handing it to the schoolteacher.

She said, "Yes?" listened a moment, and then, "Thanks, young man," and hung up.

After some twenty minutes, Chief Robles of the Tijuana police arrived, with Ruth Fagan, Thallie Gordon, and Art Wingfield in tow. They were all more or less in the typical, "You can't do this to me!" frame of mind, but the *Jefe* ushered them in with firm politeness, and stood implacably in the doorway. "Anything else, Inspector?" he offered hopefully.

"Stick around," Piper said. "This is your territory, not mine. And they're your prisoners, if any. Besides, this just possibly might be interesting."

The wiry little brown man lighted a long brown cigarette, and leaned back comfortably against the wall. Two or three attempts at conversation on the part of the prisoners were cut off sharply. Everyone waited in a stiff, strained silence, and after another half-hour the phone rang from downstairs, announcing still more visitors. And then finally Junior Gault came down the hall, followed closely by two San Diego detectives. He looked unpressed, unshaven, and more uncooperative than ever.

"What do you think you are getting away with?" the sulky young man demanded. "Dragging me into jail and then out again and down across the border—"

Chief Robles looked at him. "The border, señor, is only a line on the map," the Mexican officer said quietly. "We have one of our men permanently assigned to the San Diego police, and they have one down here. We don't like very much to have criminals jumping back and forth across the line. You want to make something?"

"I'm not talking without my lawyer," Junior said.

"That's an idea," spoke up Miss Withers brightly. "Would someone step down the hall and ask Mr. Bordin to join us? He certainly should be back by now."

So he was, but just. They found Sascha Bordin on his knees in the middle of his hotel room before an open suitcase, trying to get three cubic feet of assorted souvenirs and curios into a one-and-a-half-cubic-foot bag. "Decided at the last minute to do a little late shopping," he explained. "I'm planning to leave in the morning."

He was not at all unwilling to join the rapidly increasing crowd in Miss Withers' suite. Immediately he took his place beside his client. "Don't say a word," he advised, "unless you are charged …"

"This is my town," said Chief Robles. "You will shut up, please?"

There was a thick silence, broken at last by John Hardesty. "Well—" he said.

"It's not well at all," said Oscar Piper wearily. "But I'll handle this." He faced the group. "If you don't know," he said abruptly, "Miss Dallas Trempleau was struck over the head by a blunt instrument and fatally injured sometime last evening."

Junior suddenly rose to his feet. "*What?*" he cried.

One of the San Diego officers shoved him back into his chair. "Just listen to the man," he said.

"We have reason to think," the inspector went on, "that somebody in this room had an appointment to meet Miss Trempleau last evening—did meet her, in fact, and took advantage of the meeting to assault her. ..."

His voice trailed away as there was a sudden hammering at the door. Miss Withers pounced like a hawk, and opened it to disclose Ina Kell waiting there, wearing garments hastily thrown together, her bright young face alight. "I just remembered," she cried. "I mean, I remembered what it was I told Dallas. I heard someone coming down the hall, and it all came back to me."

"Come in, child," said the schoolteacher.

The girl entered, and suddenly froze as she saw all the expectant faces.

"Never mind all this," pressed the schoolteacher. "Tell us what you remembered. It was something about Byron's poetry. ..."

"Oh, no!" said the girl. "Just about Byron, *himself.* He limped, you remember? Well, when I heard somebody coming down the hallway just now, limping just a little, I remembered that the morning of the murder, just as I was coming out of the bathroom, I heard someone going down the hall—somebody who limped." She looked at Junior Gault. "You didn't kill him the first time, did you?" she said in almost a whisper. "You came back a second time, and *that's* the time you killed him!"

"Judas priest in a monsoon!" muttered Oscar Piper.

Ina Kell Braggioli was still looking at Junior Gault. "I'm sorry!" she said.

Junior said nothing, being suddenly involved with policemen who were trying to keep him from breaking loose and committing some overt act, presumably one that would have involved his slugging everyone on the jaw and then walking out of the place.

"Dream on," said Miss Withers softly, to nobody in particular.

"*Now you begin
When crimes are done, and past, and to be punished,
To think what your crimes are. ...*"
—BEN JONSON, *The Fox*

20

"So, that winds it up very neatly," said the inspector complacently, as he put down his coffee cup. It was nearly three o'clock in the morning, but neither he nor Miss Withers was in the mood for sleep. "Gault will be held in San Diego until we extradite him—did you see his face when they took him away?"

"Yes," admitted the schoolteacher softly. "Yes, I did—"

"The fight certainly went out of him, didn't it? Once we made it clear that he'd murdered Tony Fagan in collusion with his girlfriend, instead of solo. No wonder Dallas took such pains to get hold of the only possible witness and spirit her out of the country—she was saving her own neck as well as Junior's. Except for you she might have got by with it."

"I wouldn't say that, Oscar ..."

"I'll say it, then. You dragged the thing out into the open. When Dallas discovered that you were on her trail, and learned that Hardesty and I were both out here, she found herself on a spot that she hadn't planned for. Letting Junior out of jail was a big help, I'll admit. One time when the D.A.'s office was on the ball. When two people conspire to commit a murder, or conspire to cover one up, it's always a good idea to allow them enough rope. It worked out perfectly. He came hellbent out here and got in touch with Dallas, presumably by telephone. She came up to meet him. But he was just smart enough—or dumb enough—to figure that Dallas would eventually crack under pressure, so as soon as they met he gave her the same treatment he'd already given Tony Fagan."

"It's very neat, isn't it?" said Miss Withers, a little absently.

"Neat? It's perfect. Gault met her, knocked her on the head with a blunt instrument, and left her dying in her own car—after running it into an empty garage in a new subdivision. Then he stuck a lot of newspapers under the car and set them afire, but due to a lucky tip from a low-flying naval aviator homeward bound for North Island, the fire was reported before it could destroy any traces. Does that wrap it up, or doesn't it?"

"Exactly," said the schoolteacher. "Only, Oscar ..."

He waved his spoon at her. "This is one case you should be very satisfied with. Everybody's happy. John Hardesty is going to go to court and get a conviction against Junior Gault. Ruth Fagan feels that she had a part in revenging her husband—or ex-husband—and she's going to pay you the five thousand dollars in the morning. Art Wingfield and his Thallie have made it up—you can't blame her for refusing to have one of these phony Mexican long-distance contract marriages, and I'll bet you they do it back home the right way. Sam Bordin has his day in court and gets a big fee, and he has a good out when his client gets convicted, because everybody can see it's a hopeless case trying to defend Junior after what happened last night. Little Ina is happily married to her handsome movie actor, and I doubt that now we'll even insist on her coming back to testify." Oscar Piper yawned prodigiously. "You and your happy endings—this time you hit the jackpot."

"Did I?" said the schoolteacher absently.

"Hildegarde, you're not even listening!"

"Yes, I am. But not to you," she said.

The inspector stared at her. "What's wrong? You're not sleepy, after all this coffee?"

She shook her head.

"Well," he said, "I am. I guess I'd better be running along."

"No, Oscar. You'll have little sleep tonight."

He did a slow double take. "*What?*"

"Wrong, all wrong," she said.

"What's wrong?"

"Wrong handcuffs, for one thing. Wrong jurisdiction, Oscar. Whatever happened to Dallas Trempleau happened down here in Mexico. You should have turned Junior Gault over to Chief Robles, if anyone."

The little Irishman glared at her. "Now what ..."

"Dallas never went anywhere," Miss Withers tried to explain. "Don't you see? She didn't drive her car across the international border. A girl who was born in Virginia, as Dallas Trempleau was, would never have told the immigration man that she was born in New York."

He looked at her strangely. "Go on," he said. "Pull some rabbits out of your hat."

"No rabbits," said the schoolteacher. "And I'm taking no bows for this case. The answer was there before me all the time—I had all the proof right in my hands and didn't see it."

"You didn't see what?" he cried. "What is this? We get a case all cleaned up and you start switching!"

Miss Withers shook her head. "It hasn't worked out just as I planned, Oscar. When you arrived with the news about Dallas, and I asked you to say that her case was even more hopeless than it was, I had a purpose."

"You were fishing, weren't you?" the inspector said. "Trying to make somebody think there wasn't a chance that the girl might pull through. But for whose benefit?"

"The very walls have ears," murmured the schoolteacher. "Oscar, I'm trying to tell you, but ..."

"You're trying to tell me a lot of damn nonsense," Oscar Piper said. "You say that Dallas phoned you she was driving up here; she brought Ina along and dropped her off with a hundred dollars and a return ticket to New York, then suddenly got bashed on the head here—and wound up across the line in somebody's garage! Now what sort of talk is that?"

"Double-talk, Oscar. Only I didn't say all those things. Don't you see? The phone call was as queer as a three-dollar bill—I mean the one from Dallas, asking me to have you here at midnight. It was her voice, it was exceptionally plausible in every way, but there was a catch to it. In it she mentioned something about *Junior* Gault, and while everyone else but perhaps his mother so refers to that unfortunate young man, it happens that his fiancée never once did—perhaps one of the major reasons he loves her.

She always called him by his right name—Winston."

"Holy Saint Paul and Minneapolis!" breathed the inspector. "So you're trying to tell me that that phone call—"

She nodded. "It was made by the one person who had lived long enough with Dallas Trempleau to copy her accent, at least passably enough to fool someone over the long-distance phone. Who else but the little girl from the country who came to New York to make her fortune—and thought she had it made the first night?"

"I'll be damned," said Oscar Piper. There was a long silence, during which Miss Withers heard a door somewhere open and close again.

"Everybody wants to get into the act," the schoolteacher continued. "Just as my poor Talley did at the greyhound races."

"Ina!" he said. "Ina Kell!"

"Yes, Oscar. But you needn't rush out next door and start arresting, because it's too late. Flight is the best possible proof of guilt, and our newlyweds have flown. But, listen a moment ..."

"You're completely and utterly nuts," the inspector told her. "I think."

"You don't think. That's the trouble. Ina Kell, you see, knew all about Tony Fagan. She'd seen him many times on television. That night, her first night in New York, she came into her borrowed apartment and, of course, her first thought was to turn on the television set. She watched Tony Fagan's last show. Then she went to bed, but not to sleep. She lay awake, listening, her ears fairly flapping. Of course she knew—her cousin must have told her—who it was that had the next apartment. She listened to the noises of the party, listened hungrily."

Oscar Piper was gnawing slowly at the wreck of his cigar. "Go on," he said. "You may have something, after all."

"I have everything. You see, Oscar, the Kell girl told the truth and almost all of the truth, in her original story. She lay there in bed and heard the party end, and some time later she heard the fight. She got up and saw Junior Gault leave, and of course recognized him—he had been, after all, rather featured on the television show. Curiosity brought her down the hall, and she found what she thought was a dead body. Immediately she envisioned herself in a major dramatic role, the most photographed witness in a big murder case. Only one thing was wrong—the victim wasn't quite dead. So she attended to that, with a nearby milk bottle, something she could take back with her and wash off and leave."

The inspector shook his head. "I don't believe it."

"You can't believe that a young and innocent girl can commit a murder, driven by vanity? How about Madeline Smith, and a dozen others? The girl had already painted a picture, had written a screenplay, of a murder investigation and trial where she was the heroine. She picked up the milk bottle and corrected a minor error—the fact that Junior Gault had only knocked out his adversary, not killed him."

Oscar Piper almost grinned. "Go on—you almost make it good."

"It's the only way it could have happened. Ina went back to her own apartment to get prettied up for the photographers, and then everything was ruined. The boy came down the hall delivering morning newspapers, and found the body—her own body. Ina had missed her cue."

"That isn't it," came a voice from the bedroom behind them. Miss Withers and the inspector both whirled around to see Ina standing in the doorway, clad as they had seen her last, but with a little pistol in her hand.

"But this can't be!" gasped the schoolteacher. "You *left* …"

"Nikki left," the girl said. "He walked out on me, just because he found out that he'd married the wrong girl. … He wanted the one with money, and he thought I had it

"It's your own fault," Miss Withers began. "You spent the money, you had the mink coat …"

"Never mind that," Ina said, her voice flat and brittle as slate. "I'm still in the clear. I'm going to take care of you both—I believe that's the phrase—and then get out of here. You can't do anything about it. Neither one of you is very smart, not in front of a gun. You forgot there was a balcony out here, didn't you? A place from which anybody could hear anything that was said inside."

"You see, Oscar?" said the schoolteacher.

He nodded, and then moved a little, his hands held low. But suddenly the little .28 was centered at his midriff. "I'm not fooling," Ina said. "Stay there."

The inspector stayed, though he didn't look very worried. Miss Withers realized that as a policeman he must have had guns pointed at him many times before. "You surprise me, Ina," he said easily.

It was a cue, in a way. The girl laughed, and not pleasantly. "Oh, so I surprise you! You thought you knew it all, didn't you? I was just a dumb, innocent kid from the country, who could be scared into saying almost anything when you were so fatherly and kind and threatened to spank me! I bet you'd have enjoyed it, too!"

"I might even enjoy it now," said the inspector softly. "So now, sister, you've got the gun. It won't do you any good in the long run, but you've got it. People who try to get what they want with guns are stupid. You've been stupid all along, haven't you?"

The girl looked suddenly gaunt, hungry, and ten years older, her mouth drawn against her teeth.

"You people who always had everything you want and need don't know anything," she said slowly. "This is a world of dog-eat-dog. It never occurred to you that maybe I was hard and smart, maybe I once saw my chance to shake down Junior Gault with the gold cigarette lighter he left behind, if only I could have got hold of his phone number and talked to him before he got arrested."

"So that was it," said Miss Withers softly. "The fingermarks on Miss Joris' phone, and the calls you tried to make in the lunchroom."

"Now you're smart," Ina said easily. "You're so smart about everything that you don't realize I'm smarter. And I'm going to put you both away in a minute and get away from here—far away from here. And don't think I'll be caught. My hair can be a different shade in an hour, and all I have to do is to stand on the highway and raise a thumb."

"The way you got back to Tijuana, after you finished—or thought you finished Dallas Trempleau," said the schoolteacher. "You were listening on the balcony, of course, when you heard that she was finished. As a matter of fact, she will probably recover—with a silver plate in her skull."

"Platinum," said the inspector, who was edging slowly along the wall. "When she regains consciousness, Ina, you're dead."

"You're lying," said the slight, redheaded girl in the doorway. But she said it without conviction. Then the phone rang. It rang again and again.

"Young lady," said Miss Withers. "You're in the catbird's seat, holding the gun. What happens?"

"Answer it," Ina decided suddenly, her face set in a sort of skull-like mask. "Go on, answer it." It was obvious that the inspector had won his point, that his appeal to her vanity had worked, and that she had decided that this last hour of triumph must be wrung out to its last drop. "Answer it carefully," Ina concluded.

Miss Withers gravely picked up the phone, and said, "Yes?"

It was a familiar voice. "I am still watching," Vito said. "Was somebody once again out on your balcony, I thought you might like to know."

"Thank you," said the schoolteacher, her voice quavering a little. "Thank you very much."

"Get rid of it!" came the brittle voice of the girl in the doorway.

"Good night, Vito," Miss Withers said hastily. "I'll call you at home in the morning. The number is *Ayuda* 564, isn't it? Oh, *Ayuda* 465." She hung up.

"I know what you're both thinking," said the girl with the gun. "You think that given a chance, or even half a chance."

She waved the little pistol, and Oscar Piper relaxed again.

"Very well, Ina," said the schoolteacher. "You have two murders to your credit already, and you think you can handle two more. You've outsmarted the police and the district attorney's office and everyone. I must give you credit for the Virgin Islands thing—it was quite brilliantly planned, in its way."

Ina brightened a shade, and then her face hardened. "You're not going to get around me so easily. Stand over there by the couch, both of you." She motioned with the little gun.

The inspector looked toward Miss Withers, and moved slowly.

"Of course," said the schoolteacher, not moving at all. "But you'll not really begrudge us a little last-minute information, will you—since you hold all the trumps? Since Junior Gault was arrested before you could reach him, you thought of calling his lawyer and, failing that, of calling his fiancée, didn't you? So she could take you out of the country, and maintain you in the style to which you had always wanted to be accustomed. Isn't that it?"

"Over there," said Ina grimly. "I'm not fooling now."

"You've had a rather high time down here, haven't you? You've called the turn, you've done the heavy gambling, and you got the mink coat and the Paris nightgown. You even made Dallas leave here and rush off to Ensenada, on the threat of going back and testifying against her sweetheart. And you even convinced poor, foolish Nikki Braggioli that you were the wealthy one and that you could make all his dreams come true."

"Does that matter now?" Ina said softly. "Get over there."

"You hit her over the head right there in Ensenada, didn't you?" Miss Withers went on. "Because she was getting on to you. And then, before you tumbled her into the luggage compartment of the car and rushed her up across the line, you phoned me in a rough approximation of her voice. But you made so many mistakes—" She stopped.

The girl with the gun, obviously enjoying herself, stiffened. "What mistakes?"

"There were dozens," said the schoolteacher pleasantly. She held up her fingers, and dutifully counted them off. "You thought you had Nikki tamed, so he'd say anything you wanted him to say. You even had him so engaged in trying to get me involved in lawsuits that I could no longer be a possible menace to you. But Nikki learned tonight that he hadn't married the millions he counted on, so he left."

"The heel," Ina said slowly. "He doesn't have a contract at Metro, or anywhere."

"The next mistake," explained Miss Withers, "was when you displayed your legs in crossing the border. It was a fairly good way of making the border guards turn their attention away from your face, even concealed as it was by a scarf and by the dark glasses, plus Dallas' beaver coat you were wearing and then draped around her when you left her for dead. It never occurred to you that a girl in slacks, which Dallas was wearing, couldn't show her legs at all. And then your biggest mistake was to think that just because you had once killed somebody with a whack over the head with a milk bottle you could repeat it—was it a champagne bottle this time? Most people have good, thick, solid skulls, not at all like poor Tony Fagan's. You put Dallas in a coma, you gave her a bad case of concussion, but she'll still be able to be at your trial."

"Shut up!" cried the girl in the doorway.

"Don't, Oscar!" Miss Withers sensed that the inspector was about to make a rush for it. "It isn't necessary, really," she said hastily. "Because, you see, when I found that nasty little weapon under the other pillow in this bedroom, I made a point of taking all of the shells or cartridges or whatever you call them out of the thing and throwing them away." The schoolteacher beamed. "So, you see, Ina, you are rather making a fool of yourself."

"*No!*" cried Ina Kell, from the depths of her heart. "*Oh, no!*" But she stared down at the gun, at the glittering little symbol of her authority, her power, as if it could tell her something. She stared at it for just a moment, but in that moment the inspector moved forward to twist it out of her hand, leaving her wrist wrung and aching.

"Goddamn it," he said after a moment, one hand imprisoning the girl against the wall in an arm lock. "Hildegarde, what are you trying to get by with? This thing is loaded, as loaded as any gun can ever be."

The schoolteacher had collapsed into a chair. "Yes, Oscar. But it's not any more loaded than the guns of the lovely, beautiful, delightful Mexican policemen who ought to be—and who *are* coming down the hall. You see," she explained hastily as she went to open the door, "my little friend Vito hasn't any telephone, so he realized I wasn't making a date to call him. Besides, *ayuda*, in Spanish, means 'help'!"

And that was that.

"*Nor look through the eyes of the dead,*
Nor feed on the spectres in books ..."
—WALT WHITMAN

21

They were parked just on the southern side of the port of entry, and the television thing was over. Ina Kell Braggioli had been formally turned over to the custody of the United States authorities, with John Hardesty much in evidence and waiting to take her back to New York.

"What happens to Junior Gault?" Miss Withers wanted to know.

The inspector shrugged. "He's got a felonious assault rap over his head, but nobody is going to press it. I guess he can stick around here, as long as Miss Trempleau is in the hospital. She doesn't smell the flowers he brings, but he brings them anyway. They say she'll be all right, eventually."

"With a platinum plate in her skull," the schoolteacher said. "Everyone seems to be in the clear but me."

"What are you beefing about?" Piper wanted to know. "They dropped the lawsuit, didn't they, when your little Mexican friend proved that the father of one of the litigants was a porter who swept up the grandstand after the dog races, and that he obviously supplied the pari-mutuel tickets that the boys were offering in evidence? What are we waiting for?"

Miss Withers shook her head. "Not yet, Oscar."

"Look," he said. "I have to get back to New York. I can't spend the best years of my life sitting here on the fringe of Mexico, waiting ..."

"Oh, hush!" she said. "I'm waiting for Vito."

"So what's with Vito? You've already fixed it up for him, haven't you, so he can go back to school across the border in San Ysidro, at fourteen bucks a month, thanks to Ruth Fagan's check? And the boy is going to take care of your dog, so what …"

"This is what," said Miss Withers, looking over her shoulder. She waved in the direction of a small, brown boy who had just appeared across the park, holding a large, brown poodle on a leash. "Very well, Oscar." And she drove the little rented coupé up to the gates.

"Born?" said the first man in uniform. The inspector divulged that he was born in Brooklyn, and Miss Withers admitted she was born in Iowa. They were waved ahead.

"You again!" said the second man. He looked into the back seat, and then made Miss Withers open up the trunk compartment. "No tricks this time? No dogs anywhere?"

There were no dogs. Miss Withers was waved ahead, and drove on for perhaps a block.

"My plane leaves in half an hour—" began Oscar Piper impatiently. But she still waited.

Suddenly, wonderfully, there came a brown streak up the road, passing through immigration and customs as if they had not been there. Talleyrand was in high gear, all jets open. The big poodle put on his brakes as he came up to the little rented car, but still took a few yards farther to bring himself to a halt.

"I told Vito to hold him there until we were well across, and then let him go," confessed Miss Withers. She opened the car door, and the dog sailed in, covering her and the inspector with unwanted kisses, shaking hands with them both, and frantically waving an almost nonexistent tail. Talley was in the seventh heaven of delight.

"My plane …" said the inspector finally.

"Do you suppose," Miss Withers remarked surprisingly, "that there is another seat on the plane—and a place for a poodle?"

"New York?" Oscar Piper looked bewildered. "But your asthma—"

"What asthma?" demanded the schoolteacher scornfully. With a lurch, and a screech of gears that set the Inspector's teeth on edge, she took off.

THE END

About the Rue Morgue Press

"Rue Morgue Press is the old-mystery lover's best friend,
reprinting high quality books from the 1930s and '40s."
—*Ellery Queen's Mystery Magazine*

Since 1997, the Rue Morgue Press has reprinted scores of traditional mysteries, the kind of books that were the hallmark of the Golden Age of detective fiction. Authors reprinted or to be reprinted by the Rue Morgue include Catherine Aird, Dorothy Bowers, Pamela Branch, Joanna Cannan, Glyn Carr, Torrey Chanslor, Clyde B. Clason, Joan Coggin, Manning Coles, Lucy Cores, Frances Crane, Norbert Davis, Elizabeth Dean, Constance & Gwenyth Little, Marlys Millhiser, James Norman, Stuart Palmer, Craig Rice, Kelley Roos, Charlotte Murray Russell, Maureen Sarsfield, Margaret Scherf and Juanita Sheridan.

To suggest titles or to receive a catalog of Rue Morgue Press books write P.O. Box 4119, Boulder, CO 80306, telephone 800-699-6214, or check out our website, www.ruemorguepress.com, which lists complete descriptions of all of our titles, along with lengthy biographies of our writer